Black Sombrero

Black Sombrero

WILLIAM COLT MACDONALD

Sagebrush
Large Print Westerns

Library of Congress Cataloging-in-Publication Data

MacDonald, William, Colt, 1891-1968.
  Black sombrero / William Colt MacDonald.
     p.   cm.
  Originally published: New York : Doubleday, Doran & Co.
1940, in series: Double D. Western.
  ISBN 1-57490-442-6 (alk. paper)
  1. Large type books. I. Title

  PS3525.A2122 B57 2002
  813'.52—dc21   2002012112

Sagebrush Large Print Westerns are published in the United States and Canada by Thomas T. Beeler, Publisher, PO Box 659, Hampton Falls, New Hampshire 03844-0659. ISBN 1-57490-442-6

Published in the United Kingdom, Eire, and the Republic of South Africa by Isis Publishing Ltd, 7 Centremead, Osney Mead, Oxford OX2 0ES England. ISBN 0-7531-6697-6

Published in Australia and New Zealand by Bolinda Publishing Pty Ltd, 17 Mohr Street, Tullamarine, Victoria, Australia, 3043 ISBN 1-74030-668-6

Manufactured by Sheridan Books in Chelsea, Michigan.

Black Sombrero

WANTED—A MAN

THE GENIAL FAT MAN ACROSS THE POKER TABLE HAD scarcely started to rake in his winnings when Johnny Donne shoved back his chair and stood up. The other three players eyed him silently a moment, then one of them commenced to button up his vest. The man at Johnny's right gathered the scattered cards and stacked them into a neat deck; the player to the left touched a match to his dead cigar butt, then reached to the heap of money before him—Johnny's hard-earned money. At least it had been Johnny's money in the beginning. Now the financial proceeds of his past months' labor was divided about equally in four parts, and none of the parts belonged to Johnny.

Johnny stood there, looking down at the four. He hadn't said anything yet. A sort of puzzled expression lingered on his features. The others watched him, waiting. Johnny smiled gravely and said, "It's sure hard to beat your kind of luck."

Across the table the fat man chuckled. "Cleaned out, son?"

Johnny said, "Not quite," and touched the holstered six-shooter at his right hip.

The fat man's eyes hardened, though the smile didn't leave his face. "You're not for making trouble? You don't think we pulled anything crooked?" The other three watched Johnny closely.

"I didn't say that."

The four players looked relieved at Johnny's reply. One of them said, "I reckon it's about time for a friendly drink." He shifted in his chair to call the bartender.

1

Johnny said, "Wait," and touched his holstered gun again. "Cash can always be raised on a Colt gun. I'd like one more hand if you gentlemen will wait a few minutes while I raise dough."

The fat man said genially, "Certainly, son," and settled back.

"Much obliged." Johnny turned swiftly and strode from the Acme Saloon. He had scarcely disappeared when the four players rose quickly from the table and approached the bar. The fat man said to the bartender, "I reckon that will do it, Earnie." He and the other three commenced disgorging their winnings from pockets and piling them on the bar.

The barkeep gathered them in, nodding a slick head. "I'll see that George gets this. You'd better slope out of here. And thanks a lot for your trouble." The four laughed and said it hadn't been any trouble at all, then moved swiftly toward the rear exit. An instant later the barkeep was alone. There were no other customers in the Acme at the time. The barkeep scribbled a note on a sheet of paper to the effect that the saloon would be closed for five minutes, locked the doors, after placing the notice on the front, and hurried off down the street, carrying with him the money Johnny had lost.

The late afternoon sun was westering fast when Johnny Donne left the Acme Saloon and stepped along San Antonio Street, his high-heeled cowman's boots making hollow, clumping sounds on the plank walk. He was a tall rangy individual with good features, black hair and gray eyes, somewhere in the vicinity of twenty-seven or -eight. A rueful smile hovered about his lips as he strode along. People passing by noticed that smile and turned to look at him. It was a rather nice smile for all the sheepish look that went with it. Well, after all, it

2

wasn't any fun being broke in a town the size of El Paso, especially when you didn't know anyone.

A mule-drawn streetcar clanged past. Johnny gave it momentary attention. That mule reminded him that his horse and saddle had been stolen the previous night. That hurt more than being broke. And now, Johnny mused, I'm aiming to put my hawg leg in hock. Lemme see, that brings me right down to the denims I stand in, one shirt and a gray Stet hat. Oh yes, and a Barlow knife, some makin's and a couple of bandannas. Still, if I can just get one more whack at those hombres . . . they sure play a smooth game. I wonder if . . . Nope, they can't be crooked . . . They'd cleaned me a heap sooner if they were . . . or I'd have caught on . . .

He pushed on, eying the various stores and shops he passed. There seemed to be a saloon every few steps. This El Paso town, Johnny told himself, sure don't take any chances of a man going thirsty. There were plenty other signs of a fast-growing town, however. Both sides of the street looked busy. Coming to the corner of El Paso Street, Johnny paused a moment near a one-story brick bank building, then turned south.

There were more saloons along El Paso Street. Johnny passed a saddler's shop, restaurants; farther on he saw a sign denoting what he was looking for: a pawnshop. He entered the pawnshop and within a few minutes again emerged on the street. By now his holster was empty, as he turned swiftly back toward the Acme Saloon, his whole mind centered on one objective: one more chance against the poker-playing experts who had cleaned him out.

It was nearly dark by the time Johnny Donne reentered the Acme; only the faintest touch of golden light still lingered on the tip of Franklin Peak, rising

3

above the mountains northeast of town. Lights were commencing to shine from windows and open doorways. Earnie Clark, the Acme barkeep, was just lighting up behind his bar as Johnny pushed through the swinging doors. At the moment the Acme was without customers. Johnny stopped short, just inside, and looked around.

Earnie glanced over his shoulder. "You back again?"

Johnny nodded a bit grimly. "I see those hombres changed their minds about waiting."

Earnie looked blank, then, "Oh, them four you were playing with, eh?"

"Do you know where they went?"

Earnie shook his head. "Ain't got the least idea," he lied. "What did they do—clean you out?"

Johnny disregarded the question. "Who were they? Know where I can find them?"

Earnie lied some more. "They're strangers to me. Never saw 'em before today when they come in and invited you into their game. You figure 'em as sharpers?"

"I didn't—before. Now I don't know. They promised to wait until I got back. Shucks!" A slow grin crossed Johnny's tanned features. "Sharpers or not, it's almost a privilege to lose to a bunch like that. They're smooth. I figure I got an education."

"They busted you, eh?"

"Just about."

Earnie clucked sympathetically and put a bottle of beer on the bar, then followed it with a platter of beef sandwiches. "These just came in," he explained. "I have 'em brought every evenin'. Pitch in."

Johnny said, "Cripes! I can still buy my supper."

"No need to. Pitch in, I said."

4

Johnny pitched in, remembering now that the poker game had carried straight through dinnertime. The sandwiches were good. Between the two the platter was soon clean. They talked while the bread and meat rapidly disappeared. Faced with the facts that he was broke and without a job prompted certain queries on Johnny's part.

"Jobs?" Earnie laughed shortly. "There just don't seem to be any for cowmen. The drought the past two years has just about got everybody's back to the wall. There's no hiring being done that I know of. Course, you might find something to do in El Paso—"

"No town jobs for me." Johnny shook his head.

"I figured as much." Earnie nodded. He produced a newspaper from the back bar. "Here's the *Banner-Independent,* just out today. You might look through it. Sometimes folks put in a piece advertising for help on one job or another. You might see something that would interest you."

Johnny accepted the paper somewhat dubiously and seated himself at a small table across the barroom. Here he glanced through the pages. Inside, next to the last page, were three columns of advertisements, but none of them seemed advertising for help. There were ads for stock feed, real estate, saddles, guns. True, one restaurant did advertise for a dishwasher, but that didn't interest Johnny. And then, just as he was about to impatiently fold the paper and return it to the bartender, a small advertisement, near one lower corner, caught his attention:

WANTED: *A man of courage for dangerous enterprise. Nerve to gamble on an uncertainty for good returns is required. See Earnest Clark, Acme Saloon.*

A frown creased Johnny's forehead as he read the words. What the devil? And why see Earnie Clark? What did he know about it? Johnny glanced toward the bar. Earnie was at present engaged in serving some customers who had entered the Acme. Johnny reread the advertisement. Pshaw! Probably wasn't anything to it. Like as not the owner of the Acme was seeking capital to put into his saloon or something of the sort. It said, right in the ad, that nerve to gamble was required. That sounded like an investment of some sort might be necessary.

Johnny grinned inwardly. Well, he had the nerve to gamble all right, but the day's proceedings had proved he didn't have the luck. He reread the advertisement again. His frown deepened. Man of courage for dangerous enterprise. Nope, that didn't sound like any open-and-shut business proposition either. Johnny swore under his breath. There was something funny in the wind. There'd been something queer about the whole day's doing. Earnie had said he didn't know the four men with whom Johnny had played cards; somehow, despite a certain amount of reasoning with himself, Johnny couldn't help doubting the barkeep's statement. And all the time he'd been playing cards Johnny had sensed the game wasn't on the level; at the same time he couldn't put his finger on anything out of the way. It was just a matter of instinct, Johnny decided. The cards hadn't been shaved or marked in any way. He felt sure on that score; past experience had educated him in the way of ordinary cardsharps.

"And if they were," Johnny mused ruefully, "they weren't ordinary by a long shot."

Once more he read the advertisement in the

6

newspaper; then, acting on impulse, he rose from his seat, carrying the newspaper with him, and approached the end of the bar.

By this time several more customers had entered the Acme, and for a few minutes Earnie was kept busy. Finally the rush of business ceased for a few minutes and he came down the bar toward Johnny. "Find anything to interest you?" he asked carelessly.

"Mebbe," Johnny said noncommittally. He tapped the newspaper. "I know you're called Earnie. Does your last name happen to be Clark?"

"You've hit it. I wondered if you'd find that piece. Lots of folks don't bother to read those advertisements. But some do. I already told three fellers the job was filled—they come in while you was playing poker with those hombres today. Guess you didn't notice 'em. They wouldn't have fitted anyway. That's why I turned 'em down. Told 'em it was developing a mine up in Montana and that capital was needed to get the job. That was enough for 'em. They lost interest." He had lowered his voice as he spoke.

"Me, I've lost interest, too"—Johnny smiled—"if capital is required."

" 'Tain't," Earnie said. "Just told the applicants that to get rid of 'em. I was sort of saving the job for you."

"How'd you know I'd want it?"

"Kept an eye on you while you were playing. I saw you were being cleaned."

"It seems to me," Johnny drawled, "that us players weren't the only ones taking an interest in the poker game."

Earnie flushed. "Maybe not," he admitted, "but don't jump to any conclusions. Do you want this job or don't you?"

7

"Just what is it?"

"I ain't free to state," Earnie said slowly, "but I can give you directions—if you're interested."

Johnny smiled. "Seeing that I'm broke and that I long ago contracted the idea of eating regularly, I reckon I'd better be interested."

"Good. You go over to the Pierdon Hotel and tell the clerk you want to see Mr. Smith."

"Has Smith got any first name?" Johnny asked sarcastically. "It's so unusual that—"

"Maybe it's John." Earnie smiled thinly. "Anyway you ask for him. If he decides to tell you his name he will."

Johnny hesitated. "Is this job on the level?"

"Absolutely."

Johnny shrugged his shoulders. "Oh well, what have I got to lose? Where's the Pierdon Hotel?"

"Over on San Francisco Street—north of here—runs east and west. You'll find the Pierdon without no trouble."

Johnny said thanks and left the Acme to walk west along San Antonio. Crossing at the plaza, he found San Francisco Street and started looking for the Pierdon Hotel, his mind turbulent with speculation. A short distance down the poorly lighted street he saw a two-story brick building that looked as though it might be a hotel. Crossing diagonally, a few more steps brought him close enough to read the words "Pierdon Hotel" painted on the double window of the establishment.

Johnny opened the door and stepped into the lobby. Directly ahead was a staircase leading to the second floor. At the right wall were a few chairs. Ranged along the left was a desk presided over by a sleepy-looking clerk, who came alive enough to present a pen and ask

8

Johnny to register.

Johnny shook his head. "I'm not aiming to put up here. I want to see Mr. Smith. I understand he's staying here."

"Only one Smith here right now. Last week we had three men of that name. But there's only one here now."

"So you said. It's him I want to see."

"Room 211. Upstairs. I reckon you can find the door."

Johnny nodded and ascended the stairs. On the second floor he found himself in a long hall that reached from the front to the rear of the building. A window was raised at the front end; at the rear a door, swung back for air circulation, opened on a flight of wooden steps that might or might not have been intended as a fire escape. A gas jet burned gloomily in the ceiling, midway of the hall, its flickering light allowing Johnny to read the numbers on the doors arranged along either wall.

Room 211 was located without any difficulty. Light showed through the transom above the door. All other transoms along the hall were dark. Johnny paused a moment, then knocked on the door of 211.

From within came an instant response in a harsh, croaking tone: "Who is it?"

Johnny replied, "My name's Donne. The barkeep in the Acme told me—"

The voice broke in, "If your name ain't Donne I'm advisin' you stay outside. If it is—the door's unlocked. Turn the knob and push."

Again Johnny hesitated. There was something mighty unusual about all this. Then he shrugged impatient shoulders, turned the knob and pushed into the room. Directly opposite as he entered was an open window. A gas jet flared overhead. For a moment he failed to locate the room's occupant; then at the left side he suddenly saw an old man, sitting up in bed, a double-barreled shotgun cradled in his arms and aimed directly toward the doorway. Johnny's arms slowly raised above his head.

"Close that door and come in," the man in the bed said harshly. "And keep your mitts plenty high!"

MURDER!

JOHNNY DIDN'T MOVE. A SLOW SMILE CROSSED HIS face. "I can't do two things at once," he said quietly. "If I close the door I've got to lower one arm."

The elderly man in the bed nodded. "There's logic in that," he conceded. "All right, close the door. But move mighty circumspect, Mister Donne. I'm not taking chances." Johnny closed the door at his back. The man in the bed went on, "Come over—closer to the light, where I can get a sight of you."

Johnny came closer. Slowly the gun in the man's hands dropped to the bed. "You're all right, I reckon. I just couldn't risk anybody but you, Donne, coming through that door." He sank slowly back to the pillows propped behind his shoulders and a slow breath of relief and strain whistled through his thin lips. For several minutes he didn't speak. Johnny remained standing in the center of the room, gazing on the occupant of the bed who now lay with his eyes closed. Now that Johnny had a good look at him he didn't seem so elderly as at first. The man appeared to be in his early fifties, though his hair was snow-white and his face deeply lined. Either he had been severely wounded at some recent

10

date or he'd been undergoing a long siege of sickness.

After a time the sick man opened his eyes. "You still standing? Sit down, Donne. Don't pay no attention to me. Sorry to have greeted you the way I did, but there's some coyotes just aching to rub me out. One of the scuts dang nigh did. Got me unawares. Still carrying the bullet under my ribs. Doc claims he don't dare take it out until I'm stronger. He's been calling every day—" He broke off, then, "I suppose you were told to ask for Mr. Smith downstairs. My name's Aldrich—George Aldrich."

"Glad to know you, Mr. Aldrich. Before we go too deep into this job I understand you're offering, I'm wanting to know if it's strictly within the law."

Aldrich's bleak blue eyes bored into Johnny's. "Suppose it wasn't, but that I offered you a fifty-fifty cut on thirty thousand dollars—hey! wait a minute! Where you going?"

Johnny had already started toward the door. "I wouldn't take a fifty-fifty cut on a million if it wasn't on the level," he stated flatly.

Aldrich nodded, satisfied. "That's the talk I want to hear. I was just testing you out, son. Yeah, you sound like the Johnny Donne I was told about."

Johnny tensed. "Who told you about me? I just answered your ad in the *Banner-Independent*."

"That ad was aimed at you, Johnny. I hoped to get you. If I couldn't get you I'd had to take somebody else, but—"

"Who told you about me?" Johnny persisted.

"Steve Sharples—your old boss in the Border Rangers. Steve and I were pards, a good many years back—"

"I suppose he told you I resigned from the Rangers—"

11

certain lines had been tightening about Johnny's lips—"under pressure."

George Aldrich nodded. "He told me about it—"

"Told you I was a suspected murderer?" The words came hard for Johnny.

"Steve told me you had been acquitted. His word is good enough for me—"

"I'm not making any explanations now," Johnny said tensely.

"Nobody is asking any, son. Relax and sit down, will you? I've a story to tell you—and it doesn't have anything to do with your past life."

Somewhat reluctantly Johnny looked around for a chair. One stood beyond the door against the wall. Removing his gray Stetson, he tossed it on top of a dresser standing near the window. For the first time he noticed on top of the dresser a steeple-crowned black Mexican sombrero. He wondered if it were Aldrich's habit to wear Mex sombreros, then decided against that thought as his eyes fell on a Stetson not unlike his own, suspended from a hook on the wall above the bed. George Aldrich's eyes were again closed, and he breathed as though with an effort. Johnny waited for him to resume the conversation.

Two or three minutes ticked off, then Aldrich opened his eyes. "Don't mind me, son. I get sort of dizzy spells now and then, get to feeling kind of weak and faint, and I have to stop until my breath catches up . . . Yeah, Steve Sharples told me about you being framed—"

"There was never any proof of that." Johnny spoke honestly.

"So far as Steve was concerned proof wa'n't necessary. Like he told me, being on the wrong side of the fence politically, he couldn't have done as much for

12

you as he'd liked, but he did say there wa'n't any real need of you resigning from the force."

"I couldn't stay on," Johnny said slowly, "not with people suspecting me. It wouldn't have helped Steve's position either. He was willing to be at my back from hell to breakfast—he even wanted to resign with me. I had a tough time talking him out of that. I finally convinced him that he could do more good at the head of the Border Rangers than he could quitting because of my difficulties—cripes! you're not interested in my troubles. I'm waiting to hear about this job you're offering."

Aldrich nodded slowly. "I'll get on with it. It's this way. I needed a man to handle what I had in mind, so I took a trip over to Austin to see Steve Sharples and ask who he'd recommend. Steve thought of you instanter—said you were the best man he knew of for such a job—"

"The same being?"

"—but that he didn't know where to find you," Aldrich went on, without noticing the interruption. "Steve told me you'd refused a couple of jobs with cattle associations and a dang nice setup with the Pinkerton people—"

Johnny broke in earnestly, "Shucks! I couldn't take those jobs, not until I'd cleared my own name to my own satisfaction. Just because a jury brings in a verdict of 'Not guilty' is no sign a man is clear all around."

"Know how you felt from what Steve told me," Aldrich said. "I wasn't sure whether you'd be interested in my proposition. Anyway, Steve sent out some telegrams and we finally discovered you were at the Circle-Y in northern New Mexico."

"I just used the Circle-Y as a base of supplies," Johnny said. "I was on my own, catching wild horses.

Put in a lot of months at that, then more time breaking 'em. Brought 'em to El Paso three days ago and sold 'em. Then—then I got tangled into a poker game and lost every cent. I hocked my hawg leg—"

He broke off in sudden surprise. Aldrich was laughing—laughing weakly, it is true, but still expressing keen enjoyment over something beyond Johnny's comprehension. Johnny waited for him to grow quiet, Aldrich finally subsided, but was so winded by his efforts all he could do was close his eyes and lay silent. Johnny waited in perplexity for Aldrich to speak.

After a few minutes the sick man continued, "I sent a telegram from Austin to the Circle-Y; they answered that you were driving a bunch of horses to El Paso. I came on here, figuring to find you when you got in. However, before you arrived something came up and I had to make a short trip out of town. By the time I returned I had this slug in my body. I'm under the doctor's care and he tells me I won't be able to move much for another six weeks. That means I have to have help worse than ever. I had Earnie Clark put that advertisement in the paper. Earnies's an old friend, but even he don't know what's up. He kept an eye peeled for your arrival and arranged other matters. Lying helpless here, I had to have a man with guts. I wanted you, but if I couldn't get you I was prepared to hire somebody else—provided he suited—"

Johnny broke in, "That advertisement wouldn't have interested me if I hadn't been broke."

Aldrich smiled. "I figured on that too. I knew you'd have to be broke before you'd listen to me. I had Earnie arrange to have your horse stolen—wait! Keep your shirt on! I'll tell you what livery he's in. Then Earnie hired the four slickest cardsharps in El Paso—"

14

"By Godfrey!" Johnny exclaimed. "That game was crooked!"

A ghost of a chuckle escaped Aldrich's lips. "Don't feel put out, Johnny. Those four aren't ordinary tinhorns. They're artists. No need of cheap tricks or marked cards with them. They're smooth. They just took you on for the fun of it."

Johnny was on his feet now, his cheeks flaming. "If you care to tell me why you did this—" he commenced.

Aldrich lay back again, eyes closed. One hand lifted feebly to detain Johnny. Reluctantly Johnny sat down. Finally Aldrich opened his eyes and said, "You've already stated you wouldn't have considered my job if you hadn't been broke. Well, I had to have you broke. I have the money you lost and will return it to you. You must admit, after the trouble I've gone to, that I deserve some consideration, before you leave without hearing my proposition. And don't forget, a fifty-fifty cut on thirty thousand isn't pin money, especially when it's all legal and aboveboard."

Johnny cooled down under the persuasion of Aldrich's words. He smiled, conceding, "You're right. Even if I never got back my money that poker lesson was sure worth it. Tell your story, Mr. Aldrich. You've hired a hand for so long as things are on the square. The instant anything smells crooked I'll step out."

Aldrich nodded with satisfaction. "I figured if I could get you to listen to me you'd take the job." With an effort he pushed the shotgun to one side and reached under his pillow to produce a wallet from which he extracted a wad of bills. "Here, take this mazuma. It's your poker losses and some over to cover expenses." Aldrich seemed relieved that Johnny's good nature had been restored. He added, "I've got a hunch we might

15

become good friends."

Johnny crossed the room, accepted the bills, and slid them into a trousers pocket. Aldrich watched him closely and when Johnny resumed his chair and breathed a sigh of relief.

"I half expected," Aldrich said, "that you might just take your poker losses and then walk out on me."

"I gave my word I'd hire on with you. I aim to keep that word."

"You sound like Steve Sharples said you would," Aldrich replied. "What I'm going to ask you to do will require nerve—" He broke off suddenly. "Do you hear anybody out in the hall?"

Johnny shook his head, rose and opened the door. His gaze ran along the corridor; it appeared deserted, with all doors closed on either side. The gas jet, suspended from the ceiling, wavered in the breeze from the open door at the end of the hall. Johnny returned to the room, closing the door. "No one there," he said.

Aldrich grumbled. "I must have imagined it. I'm getting spooky as an old woman of late." His words came rather faintly and he laid aside the shotgun he had seized up.

"Take it easy," Johnny suggested sympathetically.

"This is all a mite too much for a man in my condition," Aldrich gasped, sinking back on his pillows. "Well, I'll get along with my story—" Again he stopped. After a minute his voice came stronger and he gestured toward the black Mexican sombrero on the dresser. "A man I thought a heap of gave me that bonnet—and was killed from ambush a few minutes later, a few miles outside of El Paso. The same cowardly coyote nearly got me too. I didn't dare bring the police into the matter; I had to send money and an

16

anonymous note to an undertaker to have my—my friend buried. You'll understand it all—when I—tell you."

His voice failed once more. Beads of sweat stood out on his forehead and his breathing was hard. "I'll—talk more—in a—few minutes." The words came scarcely above a whisper.

"Take it easy," Johnny said quickly. "There's no hurry. We've got all night."

Aldrich nodded weakly and sank back on his pillows. After a moment his eyes closed. His breathing came easier, but he didn't reopen his eyes. Quite suddenly it occurred to Johnny that Aldrich had slipped into sleep.

"Poor cuss," Johnny mused. "He's right close to being worn out. I wonder if I should go away and come back tomorrow. Nope, I'd better not do that. He'll probably wake up in a few minutes. I'll just wait until he feels more like talking. I'd sure like to know just what his story is."

Five minutes passed. Johnny sat, silently waiting. His eyes roved about the room. Seeing the black sombrero on the dresser, he tiptoed across to get it, then returned to his chair again. The light at the gas jet hissed and flickered, while Johnny examined the hat. It was of black felt, of the type usually worn by the higher-class Mexicans. The crown was high, dented on either side and covered with a floral design in red-and-white silk embroidery and tiny silver sequins. The wide brim, curved upward all around, was similarly embellished. The inside of the crown was lined with white silk, somewhat stained now, and the sweatband showed evidence of considerable wear at some time or other. Johnny looked the hat over, admiring the braided silk cord, in red, around the outside of the crown; then his

17

interest languished.

Ten minutes more slipped past with Aldrich showing no sign of awakening. He was breathing deep and easily now.

Johnny considered, he sure seems to need that sleep. I'd certain like to roll a cigarette, but I'm afraid the scratching of a match might awaken him. I wouldn't want to disturb him. I've got plenty of time anyway.

Johnny sat on his chair, elbows on knees, idly twirling the black sombrero between his legs. Except for the hissing gas jet and the sleeper's deep breathing there wasn't a sound to be heard in the room. Distant noises from the town carried faintly to Johnny's hearing. A streetcar clanged over on San Antonio Street. Somewhere a couple of men were yelling rather drunkenly, but their remarks couldn't be distinguished. Probably the sounds issued from that saloon Johnny had noticed two doors away from the Pierdon Hotel when he was entering the building.

Once he thought he heard a slight noise out in the hall, but when he tensed his hearing the sound wasn't repeated and he figured he must have been mistaken. Another five minutes ticked off with no change in Aldrich's position. Johnny settled back in his chair a trifle impatiently. His gaze roved about the room, then suddenly stopped at the open transom above the door.

Johnny's chair was to the left of the door, close to the wall, not within eye range of anyone peering through the transom. But at that instant he wasn't thinking of who might be looking into the room. It was the Colt six-shooter, clutched in a muscular fist, that held his attention. The barrel of the gun was just moving past the opened transom glass and being directed down toward the sleeping Aldrich.

"Aldrich!" Johnny exclaimed, coming to his feet.

The warning came too late. The six-shooter's savage roar shook the hotel room. Black smoke curled about the door. Johnny heard Aldrich groan, half rise and then sink back. The six-shooter dropped to the floor, inside the room, as the murderous hand released its grip.

Johnny whipped open the door. The hall was dark now. Someone had extinguished the gas jet. Johnny plunged into the hall—and went sprawling over the chair on which the murderer had stood to fire his killer's bullet. Even as Johnny struggled up he heard footsteps dying away in the alley back of the hotel.

Voices could be heard downstairs in the hotel now. Johnny leaped to the bed. A huge red stain was spreading swiftly on Aldrich's left breast. The man's eyes were closed. Momentarily they opened as he gasped, "Johnny—my daughter will—"

And that was all. Aldrich's head fell to one side. For just an instant Johnny stood as one stunned. Aldrich was dead. The assassin's gun lay there on the floor. In his pocket Johnny already held money that had come from Aldrich. It would look like murder and robbery both to the police when they arrived.

Johnny groaned. "And there's one murder hanging over me now that's never been cleared up."

The voices downstairs were louder now, more excitable. The clerk had probably sent for the police. Johnny was in a quandary. "They'll pin this on me sure," he whispered hoarsely to himself. "In prison I wouldn't be able to do a thing to help Aldrich—or the cause he spoke of. Free, I can work things out in my own way. I'd never have a chance to explain things. I'd better get going. I hate to run out like this—but I'd better get going."

Steps were already sounding on the staircase. Johnny whirled, closed the door as softly as possible. For just a brief instant he glanced at Aldrich. Words came to his lips. "I took a job with you, George Aldrich. I aim to see it through."

Like a flash he whirled toward the open window in the outside wall. An instant later he had dropped to the soft earth below. Above he could hear voices in the room from which he had just descended. He hesitated just a moment, getting his bearings after the shock of landing. To his right was an adobe building of some sort, dark at present, though he guessed it was a home. Anyway, it felt like a flower garden into which he'd dropped. At the rear was the alley which passed back of the hotel. In front was San Francisco Street, along which men were now hurrying, talking excitedly. A crowd had gathered about the front of the hotel.

Swiftly Johnny made his way toward the street and mingled with the crowd. If anyone saw him emerge from the passageway between the Pierdon Hotel and the adjacent adobe building no thought was given the matter. Everyone in the crowd was talking too excitedly to be interested in anyone else. Johnny asked a man in the gathering what had happened. The fellow replied shortly that he heard a man had been shot. From the entrance of the Pierdon the hotel clerk appeared and was the immediate butt of several questions.

"A man named Smith was just shot in his room," the clerk said nervously. "No—no—they didn't catch the murderer. There was a door at the end of the hall upstairs. He must have escaped that way and down through the alley . . ."

Johnny didn't wait to hear more. He turned swiftly and made his way down the street, heading in the direction of the nearest railroad depot. As he hurried along he was suddenly aware that he still clutched in one hand the black sombrero.

"Well I'll be damned," he muttered. "Imagine me holding onto this Mex top-piece all this time!"

He was about to toss it into the shadowy areaway between two buildings, when it occurred to him that it would be found and might be recognized as Aldrich's property. And then another thought struck Johnny: "I left my own Stet hat up in Aldrich's room. That will make a perfectly elegant clue for the police. Oh well, I need a hat anyway. I'd better hang onto this."

He hurried along and within a short time neared the railroad depot. The tracks were to his left, and just pulling out was a long line of T.N. & A.S. freight cars. Right then it made no difference to Johnny which way the train was headed; he intended to be on it. The locomotive snorted past, belching steam and smoke. Several boxcars rattled and lurched as the train worked to pick up speed. Johnny broke into a run. Someone near the depot yelled at him, but Johnny couldn't distinguish the words. He put an extra burst into his sprint and closed in on the nearest boxcar. His fingers felt for and found the rungs of the iron ladder at the end of the boxcar. His grip tightened, his feet were whipped from the earth, then he commenced the climb to the top as a cloud of smoke, swept back from the locomotive, enveloped his movements.

"YOU'RE COVERED!"

SIX WEEKS HAD PASSED SINCE THE MURDER OF George Aldrich in El Paso and as many hundred miles now lay between Johnny Donne and the scene of that killing. He had crossed the ridge of the Mimbreno Mountains shortly past noon, reined his roan pony down the treacherous slopes during the ensuing hours and by the time the sun was dipping low on the western horizon had started to make a dry camp on the edge of an arroyo heavily covered with thick brush. The Heiser saddle he stripped from the pony's back looked fairly new. For that matter, Johnny hadn't owned the horse long. He still wore the denim overalls, high-heeled cowman's boots and shirt he had worn in El Paso. On his head was the red-and-white embroidered black sombrero which he had found fitted perfectly. Wide cartridge belts crisscrossed Johnny's lean hips and two holsters were weighted down by an efficient-looking pair of Colt's forty-five six-shooters. The guns hadn't been new when Johnny bought them, he had preferred secondhand guns, well broken in, so long as they were in tiptop condition.

He stood, absentmindedly rubbing down the pony's back with the saddle blanket, then, after a time, staked the beast out beneath a cottonwood tree not far from where he intended to spread his camp. From his blanket roll he produced some fairly fresh biscuits and strips of beef which he broiled on sticks above a small fire. A tin can, that had contained beans at some recent date, served in lieu of a coffeepot, after Johnny had filled it from a paper sack of coffee and some water from his canteen.

With supper out of the way Johnny sat by his fire and commenced to roll a cigarette. By this time the sun had long since descended and the first stars had commenced to wink into being in the velvety black sky above. Johnny followed his first cigarette with a second and crouched closer to his fire. A cool breeze had sprung up with the coming of darkness, and Johnny was grateful for the leaping warmth of the flames as they danced briskly in the night air, reflecting dull lights on the dust-laden leaves of the scrub oak and other brush at his rear.

Johnny sighed thoughtfully and tossed a cigarette butt to the glowing embers. He shoved the black sombrero to the back of his head. By now a small dark mustache adorned his upper lip, and with the Mexican sombrero and his black hair he might have been taken for a Latin American—a rather handsome individual of that type, even though his face was somewhat lined by the strain of the past six weeks.

"Well, I reckon I might as well put out my fire and roll into blankets," he mused and then stopped, listening intently. But there was nothing to be heard but the chirping of a cricket back in the brush. He reached to his vest pocket and decided to roll a final cigarette. The cigarette rolled and lighted, he sat as before, at ease on his blanket, his mind teeming with speculation. Somewhere out of the surrounding silence a night bird sang three quick liquid notes and was quiet again.

Five minutes passed and then ten. Johnny disposed of his cigarette butt once more. He leaned forward, as though adjusting the corner of the blanket on which he was seated. When he resumed his sitting position the butt of a six-shooter was cradled in his right fist. The flames of his fire died down, the glow from the embers casting red lights on his features.

Abruptly, from the darkness at his rear, a voice drawled, "You'd better reach for the sky, Donne. You're covered!"

Johnny replied softly, without turning his head, "Maybe that works two ways, mister."

"Huh! What do you mean? You are Donne, aren't you?"

"The name's correct. But if I'm covered so are you. Your horse slipped on that rocky slope back a spell. I've been waiting to see who was coming. I've been ready too. When you started pushing through that brush back of me I sort of drew a bead on that general terrain—"

A kind of gasping sound interrupted. "But—but I'm back of you—"

"My gun barrel"—Johnny chuckled—"is pointing in your general direction from under my left armpit. I might miss my aim, but I'm betting a plugged peso I'll come mighty close, in case you decide to take a chance."

There was a momentary silence from the unseen speaker, then an annoyed clucking sound: "Tch, tch! So you knew I was coming all the time. I reckon I'll have to practice my trailing some more—I mean my shadowing."

"Whatever you mean"—Johnny grinned into the firelight—"you've got to admit we're deadlocked right now. We're both covered. What you aiming to do about it?"

"It's a problem, ain't it? I wish I could see your gun barrel and make sure it's pointing my direction."

"It is." Johnny chuckled. "It wasn't so accurate at first, but the sound of your voice has helped me to correct my range."

"By damn!" The speaker sounded dismayed. "I was

afraid of something like this when I took to houndin' you down."

"Look," Johnny pointed out; "it's a deadlock. You can't shoot me without getting potted yourself. Suppose we declare a truce. Put your gun away and come in and talk it over."

"Well, that's an idea anyway." The unseen man's voice sounded rather weary. "Besides, I'm getting plumb tired crouching in this brush. I'd like to stretch out. I'm comin' in."

"Put your gun away," Johnny warned quickly.

"It's already put away. It was getting sort of heavy to hold anyway." Steps sounded through the brush, a twig snapped.

Johnny tossed some sticks of greasewood on the bed of coals before him. The greasewood made sputtering sounds, then caught and commenced to burn briskly. In the light from the flames Johnny sized up the man who had stepped into the open, then slid his own six-shooter into holster.

The newcomer had sleepy-looking blue eyes and tousled yellow hair under his shoved-back Stetson. He was chunkily built, with a barrel-like torso and broad shoulders. His legs were bowed and his clothing was that of a cowpuncher. At his right thigh was a forty-five Colt gun and on his vest was a badge of some shiny metal. With scarcely a glance at Johnny he dropped down in a sprawling position by the fire. "Imagine" — he yawned sleepily—"getting caught like this the first time you make an arrest. Oh well"—he breathed a long sigh of relief—"I'd just have to make that long ride back with you anyway."

Johnny smiled and looked at his visitor. "May I ask to whom I'm indebted for this visit?" he queried politely.

There was another jawbreaking yawn. "I'm Detective Hartigan. If you want my full name it's Humboldt Drummond Hartigan."

"Humboldt Drummond—Say, it's a wonder folks don't call you Humdrum for short."

"They do"—lazily—"I figured you'd think of it."

Johnny said gravely, "Glad to meet you, Humdrum. My name's Donne, as you already guessed."

"Uh-huh. Johnny Donne. Some folks used to call you Johnny Don, back in the days when you were in the Border Rangers. The Mexes down in that country called you Don Johnny, didn't they?"

"Seems you know quite a bit about me," Johnny said.

"Sure, that's part of my training to become a detective. It comes under lesson two—or maybe it was lesson one. 'Students of criminology should always acquaint themselves with the past history of suspected criminals.' Of course I knew about you before I became a detective. You did right good work with the Rangers, and I used to read every word the papers said about you."

Maybe we'd better not go into that," Johnny said a trifle grimly.

"That's all right with me," Humdrum Hartigan said easily. "Though it was you that gave me the idea of becoming a detective. I used to punch cows on the Beartrap outfit, over east of Waco, but that was sort of hard work and the foreman was always pushing me to work harder. He claimed all I wanted to do was sleep—"

Johnny grinned. "Maybe he had something on his side. Right now you don't look but half awake."

Humdrum yawned. "Ain't no law against sleeping, is there? Me, I crave lots of rest. Before I was called

26

Humdrum my nickname was Horizontal. You know I like to stretch out—"

"Explanations aren't necessary," Johnny said dryly.

"So now you understand why I turned detective."

"You working for Pinkerton or some smaller outfit?"

Humdrum shook his head. "Neither. I'm on my own."

"But where do you get your authority?"

"From the correspondence course I subscribed to. You see—"

Johnny's jaw dropped, then he burst out, "You telling me you're just a mail-order detective?"

Humdrum's eyes opened a little wider and he managed to look up at Johnny. "Got my badge, ain't I? I got a dee-ploma, too, but I didn't bring it with me. Sure, it was one morning when that Beartrap foreman was riding me specially hard that I happened to notice an advertisement in the *Police Gazette,* telling how to learn to be a detective in ten easy lessons, so that night I sent my money off for the complete course."

By this time Johnny was breathing easier. He said in some amusement, "I'll bet it was interesting studying."

"Sure was. They tell you all about disguises and furnish equipment. The handcuffs are sort of heavy so I don't bother to carry 'em. This badge I got on is genuwine silver plate. The detective company sent a gun, too, but I never could get used to such a peewee shootin' iron. One day I was comparin' barrels and I shoved that peewee barrel right into the muzzle of my forty-five. Somehow, by accident, I pulled my trigger. Do you know I never could find that peewee gun again?"

Johnny was laughing openly by this time. "It's best to stick to the old forty-five, Humdrum."

Humdrum nodded seriously. "Exactly the way I

figured it. No use trying to learn too many new things at once. Once I've mastered the easy things then I can go on with the harder subjects. Look!" He came to a sitting position, turned the brim of his Stetson up in front, yanked a lock of straw-colored hair over his forehead and stuck the fingers of one hand inside his shirt. "Now who do I look like?"

Johnny grinned. "Like Humdrum Hartigan scratching his stomach."

"Shucks!" Humdrum looked disappointed. "This is one of my disguises. I'm supposed to look like Napoleon." From somewhere inside his shirt he produced a set of false Vandyke whiskers. After slicking his hair into something resembling a neat part he slipped the wire earpieces of the whiskers into place and asked, "Now who do I represent?"

"You still look like Humdrum Hartigan—only with a moth-eaten beard."

"Hang the luck," Humdrum said disgruntledly. "I was hopin' you'd tell me I resembled the Czar of Roosia."

"Maybe you do," Johnny conceded with a chuckle. "I never saw the gent so there's no telling."

Humdrum said gratefully, "That would make a difference, you not knowing him wouldn't it? I've got some more disguises in my bedroll on my saddle, but that's too far to go for 'em right now." He sank back on the earth, eying Johnny sleepily.

"If you're planning to spend the night," Johnny suggested, "maybe you want to bring your horse in."

Humdrum shook his head. "My bronc's pegged out all right. Why wouldn't I spend the night? We had a truce but I still kind of figure you're my prisoner. I tracked you down, didn't I? Anyway, the night was made for sleeping. I note you got an extra blanket."

28

"How long since you had supper?"

Humdrum wasn't sure about that. "I've been grabbing a snatch on and off. Too much trouble to cook things."

Johnny found some biscuits and beef. He cooked the latter and boiled fresh coffee, saying, "I hope this coffee won't keep you awake."

"I don't figure it will," Humdrum said seriously. He sat up and started to eat with evident relish.

"How long have you been trailing me?" Johnny asked.

"Since the night George Aldrich was killed. I was in El Paso that night, and right quick I commenced picking up clues," Humdrum said between mouthfuls of beef and biscuit. "The clerk at the Pierdon Hotel told me it was a cowman who had visited Aldrich. While the police of El Paso were running around looking for clues I did some thinking. I know a cowman wouldn't want to stay in town; he'd head for open country where he could feel at home. There was a T.N. & A.S. freight pulled out shortly after the killing. I figured you'd caught that. I was right. A man of your description was seen in Gallup. I picked up your trail there. About the time you disappeared from Gallup a train was leaving for El Paso. I swung back to El Paso and picked up more information—"

"I backtracked and hung around El Paso a spell trying to learn what I could pick up regarding Aldrich or who did the shooting."

"You didn't, eh?" A sharper tone had entered Humdrum's voice.

"I certainly did not," Johnny said definitely.

Humdrum breathed a long sigh of relief. "I couldn't believe it was you," he confessed. "Your past rep proved that to me, but I thought maybe you might know

29

something about it."

Johnny told Humdrum briefly what had happened in El Paso.

Humdrum nodded and drank the last of his coffee. "You led me quite a chase for a spell. You were always circling wide and swinging back. You stopped in various towns—Gunsight, Saddleburg, Torvo Tanks— no need of me telling *you* though."

"I was figuring to throw off anybody that might be trailing me," Johnny said ruefully. "I didn't quite succeed, I reckon. I ran down a couple of fruitless clues. Besides, I wanted to make sure of being free before I tackled the job of locating Aldrich's murderer. I wonder how many more hombres are trailing me."

"I'm the only one," Humdrum said. "They're still searching around El Paso for the murderer. Dumb clucks. Of course"—modestly—"I've got the advantage of being a trained detective . . . Anyway, a few days ago you stopped at a town named Gramma and bought yourself a roan pony. I reckon you were tired of riding railroad cars. You headed up into the Mimbreno Mountains. I followed and—well, I caught up with you tonight."

Johnny shook his head in some wonder. "Humdrum, you deserve a heap of praise. You've hung to my trail like a burr in a bronc's tail. Just because a man likes to sleep is no sign his head doesn't keep on working."

"That's exactly what I was always telling that Beartrap foreman," Humdrum said earnestly, "but he'd never see things my way. What you going to do next?"

"I'm heading for Spearhead Wells—"

"Aldrich's town?"

Johnny nodded. "Maybe I can pick up some clues there. Like I told you, before he was killed George

30

Aldrich hired me to do a job. I don't know yet what the job is, but I aim to see it through. Somebody had shot him because of the job, I feel quite sure of that. Some scut murdered him for the same reason. This black sombrero I'm wearing may have something to do with it. I've a hunch it has. But the whole business is a problem I can't work out. I've got to go to Spearhead Wells."

Humdrum nodded sleepily. "That may be risky."

"I've got to chance it."

"The papers in El Paso at the time of the murder gave your name. The evidence pointed toward you."

"Circumstantial evidence. You've probably heard I was a victim of circumstantial evidence once before. Maybe I'll tell you about that sometime. Yes, I saw copies of the El Paso newspapers. That Acme bartender, Earnie Clark, told the police my name and that he had directed me to Aldrich's hotel, but he didn't know why Aldrich wanted to hire a man. It was from what Clark told the newspapers that I learned where Aldrich was from—Spearhead Wells. Luckily the news has died out a heap. The authorities won't be so keen on my trail. Maybe I'll have some luck learning things in Spearhead Wells."

Humdrum yawned. "Let's hope so."

"Unless"—Johnny smiled thinly—"you're figuring to take me back to El Paso as your prisoner."

Humdrum stated drowsily, "I'm aiming to do just that, but we'll make the journey by way of Spearhead Wells. You're in my custody, but I ain't in no hurry to make that long trip back. I've lost a heap of sleep, trailin' you around, and I've got to make it up someplace. It might as well be in Spearhead Wells."

"But what are you going to do?"

31

"Me?" A certain indignation filtered through Humdrum's torpid manner. "Cripes! Ain't I lending you the advantage of my valuable detective training? What more do you want?"

Johnny put out his hand. Humdrum grasped it firmly.

"I'm glad we've got that settled," Humdrum drawled lazily. "Next time you shove your hand over this way put a blanket in it. I feel a nap coming on. Goo' night."

Less than five minutes later Humdrum was snoring in one of Johnny's blankets. Johnny sat by the dying fire a short time longer, then spread his own bed. The last thought in his mind as he drifted off to sleep that night concerned Humdrum Hartigan: the mail-order detective wasn't such a sleepy clown as he pretended to be. "And," Johnny mused with some satisfaction, "I may need a man like that at my back before long."

SHEER NERVE

THE TWO RIDERS WEREN'T MORE THAN TEN OR TWELVE miles out of Spearhead Wells by the time the following day's sun had wheeled far to the west and started to dip toward the higher peaks of the Sangre de Santos Range. The Mimbreno Mountains were far to their rear now, only dimly visible in the grayish-purple range haze. Johnny and Humdrum were covered with dust. The day had been hot, and Johnny's roan and Humdrum's wiry gray pony were streaked with rivulets of sweat. Johnny's features appeared rather drawn; he wondered what lay ahead of him. Most of the day Humdrum had sat slumped in his saddle, apparently dozing.

It was rolling grass country through which the two were passing. There was a well-defined trail leading to

Spearhead Wells, easy to follow, though now and then huge outcroppings of granite barred the way and forced the riders to swing in a wide arc on the trail. Occasional clumps of prickly pear and gray-green sage dotted the surrounding country. Off to the south a few miles lay the Mexican border line. To the north stretched a long valley laying between the Mimbreno Mountains on the east and the Sangre de Santos Range on the west. Once Johnny spied, a short distance away, a bunch of white-faced Hereford cattle, bearing the Rafter-N brand. The two men hadn't passed a rider all day long. It was plain the country hereabouts wasn't thickly populated.

The ponies trotted on, kicking up occasional clouds of dust to float away in the hot air. Once as the riders climbed a long slope and finally reached the crest Johnny saw, several ridges beyond, a couple of roof tops.

"That must be Spearhead Wells," he observed.

By the time Humdrum aroused himself and opened his eyes the horses had once more started down a long slope, heading toward the next rise of ground.

"Probably is," Humdrum grunted with no great show of interest. He yawned and stretched, eyed Johnny sleepily a moment and observed, "No need of you waking me up. It's likely just the same as a lot of other towns."

"I don't figure it will be the same for me," Johnny said grimly.

Humdrum didn't reply. After a moment he unpinned the detective badge from his vest and stuck it into a pocket.

Johnny said "Getting ready to put on another disguise, or afraid your authority won't be recognized?"

"I figure a disguise is necessary, but there won't be

any make-up needed. I'll just pretend I'm a cow poke, traveling through the country. That'll do for both of us."

"I hope it will do for me." Johnny frowned. "I still don't know exactly what I intend to do when we hit Spearhead Wells. Somebody will spot me as Johnny Donne and I'm sure to be arrested. Or something worse. Aldrich's murder may have been forgotten by this time in a lot of towns, but his own town will still be remembering—"

"I've been thinking—" Humdrum commenced.

Johnny interrupted ironically, "Now I could have sworn you were sound asleep most of today."

"Thinking and sleeping is something I can do at the same time," Humdrum said placidly. "It's this way, in all the newspaper accounts covering Aldrich's murder I didn't see any pictures of you—"

"Haven't had a picture taken since I was a kid about ten years old."

"That's fine. The newspapers gave a description, of course, but that same description could have fitted any number of men. I know I'd never have known you. That mustache you've raised probably changes your appearance a heap. I figure you look a few years older than the description said. Of course if we ride into town and you give out your name as Johnny Donne you'll run smack dab into trouble. Suppose I just call you Don Johnny. Folks will maybe think you're a Mex. You sort of look like one of these good-looking Mex boys I've seen down below the border—specially with that black sombrero."

Johnny scowled. "Mexicans don't generally have gray eyes."

Humdrum qualified that statement. "Over Tucson way," he said, "I've seen some right good-looking

34

Mexican girls with gray and blue both. Anyway"—he yawned widely—"you got any better plan to offer?"

Johnny thought a time and finally sighed. "I reckon I haven't. I could take a completely different name, of course, but I'm danged if I like the idea. Never did like sailing under false colors. We'll let it ride as is."

Humdrum nodded and again slumped in his saddle. "Wake me up when we hit town," he said drowsily, his eyes dropping shut.

The ponies jogged on for another three quarters of an hour. Abruptly, rounding the shoulder of a hill, Johnny saw a squat adobe house. The trail looked more traveled now. Farther on more adobes appeared, and then a whole string of them on either side of the road. The riders passed a frame shack with a couple of Mexicans squatted near the doorway. Lights were shining from doors and windows now. The sun had dropped behind the Sangre de Santos.

"Prop those eyelids open, Humdrum," Johnny announced. "We're here."

Humdrum straightened in his saddle. "I know it. I smelled food cooking in a couple of those places we passed. Y'know, I like to eat almost as much as I do to sleep."

"Cowboy, what an eater you must be!" Johnny grinned.

They were traveling along the main street of Spearhead Wells now. On either side were high, false-fronted wooden buildings, separated here and there by structures constructed of rock and adobe. There were several saloons, a couple of general stores, a gun-and-saddle shop, a small place whose sign proclaimed it to be the Boston Tonsorial Parlor, a photo gallery and several other houses of commercial enterprise. A hotel

35

termed the Cowman's Rest Hotel caught Johnny's eyes. A couple of cross streets intersected the main thoroughfare, and Johnny guessed the back streets were given over to the residential district. Lights shone from doors and windows all along the way. It was quite dark by this time.

"Larger town than I expected," Johnny commented to his companion. "Quite a number of horses and wagons at the hitch racks. Looks plumb busy."

"That suits me," Humdrum commented. "The larger and busier the town the less notice folks will take of you. At the same time there should be more folks to tell what they know."

"About what?"

"About Aldrich, of course. What did we come here for?"

"You're right, Humdrum. I just thought you were talking about something in particular."

Humdrum frowned. "You keep acting like I know more than I do all the time."

Johnny grinned through the darkness. "You couldn't."

"I couldn't what?" Humdrum sounded puzzled.

"Know more than you do. Cripes! Can't you stay awake long enough to remember what we're talking about?"

"I ain't sure if I can or not unless I get a drink and something to eat right soon. I hope that hotel we passed has good beds."

"You figuring to stay there?"

"I'm figuring to get a drink and chow first. Steer your bronc over to the left there. See? Where it says Continental Saloon. Looks like it might be a good place to sluice down."

The two reined their ponies toward the tie rail Humdrum had indicated, dismounted and tossed the reins over the rail. Then they mounted the short flight of steps to the entrance, crossed a wide plank porch and pushed through the swinging doors. Within the Continental Saloon the bar ran along the left side of the room. The opposite side was given over to several round wooden tables and chairs. Above the tables the wall was decorated with a large number of pictures of burlesque actresses, race horses and prize fighters, the pictures having been torn from a pink-sheeted magazine quite popular in that day.

There weren't many customers in the saloon when the two entered. Three men in citizens' clothing stood talking real-estate values at the far end of the bar; at one of the card tables four cowpunchers played seven-up and consumed bottled beer. The bartender, a tall thin man with a sort of twisted build, left the conversation regarding real estate values and came quickly up the bar when Johnny and Humdrum entered.

"What'll it be, gents?" he asked.

Humdrum ordered a glass of whiskey; Johnny asked for beer. Bottles and glasses were set out. Johnny tasted his beer and decided it was good after the dusty day's ride. Humdrum sipped his whiskey.

"Strangers in town, aren't you?" the barkeep asked.

Johnny shook his head. "We're not strange. The town is though."

The barkeep smiled genially. "Just passing through?"

Humdrum nodded and yawned sleepily. "Been out seeing the country a mite. Sort of a vacation, y'know. We wouldn't mind resting up here a couple of days, if there was a good place to stay."

"You'll like Spearhead Wells," the bartender said.

"The town is growing fast. It's new country, hereabouts, to some extent. Stockmen are just finding out how good the grazing is. If you stay I can recommend the hotel. There's a few boardinghouses too. Most folks like the hotel restaurant, though we got some restaurants all along Main Street that can't be beat—"

Humdrum chuckled. "You sound like a chamber of commerce."

"I'm the president of our local town-improvement-and-business society," the bartender said proudly. "My name's Jones—Corkscrew Jones, they call me. Sort of got cracked up in a railroad accident one time, and when I left the hospital my whole frame had took on a sort of twisted look. That accident kind of knocked me out for hard labor, so I figured I might find me a good saloon to run. I found it here in Spearhead Wells. Course"—modestly—"my being president of the town improvement society don't mean anything. I just took the job 'cause nobody else wanted it. But I aim to do my part in building up this town to be a respectable community." Corkscrew Jones had sparse gray hair and a lined face. He extended a thin, bony hand across the bar.

"My name's Hartigan," Humdrum said, shaking the proffered hand. "Shake with my friend, Don Johnny."

"Glad to meet you, Mister Donshawnee," beamed Corkscrew Jones. "Now if you two are interested in going into business here in Spearhead—"

"My name—" Johnny commenced a correction, then paused abruptly as Humdrum's booted toe came into violent contact with his shin.

"Just call him Johnny." Humdrum was smiling sleepily at the bartender. "He don't care to be mistered."

"Sure, Johnny. Sure, Mister Hartigan—"

38

"My friends call me Humdrum," Hartigan said. "But I'm danged if I know why."

"Stay in town long enough," Jones suggested, "and maybe we'll find out. How about a drink on the house?"

Johnny shook his head. "I've had enough before supper. Humdrum, what say we drift along and sample the chow at the hotel restaurant?"

Humdrum nodded. They said "S'long" to Corkscrew Jones and turned toward the doorway. At that moment the swinging doors parted abruptly to allow the entrance of a wiry, medium-sized man in denims, high-heeled boots and a slouch-brimmed sombrero of indiscriminate color. His face was hard and lined; a tousled wisp of iron-gray hair fell across his right eyebrow. A well-worn cartridge belt slanted across the man's lean hips; a brown paper cigarette jutted from one corner of his thin mouth. A certain unsteadiness in the man's swaggering entrance attested an overindulgence in strong drink as he rocked toward the bar.

Johnny and Humdrum were halfway to the door when the newcomer spied them. He stopped directly in their path, peering at them from small, bloodshot eyes. "You two is strangers here, ain't you?" he growled abruptly.

Cockscrew Jones called quickly from the bar: "They're friends of mine, Ogallala. Let 'em be."

"Yes, we're strangers here," Johnny said quietly. "What about it?"

"None of yore lip, young feller," the man snapped. "We just like to know who is coming and going—" He stopped short, his gaze falling on Johnny's steeple-crowned black sombrero. His small eyes opened wider. "Sa-ay, where did you get that hat?"

Johnny tensed. "Does it make any particular difference to you, mister?"

"Maybe it makes a hell of a lot of difference," the man snarled belligerently.

Corkscrew Jones cut in, "Don't you start any trouble, Ogallala. You know what Kane told you."

The man called Ogallala relaxed a trifle. "I ain't startin' any trouble, Corkscrew. If these hombres are friends of yours I'll buy 'em a drink."

Humdrum drawled, "Thanks, we've had our drink."

"I can stand another one," Johnny said suddenly. He was interested to know why the man was so inquisitive about the black sombrero. "I'm buying the drinks though."

The three returned to the bar. Johnny put down some money and said, "Call your shots."

Corkscrew Jones performed introductions: "This is Ogallala Mitchell. Ogallala's brother, Kane, owns the Spur-Bar outfit, west of here. Ogallala, shake hands with Humdrum Hartigan and Johnny Donshawnee—"

"My name—"Johnny again attempted to correct the barkeep.

Once more Humdrum interrupted, "Donshawnee and I are glad to know you Ogallala," he said with unusual quickness.

Ogallala Mitchell grunted a surly "Howdy" without offering to shake hands, then snapped at Corkscrew, "Trot out the bottle, Jones. You know my brand."

Corkscrew set out bottles and glasses. Johnny and Humdrum took cigars which they put into vest pockets. Corkscrew leaned across the bar while Ogallala was pouring a drink and whispered to Johnny: "Don't pay any attention to him. He gets on the prod easy and is considerable of a troublemaker around town. If it wasn't for his brother, Kane Mitchell—" He broke off suddenly.

40

Ogallala had downed his drink and was staring at Johnny's black sombrero. "I'm asking where you got that bonnet, Donshawnee," he growled.

Johnny shrugged his lean shoulders. It was none of Mitchell's business where he had procured the black sombrero—at least he didn't think it was. "Well, if you must know," Johnny said easily. "I bought it down in Chihuahua last year."

"That right?" Mitchell demanded.

"I'm telling you."

Ogallala Mitchell glared uncertainly. "Lemme see it," he snapped.

Johnny hesitated, then reluctantly gave in. After all, there was no sense in creating trouble now if it could be avoided. "Sure, look it over," Johnny said carelessly. He removed the black sombrero and handed it to Mitchell.

Mitchell seized the hat eagerly and commenced a close examination. He looked over the brim and crown, then bent his scrutiny on the braided silk band around the crown. He looked up suddenly at Johnny. "You say you bought this in Chihuahua?"

Johnny nodded.

"Where?"

"I don't remember exactly. Got it in a shop down there."

Mitchell said bluntly, "I think you're a liar."

Johnny flushed but kept his voice quiet. "You've been drinking, Mitchell, or you wouldn't talk like that. I'll take that hat now."

Mitchell drew back. "I'll buy this hat from you."

"I don't want to sell it."

"I'll give you twice what you paid, Donshawnee."

Johnny shook his head, put out one hand and took the sombrero from Mitchell's reluctant grasp. "I'm not

41

selling, Mitchell."

Johnny replaced the sombrero on his head and started toward the door, followed by Humdrum. And then he stopped short at Mitchell's next words:

"You'd better let me have that hat, Donshawnee. It was stole from me. I'm warning you!"

Turning, Johnny saw that Ogallala Mitchell had drawn his forty-five. "I'm warning you, Donshawnee," Mitchell repeated. "You give me that hat or else—"

"Ogallala!" Corkscrew exclaimed, "Put that gun away!"

"You keep out of this, Corkscrew," Mitchell snarled.

Humdrum spoke swiftly to Johnny, "Spread out. I'll get the drop on him while he is—"

"I'll handle this," Johnny said shortly. "It's my problem, Humdrum."

By this time the other customers in the saloon had moved quickly toward the back of the room, expecting shooting to break out at any instant.

Johnny was moving toward Ogallala now, his face stern and determined. Ogallala stood, back to bar, legs spread out a trifle, the gun in his right fist bearing directly on Johnny's middle.

Johnny advanced slowly, arms swinging at sides. He spoke quietly, "You'd better put that gun away, Mitchell. You're acting like a fool. If my hat was stolen from you you don't have to do this to get it back. Prove it was stolen from you and you've got the law on your side."

He was two steps nearer now, his eyes boring into Ogallala's. "If you weren't drunk you wouldn't try anything like this. Sure, you've got the drop on me. Maybe you could shoot me. You probably could. But you couldn't save yourself, Mitchell. You couldn't drop

42

me fast enough to prevent me drawing a gun. I'd get you sure before I went down. You know that. *You know that, understand!*"

The last four words cracked like shots from a Winchester. The forty-five in Ogallala Mitchell's hand wavered a trifle. One foot edged back. Johnny kept advancing, his eyes holding Mitchell's. Mitchell's eyes shifted sidewise, then back to meet Johnny's gaze.

"You know I could get you," Johnny said coldly. "You'd wish you hadn't pulled on me, when you felt my slug tearing through your middle, Mitchell—and it would, sure as hell!"

He was holding Mitchell's eyes with all the strength of his will now. Mitchell tried to look away, but something in that inexorable gaze boring into his own prevented such movement. He hadn't realized before how hard Johnny's eyes were. Deep in their depths cold blue flames flickered and leaped and seemed to burn all resistance from Mitchell's will.

"You'd better put that gun away."

Johnny's words drilled relentlessly into Mitchell's brain, beating down all opposition. Mitchell's mouth hung slack now. He tried to look away but found that impossible. A sort of choking gasp left his lips. He shrunk back against the bar, the gun in his hand slowly lowering to his side. He tried to speak, but words wouldn't come. He stared back at Johnny as though hypnotized. A strange shivering coursed his spine; his legs felt weak as though they might let him to the floor.

"Dammit! Put that gun away!"

The words snapped like the blows of a trip hammer against Mitchell's senses. He jumped as though shot, flung himself to one side, trembling all over, and slid his six-shooter back into holster. "I—I was just jokin', " he protested hoarsely.

Johnny laughed contemptuously. "Well, let's get serious then. We're all even now. Pull that iron and get to work."

Ogallala Mitchell shook his head, apparently unnerved for the time being. "I—I—I—" he stammered.

"Get out of here," Johnny snapped. "And don't pull any more guns on me. You won't get off so easy the next time you try it."

Mitchell turned and half staggered, half ran, toward the street. He almost fell through the swinging doors and within a moment had disappeared.

"That"—Corkscrew Jones breathed a long sigh of relief—"was an exhibition of sheer nerve, Johnny, if I ever saw one!"

WARPATH TALK!

CORKSCREW'S WORDS BROKE THE SILENCE THAT HAD followed Ogallala Mitchell's sudden exit. The other customers in the Continental gathered about Johnny at the bar. Expressions of admiration for Johnny's courage suddenly found voice. Two men wanted to buy drinks for Johnny.

Humdrum drawled lazily, "That, pardner, was handled mighty neat. You got my congratulations."

"Thanks, Humdrum." Johnny flushed with pleasure. He wasn't missing that word "pardner." It sounded mighty good to him. "There really wasn't anything to it though," he said modestly. "Mitchell could have bored me if he'd kept his nerve, but I've found you can shake a drunk's nerve right easy sometimes. The minute he got to thinking I might shoot him he couldn't think

44

straight. When he didn't pull trigger right off I knew I had him."

"Bravest thing I ever see," one of the customers commented. "There Ogallala was, a pointin' that gun at yore belly, and you walkin' right inter it and a tellin' him to put it away. An' he shore put it away!"

"I wonder what gave Ogallala the idea you had his hat," another man said. "I can't say I ever saw him wearin' a hat like that."

"Cripes!" Corkscrew said. "Those hats are turned out by the dozen down in *mañana* land. I've seen plenty of 'em. But you know how Ogallala is always lookin' for some excuse to make trouble."

One of the customers in citizens' clothing nodded. "Yes, and Kane Mitchell is largely responsible for that. Ever since Ogallala got out of the penitentiary Kane sort of babies him and lets him have his own way."

"I don't like that either," Corkscrew said seriously. He spoke directly to Johnny and Humdrum: "Kane Mitchell runs a pretty rough outfit. He'd run this town if he could. He's not going to take kindly to the way you treated Ogallala. Maybe you two had better get your broncs and drift pronto."

Humdrum looked at Johnny. "Me, I'm not driftin' sudden for anybody. I aim to get my night's sleep."

Johnny nodded. "I reckon we can take care of ourselves, Corkscrew. Thanks for the warning just the same. Did I hear somebody say that Ogallala had served a term in the pen?"

"He was in for holdup activities." Corkscrew supplied the information. "He's only been at liberty a couple of months. They let him out before his sentence was completed. I reckon Kane Mitchell spread some money in the right places. He claimed his brother was in poor health and would die if he wasn't released. He may be in poor health, but he's just about the toughest old root I ever saw—and plenty cantankerous. I wouldn't trust him any further than I could toss a adobe house."

"The third brother is just as bad," a man interposed.

Corkscrew nodded. "Yes, Vink Mitchell is snake dangerous, the three of 'em—Kane, Vink and Ogallala—make a bad trio to buck. I hope you won't have any trouble with 'em, Johnny."

Johnny shrugged lean shoulders. "I hope not. We didn't come here looking for trouble, but if it heads our way we're not aiming to dodge either."

"Too much trouble to dodge," Humdrum grunted lazily. "A feller has to move too fast. C'mon, Johnny, let's go eat."

They left the Continental after thanking Corkscrew for his invitation to "come in often if you stay" and got into saddles at the hitch rail. Five minutes later Johnny was putting up the horses at the Red Star Livery, located just back of the Cowman's Rest Hotel, while Humdrum entered the lobby of the establishment to register for rooms. Humdrum was chatting with the clerk, a thin-faced, elderly man, behind the desk, when Johnny entered the small lobby.

The clerk nodded to Johnny, addressing him as "Mr. Donshawnee," so Johnny knew how Humdrum had entered his name on the registry book. Humdrum said, "I got us two rooms on the second floor. I like a bed all to myself so I can sprawl out in comfort. Let's eat."

To the left of the lobby was a door leading to the hotel bar; Johnny and Humdrum passed through a door to the right and found themselves in the dining room. There weren't more than eight or ten tables in the dining room; only two of these were occupied and by diners

46

who looked as though they might be traveling salesmen for saddlery or feed companies. The place was lighted by oil lamps placed in brackets about the walls.

Johnny and Humdrum found a table at the back of the room, placed their hats on hooks screwed into the wall and sat down. Within a few minutes a tall, slim girl with light hair came up to take their orders. She smiled at Johnny and Humdrum, and Johnny noted with approval her neat gingham dress and apron. He noticed other things, too, about the waitress: she had dark blue eyes with long black lashes; her skin was a creamy tan; her hair a pale golden shade. After a few moments he became conscious of her voice.

" . . . and it's a bit past the supper hour now, so there's nothing left but roast beef," the girl was saying.

"That—that will be fine," Johnny stammered, his face flushing, as he realized the girl had colored a trifle under his close scrutiny.

"Just so long as there's lots of beef and potatoes and biscuits and coffee and pie," Humdrum said, "I don't care for much else to eat anyway. Any little snack like that will do, miss."

The girl disappeared through a doorway leading to the kitchen. Humdrum drawled lazily, "If the hotel food compares to its help I figure I'll make my home here."

Johnny nodded, eyes still on the doorway through which the waitress had made her exit. "Yeah, it's sort of a nice place. I reckon I could like this town, under different circumstances."

"The *town*," Humdrum observed dryly, "seems to have caught your eye. From the way you looked at the girl I was commencing to think you knew her. I almost asked for an introduction."

"Well—well, she is kind of pretty." Johnny grinned

sheepishly. "You can't blame a man for looking."

"Kind of pretty?" Humdrum snorted sarcastically. "That's an understatement if I ever heard one. Must be all the cow hands in this neck of the range are either married or blind, or that girl wouldn't be juggling dishes for a living. I'm danged if I can understand it."

"That's easy," Johnny said promptly. "She hasn't found anybody to measure up to her requirements."

"Or," Humdrum said slyly, "she's already married. Maybe her husband owns this hotel."

Somehow Johnny didn't just like that thought. Hitherto he had been more or less immune to feminine charms, but there was something about this girl that was different. The girl returned with steaming platters of food in a few minutes. For the sake of making conversation Johnny asked. "Do we pay you now, miss?"—and hoped "miss" was the correct form of addressing her.

"Pay at the desk as you go out," she replied. "Either the man behind the desk or his wife will take your money. They own the Cowman's Rest, you know." She moved back toward the kitchen.

Humdrum chuckled. "Now you can eat in peace, cowboy."

They fell to over the food. A half-dozen more diners straggled in and found tables. The girl seemed on pleasant terms with everyone. Johnny could scarcely keep his gaze from her as she busied herself about the various tables.

"Look," Humdrum said finally, "if you don't want that roast beef I'll take it."

Johnny flushed and resumed eating. After a time he said, "Y'know, I wouldn't mind going to work for some outfit hereabouts if we could get a job. Of course maybe you wouldn't want to take a job."

Humdrum grunted between mouthfuls of food. "I don't like jobs. There's always some sort of work connected to 'em. Anyway, there's no reason for you to take a job in this country, unless you wanted an excuse for being here while you checked into things. Incidentally"—he lowered his voice—"I haven't heard anybody mention Aldrich's name, have you?"

Johnny shook his head. "No, I haven't. But, like you say, a job would give me an excuse for being here—"

"Only, of course," Humdrum said ironically, "for the purpose of checking into the Aldrich affair and carrying out your promise to him."

"Naturally." Johnny felt his face growing red.

"Working in a hotel like this," Humdrum said idly, "a girl might hear of any jobs that were open."

A few minutes later when the girl came to their table to bring fresh coffee Humdrum asked, "You don't happen to know of any jobs around here, do you, miss?"

"If you mean cow punching jobs," the girl replied, "I don't; at least there are none that would interest you. The only one I know of can't pay wages. The outfit's rather in the hole at present. The owner is stony-broke."

"Just where—" Johnny commenced.

"I reckon that wouldn't do," Humdrum broke in.

"I didn't think it would," the girl said coolly and walked away.

Johnny said irritably, "You didn't give her any time to tell us about it. It would give us an excuse to stay here—"

"And work for nothing?" Humdrum grunted. "We'd probably be too tied up to get around and learn things. You take any outfit that can't pay wages and it's probably broken down and way off in the hills

49

someplace, where we never would be able to get to town."

At that moment a broad-shouldered, grizzled man stepped into the dining room. He had sweeping gray mustaches and bushy eyebrows. He wore corduroys, high heeled boots, and on his vest was a star-shaped badge. He glanced about the room a few moments, then came directly to the table at which Johnny and Humdrum were seated.

"You fellers named Hartigan and Donshawnee?" he asked.

"I'm Hartigan," Humdrum nodded. "He's Donshawnee. What's on your mind?"

"I'm Sheriff Pritchard—Nick Pritchard." He put out a hand which both shook, then drew up a chair. "I've had a complaint against you. Ogallala Mitchell claims you stole his hat, then when he asked for it pulled a gun on him and ran him out of the Continental—"

"That's not true," Johnny interrupted quietly. "I'll tell you just what happened."

"You needn't take time." Sheriff Pritchard smiled. "I've talked to Corkscrew Jones. He gave me the whole story. Corkscrew's word is always good enough for me. And I talked to a couple of others who saw the whole business. Donshawnee, you've got nerve."

"Aw, it wasn't anything," Johnny protested.

"Anybody who faces a gun in Ogallala Mitchell's fist is facing plenty," the sheriff said earnestly. "My congratulations on the way you handled it. Ogallala is one mean hombre when he sets out to start trouble. I know! All those Mitchells are." Nick Pritchard sighed. "It's kept me busy nigh every minute to keep them Spur-Bar hombres from starting trouble in Spearhead Wells. Kane Mitchell, himself, knows that Ogallala is a

50

problem, and he's warned his brother to move more gentle. At the same time them Mitchells stick together, and Kane will back any move Ogallala makes."

"You didn't come here to arrest us then?" Humdrum queried lazily.

Pritchard shook his head. "So long as Ogallala made a complaint I had to carry out the law and handle things as fair as possible. That's one reason I came here. I wanted to shake the hand of the man who made Ogallala back down. Lord knows I wish there were more men in this town with that kind of nerve. All I want is to ask one question, Donshawnee: did you steal Ogallala's hat?"

Johnny shook his head. "That hat was given to me," he said evasively. "As a matter of fact I never saw Mitchell before."

"That's all I want to know," the sheriff said. "I know you didn't pull a gun on Ogallala, so I'll just go back and lay the facts before him. From now on it's up to you. Of course if him and Kane and Vink want to get nasty about this business I'll do everything in my power to protect a fight. But, naturally, I can't be every place at once. The Mitchells generally pick out some time when I'm at the other end of town to start trouble. Then all I have to depend on is the word of witnesses. And most witnesses is so afeared of the Mitchells that the evidence ain't always reliable." The sheriff got to his feet. "I'll go back and tell Ogallala it's not his hat you're wearing."

"Where is Mitchell now?" Johnny asked.

"In the Continental Saloon, with his brothers, Kane and Vink. Kane is really the big boss of the three. I won't tell 'em where I found you."

"I reckon," Humdrum drawled, "that we don't care

much whether you do or not."

The sheriff smiled thinly. "It's plain to be seen you haven't yet encountered Kane Mitchell. There ain't many folks around feel that way, Hartigan." He stood at the table, looking down at Johnny and Humdrum. "There'll be plenty of people, though, who will be glad to see any of the Mitchells meet their come-uppance. Especially Susan. She ain't no use for any of the Spur-Bar."

"Who did you say?" Johnny queried.

"Susan Aldrich—the girl who waits on table here. She's a dang nice girl—if you haven't already noticed it. She owns the Rocking-A ranch, fifteen miles northwest of town. Her father was murdered a spell back. Susan found herself in a bit of a tight. There was interest to meet on a loan on her ranch. This job here happened to be open, so Susan took it, to raise money—"

"Who's running her ranch?" Johnny managed to hold his voice to a normal tone.

"Her father's old foreman is there, carrying on with the help of one hand. It looks like a pretty hopeless sort of situation to me, but Susan has loads of courage—there she is, now." Pritchard raised his voice, "Susan, drift over this way a minute."

Susan Aldrich had just entered from the kitchen. She replied to the sheriff's summons by approaching the table. "What's up, Sheriff Nick?" She smiled.

"Susan, you've fed these two hombres, but I didn't think you knew who they were. This is Susan Aldrich—Humdrum Hartigan and Johnny Donshawnee."

The girl said something in a polite tone to acknowledge the introduction. Humdrum and Johnny were on their feet now. The sheriff went on, "Susan, awhile back Ogallala Mitchell pulled a gun on Johnny.

Johnny told him to put his gun away and clear out of the Continental. The queer part about it is Johnny didn't even draw his iron, but Ogallala got!"

Susan Aldrich extended one slim hand to Johnny. There was a new light of interest in her blue eyes now. "That," she said, "must have been nice to see, Mr. Donshawnee."

"Well, I've got to be pushing along," Pritchard cut in. "I'll see you men again"—he smiled a trifle—"if you decide to stay in town. I hope you do."

"I have a hunch we will," Johnny said.

The sheriff nodded and strode away.

Johnny turned back to Susan: "Miss Aldrich, a bit back you mentioned an outfit that could use some help. Were you referring to your Rocking-A?"

Susan nodded. "I see Sheriff Nick has been doing some talking."

"He told us a little bit. Miss Aldrich, you've hired a hand."

"You don't understand," the girl protested. "I can't afford to hire any help. I can't pay wages—" She paused, then, "Eventually, when the Rocking-A gets on its feet, I'll be willing to pay double—"

"Let's forget wages," Johnny said earnestly. "I'm asking for a job. I don't know about Humdrum—"

Humdrum grunted, "I don't like work, but I go where Johnny does, Miss Aldrich. I'll watch, while he works—"

"But look here," Susan said dubiously, "you don't know what you might get into. You don't know conditions around here. You've already made an enemy of Ogallala Mitchell—that means you'll have the whole Spur-Bar outfit against you—"

"Would that endanger your interests?" Johnny cut in

53

quietly.

Susan shook her head. "No more than they're already endangered."

Johnny asked flatly, "Do we get jobs?"

Susan hesitated, frowning. "I scarcely know what to say. You see—" She broke off, smiled, said impulsively, "Cowboys, you're hired. If you'll wait a few minutes I'll write a note to my foreman. You can take it out to him in the morning." She turned to leave the table, then swung back, her eyes looking a trifle moist. "And thanks a heap," she said earnestly. "The Rocking-A really does need help."

Johnny wasn't sure of his reply. He only knew that more than anything else he wanted to help Susan Aldrich. He watched her hurry back to the kitchen, then turned to meet Humdrum's cynical gaze. Humdrum smiled sleepily. "It's sure funny what a pretty girl can do to a man," he observed, sitting down again.

"Aw, shucks," Johnny protested, "you know I'm just doing this so I can carry out my promise to her father."

"Oh, of course," Humdrum said in exaggerated tones.

Johnny fell silent before Humdrum's ironical smile. Five minutes passed while they waited for Susan's return. By now all the other diners had left the dining room. It was getting along toward eight-thirty. Johnny settled back in his chair.

Suddenly Corkscrew Jones appeared from the hotel lobby. He hesitated a moment in the doorway, then, seeing Johnny and Humdrum, hurried across the room. "Gosh, I'm glad to find you still here," he said a bit breathlessly.

Johnny said, "What's up?"

"The three Mitchell brothers are on the warpath. Kane Mitchell swears no man can handle his brother the way

54

you did, Johnny, and get away with it. Hell is due to pop!"

"LET 'ER POP!"

HUMDRUM SMILED LAZILY. "HELL'S DUE TO POP, IS she? Well, let 'er pop! Just plain poppin' won't disturb my peace. It's these loud explosions I don't like."

Johnny said more seriously, "Where are the Mitchells now, Corkscrew?"

"Around town someplace, looking for you. Sheriff Nick came in the Continental and told Ogallala he had seen you, but refused to say where. He told Ogallala and the other two Mitchells that you hadn't stolen that hat, but the Mitchells are spoiling for trouble. I didn't tell them you were coming here for supper. I imagine they're searching the saloons around town for you—"

Humdrum cut in, "What's the matter with Sheriff Pritchard? Can't he prevent trouble?"

Corkscrew replied, "I suggested to Pritchard that he toss the Mitchells in the cooler until they had calmed down, but Sheriff Nick didn't see it that way. He keeps trouble down when possible, but, after all, the Mitchells have a lot of influence around town, and Pritchard tries to be as neutral as possible. You've got to look at it this way, of course—you two are strangers in town and you had a ruckus with Ogallala right off. For all the sheriff knows you may have come here with the intention of making trouble. On the other hand, the sheriff can't make an arrest every time a man makes threats. In a town like this that sort of thing goes on all the time. If any actual gun fighting breaks out then you'll see that Sheriff Nick is plenty efficient."

At that moment Susan Aldrich reappeared from the kitchen, bearing a folded sheet of notepaper in her hand. She crossed the dining room and handed it to Johnny who had gained his feet at her approach. "Oh, hello, Corkscrew," she smiled. "You over here for your supper?"

Corkscrew shook his head. "I had to see Johnny and Humdrum on some business," he evaded.

Susan turned to Johnny. "Just give that note to my foreman, Mecate Bowen. Maybe he'll put you down as crazy—working without wages. I think you'll like him though."

"If you do," Johnny replied, "I know I will."

Corkscrew asked curiously, "You two going to work for the Rocking-A?"

Humdrum nodded. "At least Johnny is. Me, I'm not so familiar with work. I reckon I'll just watch him and see how it goes for a spell."

"We'd better be getting along on that business Corkscrew told us about," Johnny put in. "We'll head out to your place first thing in the morning, Miss Aldrich."

"If you're able to do so," Corkscrew said in a dubious undertone.

Susan looked queerly at him, then back to Johnny and Humdrum. "The trail to the Rocking-A runs northwest from Spearhead Wells," she said. "It's about a fifteen or sixteen mile ride. And I don't know how I'm going to thank you—"

"Let's not talk about that now," Johnny said awkwardly, "We'll be seeing you again, Miss Aldrich." Cutting short the girl's thanks, he and Humdrum removed their hats from hooks and started for the exit, followed by Corkscrew.

Once more on the street Corkscrew said, "I've got to get back to my bar. I left my assistant in charge, but there's a heap of customers on hand and we've been right busy."

"Thanks for the warning anyway," Johnny said.

"Don't mention it," from Corkscrew.

"All right, we won't." Humdrum chuckled lazily. "C'mon, Johnny, it looks like we got a job to do."

Corkscrew looked anxiously at the two, then hurried off in the direction of the Continental Saloon. Johnny and Humdrum turned the opposite way and sauntered, side by side, along Main Street, eyes alert for the first sign of Ogallala Mitchell and his two brothers. There weren't many people on Main Street now, though all the saloons they passed sounded as though they were crowded. A few ponies stood at hitch racks along the way. Lights gleamed from many of the buildings; others were in total darkness.

Humdrum said idly, "Well, them hombres may be looking for us, but it don't appear like they were looking real careful like."

"Might be they were just throwing out a bluff, hoping to scare us into leaving town," Johnny commented. "Let's cross over and head back."

Humdrum nodded. They had covered some four blocks by this time and the buildings were commencing to thin out. Crossing the street diagonally, they headed back in a westward direction again. Within a short time they were standing across the road from the Cowman's Rest Hotel.

"Maybe," Humdrum said plaintively, "it would have been better to just sit tight and let them coyotes find us. My feet are commencing to hurt. I never did care for walking—"

"Wait!" Johnny interrupted. He was peering across the street toward the hotel. Through the broad lobby window he had caught sight of the clerk behind the desk in conversation with a man who, from a distance, looked like Ogallala Mitchell. "Come on," Johnny said grimly, "it looks like they've tracked us down. Probably the Mitchells have been waiting in saloons for us to put in an appearance while we were looking for them on the street. You ready, Humdrum?"

"I'm ready for bed," Humdrum grumbled. "And my bed's at the hotel. Let's not waste too much time in the lobby."

They crossed the street with swift strides, mounted the steps to the hotel porch, then paused a moment to glance through the glass into the interior of the lobby. Ogallala Mitchell was in conversation with the clerk and had apparently been examining the hotel register to learn if Johnny and Humdrum were staying there. Johnny glanced about the lobby. Two men were standing close behind Ogallala Mitchell. Susan Aldrich was nowhere in sight. Johnny hadn't expected she would be; the girl had probably retired to her room for the night by this time. The door leading from the lobby to the dining room was now closed.

Of the two men accompanying Ogallala Mitchell there was no doubt in Johnny's mind as to which was Kane Mitchell. While Ogallala was undoubtedly the oldest of the three, Kane looked to be the born leader, even though his pursuits might not always have been morally impeccable. He was a big rangy man of about thirty-five, with sharp eyes and a lean muscular jaw. His coloring was dark and when he moved slightly behind Ogallala, Johnny could almost visualize the man's supple muscles rippling under his skin. No doubt about

58

it, Kane Mitchell was an enemy to be reckoned with. A pair of six-shooters were slung from a single belt about his lean middle, but, Johnny decided instantly, Kane Mitchell wasn't the type to depend on force alone. The man's eyes looked crafty, cunning; there was sure to be some intelligence behind any move he made. He wore cowman togs and his sombrero was an expensive gray Stetson.

Vink Mitchell, the younger brother, was different. Probably about thirty years old, there was a mean, treacherous something about him which Johnny instantly disliked. He had a rather dandified appearance and, by women of a certain type, might have been considered handsome. A snakeskin band encircled the crown of his sombrero; there was a brightly colored silk neckerchief about his throat. His twin forty-fives were mother-of-pearl butted; on the fingers of his left hand were two silver-and-turquoise rings.

Johnny hesitated but an instant more. Humdrum grumbled, "We going to stand here all night? Let's get this over with. I'm sleepy."

Johnny said grimly, "Before this is over you may take a long sleep, Humdrum. After all, it's me Ogallala is fighting. He didn't have any quarrel with you. You'd better stay out of this and let me—"

"Look"—Humdrum yawned—"I ain't intendin' to be chased any farther from my bed. Make your play. Maybe I can stay awake long enough to help out."

Johnny said shortly, "Come on," and turned the knob of the door.

As he stepped inside the small lobby, followed by Humdrum, the three Mitchells turned around. Then all three spied Johnny's steeple crown black sombrero at the same moment.

59

"That's him now!" Ogallala exclaimed angrily.

"Gentlemen, gentlemen," nervously implored the man behind the desk. "Let's not have any trouble in my hotel. I—"

No one paid the man any attention. Kane Mitchell had swung around, eyes boring into Johnny's. Johnny had come to a halt a few feet away. Behind him Humdrum carefully closed the door.

"That's him!" Ogallala snarled again. "Kane, make him—"

"Leave be, Ogallala," Kane Mitchell snapped. "I'll handle this." His eyes still drilled into Johnny's, as though hoping to instill a certain fear by the look.

Johnny said quietly, "I take it you hombres are the Mitchell brothers."

"Yo're damn right." Vink Mitchell spat angrily. His hand was already dropping close to gun butt.

Johnny nodded calmly. "Keep your hand away from that gun, Mitchell, or you'll get hurt—"

"By Gawd!" Vink Mitchell commenced.

"You, Vink," Kane Mitchell snapped suddenly, "keep your trap shut. I'm handling this." Vink was silent. Kane Mitchell continued. "Donshawnee, nobody can buck us Mitchells and get away with it. You stole my brother's hat—that hat you're wearing—and you run him out of the Continental at the point of a gun—"

"Your brother," Johnny said coolly, "is a liar on two counts if he told you that—"

"No man can call me a liar!" Ogallala half yelled.

"If I wasn't so tired," Humdrum commented indolently, "I'd call you a liar. I saw the whole business. Your brother showed a wide trace of yellow, Kane Mitchell, and did some backing down. Johnny didn't even pull a gun. There's witnesses to prove that."

60

Kane Mitchell's eyes flickered restlessly. Johnny guessed he was already aware of the part Ogallala had played but was determined to back his brother up at any cost. Kane Mitchell turned angry eyes on Humdrum. "You keep out of this, Hartigan, and you won't be hurt. I haven't any business with you."

"That's fine," Humdrum said lazily. "I was afraid you might have. All right, settle your business with Johnny." Humdrum yawned widely and dropped into a chair near the door. He sat listening to the proceedings with his eyes half shut. Kane Mitchell bent a look of extreme contempt on him and turned back to Johnny.

"Donshawnee," Kane Mitchell said coldly, "I don't like to make trouble if it can be avoided. You hand that black sombrero over to Ogallala and get out of town. That's your only chance."

"Suppose I refuse?" Johnny said steadily. He'd noticed now that both Ogallala and Vink Mitchell had their hands on gun butts. Behind them the desk clerk was still begging that no trouble be started in his place. No one heard his words. "Suppose I refuse?" Johnny repeated. "This is my hat and I intend to keep it."

"Samuel Colt," Kane Mitchell said harshly, "invented a device for taking care of such arguments. You'll do as I say or—"

"Oh hell, let him have it," Ogallala Mitchell burst out impatiently, jerking his gun from holster. "He's got an iron. Let him yank it if he wants to keep my hat."

"My sentiments to a T," Vink Mitchell rasped, his own right weapon coming into view.

Johnny made no attempt to draw. He knew both Vink and Ogallala would get him if he did. Kane Mitchell smiled thinly. "You see what you're up against, Donshawnee. You'd better listen to reason. A man

61

hasn't a chance when there's a gun pointed at his middle."

"I'm glad to hear you bring up that point." Humdrum's listless tones unexpectedly interrupted the conversation. "Seeing you agree with me is certain to make you realize the force of my argument—"

"Why, dammit—" Kane Mitchell commenced, then stopped short as his eyes fell on the gun in Humdrum's hand. The gun was pointing squarely at Kane Mitchell's middle.

"Uh-huh." Humdrum chuckled. "I've had you covered ever since I sat down, Mitchell. If I'd drawn while I was standing you'd have noticed it, but when I sat down you figured I was out of things and didn't want any part of your argument."

"Look here—" Kane Mitchell said, backing a step.

"I've been looking too long now," Humdrum cut in plaintively. "It's way past my bedtime. I'm tired of all this shilly-shallying. Tell your brothers to put their guns away, Mitchell. If they start shooting I'll sure as hell bore you."

"Put 'em away, boys," Kane Mitchell ordered reluctantly.

Vink and Ogallala cursed but obeyed the order.

"That's better." Humdrum yawned. "Now unbuckle your belts—all three of you—and let that hardware drop on the floor. It must be getting sort of heavy to carry anyway, and you—"

Three violent protests filled the air. Johnny spoke sternly, "Go ahead, unbuckle those belts. You pulled first. We could have put the drop on you when we first arrived here, but we thought this might be settled peacefully. Maybe we we're wrong, but we're still trying. Do as Humdrum ordered."

"Damned if I will," Kane Mitchell snapped. "Now look here—"

He paused. Something had dropped with a tinny, metallic clatter to the floor near Humdrum's chair. Humdrum said lazily. "Cover these hombres, Johnny, while I get something I dropped."

There was no necessity for Johnny to keep the three men covered: the gaze of all three Mitchells was intent on the object Humdrum retrieved from the floor and replaced in his pocket. To the Mitchells the object appeared to be a law officer's badge.

Kane Mitchell's eyes narrowed. If that was a law officer's badge it might place a different aspect on things. What were law officers doing in Spearhead Wells? Mitchell decided to employ diplomacy. "All right, boys," he said, suddenly agreeable to Humdrum's suggestion. "Let's unbuckle our belts. There's been a misunderstanding all around, but I like to see things settled peaceable when possible." He set the example by unbuckling and allowing his own guns to slip to the floor. Reluctantly Vink and Ogallala followed suit.

"Now clear out of here." Humdrum yawned. "You can get your guns from the clerk tomorrow mornin'. We can continue the discussion then, if you still feel like it. Good night."

"Well now, wait a minute," Kane Mitchell protested, his face darkening.

"Clear out," Johnny said sternly. "You've made your talk, Mitchell, but you couldn't back it up. And I'm not surrendering this black sombrero. Get that straight. I'm not looking for trouble, but I'm not avoiding any either. Anybody that wants this hat will have to come with his guns smoking."

Kane Mitchell smiled thinly. "That's war talk,

Donshawnee."

"It's meant to be—"

At that moment the door to the hotel opened and Sheriff Pritchard stepped in, followed by Susan Aldrich. "What's up?" Pritchard demanded.

"These men—" Kane Mitchell commenced.

Humdrum cut in, "The Mitchells wanted to know if they could leave their guns here overnight, Sheriff. Johnny and I persuaded the clerk to take care of them. No, we weren't having any trouble—leastwise, Johnny and I weren't."

Johnny explained briefly what had happened. The sheriff then turned to Kane Mitchell. Mitchell said, forcing a laugh, "I reckon it was just a misunderstanding all around, Nick. Things didn't happen exactly as Donshawnee says, but we won't argue the matter now. Ogallala could be mistaken about that hat. It's just that I'm a heap mistrustful of two strangers in Spearhead Wells and I thought they should be investigated."

"I'll do all the investigating necessary," Pritchard said shortly. "These men aren't exactly strangers. They're working for the Rocking-A, so Miss Aldrich tells me."

Exclamations of surprise broke from the Mitchell brothers. They looked to Susan for confirmation. Susan nodded coldly. The sheriff continued, "Miss Susan heard you three inquiring for Donshawnee and Hartigan in the office here. She figured trouble might be afoot, so she slipped out the rear door of the hotel and came down to my office—"

Vink Mitchell laughed sarcastically. "Nothing like working for a lady boss who looks after her help."

Susan smiled. "From all I can gather, Vink Mitchell, my help didn't require any looking after."

Vink Mitchell's face reddened and he fell silent.

Ogallala muttered curses under his breath. Kane Mitchell glanced at the guns and belts on the floor and asked the sheriff a question. Before Pritchard could reply Humdrum drawled genially, "Sure, let 'em have their guns, if it'll make 'em more content. I was just makin' certain I wouldn't have my sleep interrupted tonight. Now it's up to you, Sheriff, to make 'em keep the peace. I'm going to bed. Goo' night." And without another word he sauntered toward the stairway that ascended from the hotel lobby to the second floor.

The Mitchells gathered their guns and, with a last hateful glance at Johnny, departed. The sheriff looked anxiously after them, then turned to Johnny. "I'm afraid you haven't heard the last of this."

"I hope not," Johnny said grimly. "I've a hunch that bucking those Mitchell hombres may prove plumb interesting." He turned to Susan Aldrich. "Thanks a lot for going after Sheriff Pritchard. For a time it looked as though he might be needed."

Susan smiled. "A ranch owner has to protect her crew, you know."

Johnny said boldly, "I sort of figure, from now on, it should be the other way about."

A few minutes later Susan said good night and ascended the stairs to her room. Johnny remained to talk to the sheriff and the hotel clerk who was, by now, recovering somewhat from his fright. Finally the sheriff took his departure and Johnny went upstairs. As he sat on his bed, smoking a final cigarette, he could hear the steady snoring of Humdrum in the adjoining room. "That hombre sure likes his rest"—Johnny chuckled—"but he's always awake when he's needed most."

Sleep eluded Johnny for some time, but it wasn't the Mitchells who occupied his mind; it was a vision of the

65

slim, blue-eyed Susan Aldrich that stayed with him, even into his dreams.

OGALLALA COMES CLEAN

TWENTY MINUTES AFTER THEY HAD LEFT THE Cowman's Rest Hotel the three Mitchells were still cursing. They had walked from one end of the town to the other and finally come to a pause in front of the Mecca Saloon where their horses were tied.

Vink Mitchell growled, "You two figuring to head back to the ranch?"

Kane Mitchell snapped, "Ain't you?"

Vink swore some more. "I ain't intending to leave town until I've squared with those hombres."

"Them's my sentiments," Ogallala rasped, "I want my hat."

Kane turned fiercely on his older brother. "Damn you and your hat," he snarled. "You got us into this. A pretty spectacle we made, being outfoxed by Donshawnee and that sleepy pard of his. By tomorrow it will be all over town how they made us back down—"

"Nobody better let me hear 'em boastin'—" Vink began.

"Will you shut up?" Kane snapped. "I want to think. There's something queer about the whole business. The most important thing is to learn something about that badge that Hartigan dropped. You both saw it as well as I did. Who is he? Who sent for him? Cattle Association detective or what? I don't like it."

Vink said slowly, "I don't figure that was a Cattle Association badge. I've seen them. They don't look like that badge Hartigan dropped."

"Might be," Ogallala proposed, "he's a deputy U. S. marshall!"

Kane Mitchell vetoed that. "If that was the case he'd have a gold badge. That badge we saw was silver or nickel."

Vink said slowly, "I wonder if our Wagon-Wheel activities are bearing fruit."

"Might be," Kane conceded. "Maybe the Aldrich girl has applied to some detective organization for a man. It fits in, her hirin' those two."

"You figuring Donshawnee is a cattle dick too?" Vink asked.

"Don't you?" Kane growled. "They came here together."

Vink agreed, "Probably. Of the two I figure Donshawnee as the most dangerous. That other hombre is too sleepy to—"

"He wasn't too sleepy to get the drop on Kane," Ogallala said with a curse. "Look, I figure we can wait an hour or so and then force the hotel door—"

"And then what?" Kane asked coldly.

"We'll go up to them fellers' rooms, polish 'em off and get my hat."

Kane and Vink burst out with a tirade of abuse directed at the older brother. "By God!" Kane finished, "you'd think that hat was the most important thing on earth."

"Maybe it is," Ogallala said sullenly.

Vink snapped, "What gives you that idea?"

Ogallala shrugged his shoulders and half turned away.

Kane eyed his older brother curiously for a moment, then said, "I'm going to get a drink before we head back." Without waiting for a reply he turned toward the

Mecca Saloon. Boisterous sounds emerged from within. On the porch Kane paused. "Too many in there," he said. "Vink, you go in and get a bottle and glasses. Ogallala and I will wait out here for you."

Vink nodded and entered the saloon. There were several straight-backed wooden chairs on the saloon porch. Kane and Ogallala found two and sat down where they could put their feet on the railing. A big moon was arcing above the distant peaks of the Sangre de Santos Range, but where the Mitchells sat the porch was in deep shadow. Within a few minutes Vink emerged, bearing a bottle and glasses. He pulled the saloon door closed behind him, shutting off the laughter and loud voices from within, then pulled up a chair beside Kane.

Drinks were poured. Kane rolled a cigarette and puffed meditatively. Finally he asked, "Ogallala, what makes you think that's your hat Donshawnee is wearing?"

"Huh?" Ogallala stirred uncomfortably. "What do you mean, Kane?"

You know what I mean," Kane said impatiently. "Don't stall, Ogallala."

"Oh, that hat. Oh yeah," Ogallala said. "What about it?"

"Dammit," Kane snapped. "You heard me the first time. I said not to stall."

"We-ell," Ogallala said lamely, "I'm right sure that's my old bonnet. I examined it close today. There's one spot on the band that's frayed, just like mine was. It's the same color and—"

"Geez!" Vink exclaimed disgustedly. "You could get another hat like that for twenty or thirty bucks. Suppose it was your hat? I'm damned if it was worth the trouble

68

it made for us tonight. Kane, I'm getting right sick of backing up Ogallala's dumb moves. Tonight's the end! He's always pulling us into trouble and—"

"Hush up, Vink," Kane said coldly. "I know what I'm doing. I feel the same way you do about Ogallala. We're brothers and we've got to do a certain amount of standing together, but not unless Ogallala comes clean with us—"

"I don't understand—" Vink commenced an interruption.

"Keep quiet and you will in a minute," Kane said. "I've been doing some thinking—"

"Well"—Ogallala arose nervously and stretched, yawned—"let's get headed home. I'm plumb weary. We'll say no more about that black sombrero. Maybe I was mistaken." He started around his chair, preparatory to heading for the hitch rack.

Kane swore and put out one hand, seizing Ogallala's wrist and jerking the older man back to his chair. "You sit down," Kane growled. "I aim to get to the bottom of one or two things."

"What's wrong, Kane?" Ogallala asked nervously. "Sure, I'll set a spell longer if you like."

"I do like," Kane snapped. "Ogallala, we've sort of babied you since you were released from the pen. We've risked our own lives backing the dumb plays you've made from time to time. You've done pretty much as you like. You never lift a hand to help about the outfit—"

"Why should I?" Ogallala said indignantly. "You two swindled me out of my third of the Spur-Bar—"

"Swindled?" Vink spat. "Do you hear that, Kane? He says we swindled him. He knows bloody well his third interest went where it would do the most good in getting

69

him out. If we spend our money why shouldn't we—"

"Yaah!" Ogallala snarled. "You only got me out because you figured I'd turn up that gold for you. I tell you I don't know where it is."

"I believe that much anyway," Kane said wearily. "If you knew you wouldn't be here. Now quit scrappin', you two. I'm going to do some talking."

Vink sat in interested silence. Ogallala slunk sullenly down in his chair. He always had been afraid of his brother Kane, and when Kane cracked the whip Ogallala knew enough to look sharp and obey orders.

"Like I say," Kane commenced heavily, "I've been doing some thinking. Ogallala, George Aldrich was murdered in El Paso. You left town here the same day he did, only you caught that night freight that passes through—now, wait a minute, I'm doing the talking. Yes, I know, you told me you'd suddenly decided to visit a pal in Albuquerque. I didn't believe that story then. I don't believe it now. The next thing we heard George Aldrich had been killed. The newspaper that carried the story that I read told how the murderer's six-shooter was found on the floor in Aldrich's hotel room. When you returned from visiting your old pal in Albuquerque"—Kane's voice took on a sarcastic tone— "you didn't have any gun. You claimed it had been stolen and I had to buy you a new one, even if I didn't believe your story. Ogallala, you killed George Aldrich!"

"Judas priest!" Vink burst out, sitting straighter in his chair.

"Yo're crazier 'n a bedbug," Ogallala protested weakly. He didn't sound convincing. "That there's a batty story if I ever heard one. Vink, don't you pay him no attention."

70

"It does sound sort of cuckoo, Kane," Vink said. "Of course if you've got any proof—"

"Proof? Proof?" Kane turned savagely on his younger brother, though keeping his tones below normal, "Good cripes! look at the facts! George Aldrich's brother Tony and Ogallala rob the Little Bonanza Mine Payroll. Tony and Ogallala get away with thirty thousand gold. A posse gets on their trail. Ogallala gets wounded and captured and sent to the penitentiary. Tony Aldrich makes an escape and hasn't been heard of since. Ogallala says that Tony buried the gold, but he claims he don't know exactly where. I figure he does know but wants to keep it all to himself—"

"That's a pipe dream," Ogallala jeered. "Do you think I'd be sticking in Spearhead Wells if I knew where that gold was?"

"Anyway," Kane growled, "you know more than you've told Vink and me. Apparently nobody knows what became of Tony Aldrich. He was at liberty while you served a prison sentence, Ogallala. Suddenly George Aldrich left for El Paso and you were right on his trail—going to Albuquerque, I suppose. All right, I'll take your word for that, but Albuquerque is a mighty short distance from El Paso. I figure you followed George Aldrich. And why did Aldrich go to El Paso in the first place?"

"All right, you tell me," Ogallala said defiantly.

"I figure he had heard from his brother Tony," Kane said promptly. "That occurred to me after I'd thought things over. Maybe it occurred to you right away. Tony Aldrich wouldn't dare come to Spearhead Wells. He's still wanted by the law. But George could meet his brother and—"

Ogallala's short laugh wasn't nice to hear. "Have

71

yore dream," he snapped sarcastically. "I'm maintainin' yo're crazy. Now you prove I'm wrong."

"I figure to do just that," Kane snapped. "Ogallala, that six gun you carried to El Paso used to be mine—remember? I gave it to you after you got out of the pen."

"Sure, what's that got to do with the question?"

Kane smiled thinly. "I always keep a record of the number of any gun I own, Ogallala. According to the El Paso newspapers the number on the six-shooter found in Aldrich's hotel room, the night he was killed, is the same as on the gun I gave you. They're still looking for the owner of that gun. I've heard that in the East dealers are commencing to keep a record of who guns are sold to, but that idea hasn't worked West yet. However, I could telegraph the El Paso police the name of the man who owned that six-shooter—"

"My Gawd, Kane!" Ogallala leaped from his chair and raised one shaking hand in protest. "You wouldn't do that! Not to your own brother. You couldn't treat your own blood brother—"

"Sit down," Kane said harshly and pulled Ogallala back to his chair. Ogallala renewed his protestations. Kane told him to shut up. "You haven't been as square with me as a brother should be, Ogallala," he said coldly. "I don't figure you deserve any consideration."

"If Ogallala knows where that gold is and hasn't told us"—Vink's voice was shaking with anger—"I figure we might as well turn him up, Kane. We're not so popular in Spearhead Wells, anyway, but what such an act of justice wouldn't boost our stock. It would prove we were honest, tipping off the police to our own brother . . ."

"You wouldn't dare," Ogallala said in a trembling voice. "I'd tell what I know and—"

72

"Anything that might happen to us," Kane interrupted frigidly, "wouldn't put a rope around our necks. Now in your case, Ogallala—"

"My Gawd, Kane"—Ogallala was shaking like a leaf—"give me a chance. I don't see how you can be so hard with me. I'm willing to play square with you and Vink. I didn't think that you would treat your own brother like this—"

"Cut out the bellyaching," Kane said harshly, "and get down to cases. Did you kill George Aldrich or didn't you?"

Ogallala sat, head bowed in his hands now. He didn't reply at once. Vink poured himself a drink of whiskey. His hand trembled, knocking the bottleneck against glass. Hoof beats drummed along the roadway and a cowhand passed, his loping pony kicking up puffs of dust to float in the moon-bathed street.

Kane said cruelly, "Come clean or think fast, Ogallala. We've got you where we want you. I've been thinking all this out ever since Aldrich was killed. I didn't say anything before. I wanted to be sure before I accused my own brother of the double cross. But you do know things you haven't told me. Now I'm putting on the pressure."

Fear was etched deeply in Ogallala's features when he raised his head to face Kane. He seemed to shrink deeper into the shadow that enveloped the saloon porch. "All right, damn you," he quavered. "You always could figure things out. Maybe it's best this way. I'll need your help if we're to get that gold. I've been intending right along to ask yore advice—"

"Don't lie, Ogallala," Kane interrupted. "Come clean."

Ogallala nodded. "Yes, I killed George Aldrich. I

73

rubbed out Tony too."

"You killed Tony!" Vink exclaimed.

Kane said shortly, "Hush up, Vink. Ogallala's telling us."

Ogallala went on: "George Aldrich went to Austin first. I was down to the railroad depot the morning he bought his ticket. I got a hunch that maybe he had heard from Tony and was to meet him there. I played my hunch and followed along."

"Did he meet Tony in Austin?" Vink asked eagerly.

"I don't know," Ogallala said. "By the time I got to Austin I couldn't see any trace of George Aldrich. Finally I gave it up as a bad job and went to the railroad station to catch the train home. Aldrich was waiting for the same train. He didn't see me, but when the train pulled out I was on it, in another car. Aldrich got off when the train reached El Paso. So did I. He went to the Pierdon Hotel and got a room there. There was a saloon a couple of doors away. I sort of made that my headquarters; it was open night and day, and I grabbed naps when I could. The clerk of the Pierdon came in the saloon right frequent to get what he called his tonic. I got acquainted with him and managed to find out things."

Ogallala paused and reached for the bottle of whiskey at Vink's feet. He drank deeply and resumed: "Nothing happened for a couple of days; then one morning I saw a Mex boy enter the Pierdon with a note. A few minutes later George Aldrich came hurrying out. I trailed him to a livery where he hired a horse. I hired a horse and followed him. About four miles out of town, in an old dry wash, he met his brother Tony. They sat and talked for a long time, so I reckon it was the first time they'd met in years. I crept up pretty close through some brush, but I couldn't hear what they were saying. Then I see Tony give his brother that black sombrero—"

"That damn hat again," Vink swore. "Get on with your story."

"Hush your mouth," Kane said impatiently. "Let Ogallala tell this his own way."

Ogallala went on: "I figured that was as good a time as any to do business, so I yanked my six gun and let Tony Aldrich have it under the left shoulder blade. From the way he dropped I know I got him instanter. Then I cut down on George Aldrich. He dropped, too, but jerked his iron and went to work on the brush in my direction. He made things so hot that I fanned my tail out of there, figuring I hadn't hit him so serious as I thought at first—"

"Showed yellow, eh?" Vink sneered.

"You'd show yellow too," Ogallala replied resentfully, "if you'd had that coot fanning his lead at you the way he was me. I got back to El Paso. That night I saw George Aldrich come dragging in on his pony. He looked about finished, but he managed it. Later I saw a doctor enter the hotel. There weren't any police around, so I figured George Aldrich didn't want any help in that direction."

"You're sure he didn't see you at any time?" Kane asked swiftly.

Ogallala shook his head. "Ain't I told you I was screened by brush when I did my shooting? Anyway, I wanted to finish the job I'd started. At the rear of the hotel there was a flight of stairs leading to the second-floor corridor. I used them to get close to Aldrich's room. There was a chair in the hall. I stood on that to peek over the transom at Aldrich. But I could never get the right chance at him. Either somebody was there,

75

talking to him, or he was mighty alert, with a shotgun in his hands. I couldn't run too many risks. A couple of times the hotel clerk come upstairs and nearly caught me; I had to duck down the back way."

"According to the newspapers," Kane said slowly, "a man by the name of Donne called on Aldrich the night he was murdered."

Ogallala cursed. "It must have been him that was there that night. I could have sworn Aldrich was alone. I'd heard voices in the room earlier in the evening and went away. Later I came back and it was all quiet. I peeked over the transom and Aldrich was sleeping. I could just see the corner of the room where his bed was. I listened. There wasn't a sound in the room. I figured him alone. Just as I pulled trigger I heard a voice yell a warning. To throw suspicion on whoever was in that room I dropped the gun through the transom. But I reckon they never caught the feller. I tore down the back stairway and kept going from then on."

There was a moment's silence. Vink heaved a long puzzled sigh. "I still don't see why you wanted to kill George Aldrich."

"Dammit," Ogallala said impatiently, "I wanted my hat that Tony had give to George Aldrich—"

"That blasted hat!" Vink swore disgustedly. "I'm commencing to think you're cracked on the subject, Ogallala."

"*You* would," Ogallala replied scornfully. "Don't forget that was my hat. That night when the posse was on our heels and Tony buried the gold I was bad hit but I wasn't unconscious all the time. And then Tony tore off and took my hat . . ."

The door of the Mecca Saloon opened and three cowpunchers from the Rafter-N outfit strolled out of the place. They spoke to the Mitchells and stood talking on the porch. Kane rose to his feet. "C'mon, let's slope for home. We can finish our *habla* there. Bring that bottle, Vink."

He strode out to the hitch rack, followed by Ogallala and Vink. The three men got into saddles and wheeled their ponies away from the tie rail. Vink crowded his pony close to Ogallala's mount. "I still don't see," Vink persisted, "why that hat is so important you kill a man in your attempt to get it."

Ogallala snorted derisively. "You blame fool," he snarled, "the man who owns that black sombrero has a good chance to find that thirty thousand gold!"

A HINT OF MISSING CATTLE

IT WAS STILL A BIT EARLY FOR MANY TO BE FOUND IN the hotel dining room the following morning when Johnny and Humdrum sat down to order their breakfasts. Humdrum appeared only half awake—as usual. Johnny was alert for his first glance at Susan Aldrich, though he half expected not to see her.

Humdrum grumbled as they sat down to a corner table. "Do you have to keep your eyes glued to that kitchen door every minute?"

Johnny grinned. "I don't want to miss a thing."

Humdrum grunted, "Talk about the early bird catching the worm. You won't miss anything. Me, I often wondered why the worm was such a damn fool as to get up and be caught. Cripes! Seven o'clock you was knocking on my door. What's the idea of getting me up in the middle of the night?"

Before Johnny could reply Susan emerged from the

kitchen, radiant in neat blue gingham and a checked apron. The morning sunlight, shining through windows, picked out pale golden glints in her neatly coiled hair. The girl came straight to their table and smiled "Good morning." That smile did things to Johnny's heart. He gulped a reply and Humdrum nodded rather sleepily. Susan told them what was to be had for breakfast. Johnny didn't know exactly what he asked her to bring.

Humdrum brightened a trifle. "It's too early to eat much," he drawled, "but for the good of my constitution I suppose I should take a mite of nourishment. I'll just have those pancakes and sausage you mentioned, Miss Aldrich. And some ham and eggs on the side and coffee and biscuits. Sa-ay, is there any of that dried apple pie left, like we had last night? Yeah, some of that too. And if there was just a small bowl of oatmeal handy . . ."

"It hardly seems enough," Susan said dryly. "Didn't you sleep well last night, Humdrum?"

Humdrum managed to shake his head. "Do you know, I could hear the bed ticking all night long."

Johnny grinned. "Maybe it was the snoring I heard in your room that kept you awake, Humdrum."

"You've probably guessed it, Johnny." Susan smiled and hurried off kitchenward. Within a short time she returned with their breakfast, but by this time more people had entered the dining room and there was no opportunity for further conversation.

Johnny and Humdrum had completed eating by the time Susan again approached their table. "Still got that note I gave you for my foreman, Johnny?"

"Yes, Miss Aldrich."

Susan paused. "Anybody that works for me, without wages, forgets the 'Miss.' Let me have that note. I wrote another for Mecate Bowen, telling him of your

78

adventures with the Mitchells. Mecate is inclined to be sort of crusty with strangers, but it will be as good as a personal introduction when he learns you've come off first-best against the Spur-Bar. Mecate hasn't any use for that crowd."

"I figure I'm going to like Mecate Bowen," Johnny said, giving up one note and receiving another in exchange. Susan hurried off to take care of a fresh customer and Johnny and Humdrum headed for the livery to get their ponies.

Twenty minutes later they were mounted and loping their ponies along the trail that ran northwest to the Aldrich Rocking-A. The trail was wagon rutted and hoof-marked and not hard to follow as it wound through the hilly grass country, which lifted gradually toward the Sangre de Santos Range. Overhead the sky was an inverted turquoise bowl, flecked here and there by soaring buzzards that wheeled and dipped in search of food. Mesquite trees, cactus and yucca were seen along the way. Now and then a jagged spur of granite lifted abruptly from the rolling plains.

The sun lifted higher above the Sangre de Santos, its heat causing the riders to draw their ponies to a slower gait. Humdrum mopped his brow with a bandanna and settled, heavy-lidded, in his saddle. Johnny broke the silence after a time. "Susan said the Rocking-A is sort of up against it. Do you suppose her father's killing had anything to do with it?"

Humdrum shrugged listless shoulders. "We'll probably learn the reason in time."

"Probably," Johnny agreed. "One thing seems certain to me—if Mecate Bowen doesn't like the Spur-Bar outfit it may be he figures they have a hand in the trouble."

"Maybe." Humdrum nodded. "Still, I don't know how they could—unless they've been rustling Rocking-A stock."

"Susan didn't say anything to that effect," Johnny pointed out.

"There's this much to it"—Humdrum roused himself to longer speech with an apparent effort—"if Mecate Bowen suits Susan he's probably a right good hombre. And if Mecate Bowen doesn't take to the Mitchell crowd he's probably got good reasons. Off-hand, without knowing why, I'd say Mecate Bowen was on the right course. Me, I don't go for those Mitchells nohow."

Johnny grinned reminiscently at thoughts of the previous night's encounter. "I'm bettin' a plugged peso they don't like you either, Humdrum."

Humdrum chuckled drowsily. "Their eyes sure opened wider when I dropped that detective badge of mine last night. I'll betcha they've done a heap of wondering about me and what I came to Spearhead Wells for. I kind of figured if I let that badge slip to the floor it would check 'em up a mite. I noticed, right away, that Kane Mitchell sort of softened his voice. I don't figure we'll have any more trouble with 'em until they get me straightened out in their minds."

"Unless," Johnny suggested, "Ogallala Mitchell insists on trying to get this black sombrero of mine. He's so danged sure this hat is his that sometimes I wonder if maybe he didn't own it at some time. On the other hand, even if it was his, I can't see a good reason for him making so much trouble to get it."

"Aw, he's just a spoiled, cantankerous ol' hellion who's so used to having his own way that he can't abide anybody opposing him. That's the way I figure it."

"You're probably right."

"If you got that settled in your mind," Humdrum said languidly, "suppose you keep your trap shut a while and let me rest. I'm sort of weary of talking."

They rode on, Humdrum slouched in the saddle, eyes closed, his solid figure rocking easily to the motion of the horse. Johnny was alert to see the country through which he was passing. Once, off to the south a distance, he saw a bunch of cows burned with what appeared to be the Spur-Bar brand, though he couldn't be sure. Later, to the right of the trail, a mile or more away, he saw more white-faced cattle. These he took to be Susan's, though the distance was too great to read brands.

The trail wound on and finally approached a long line of cottonwood trees marching along the banks of a stream. Johnny wondered how deep the fording would be, but another turn in the trail obviated the necessity of wading across: a sturdy plank bridge, with a railing on either side, wide enough to allow the passage of a wagon, crossed the stream. Several cows were strung along the banks, bearing the Rocking-A brand.

Humdrum sat straighter in his saddle as they approached the river. "Huh! Water, eh? I wonder if this creek has got a name."

Johnny nodded. "I remember that hand in the livery stable mentioning it. This must be Rio Arenoso— Arenoso Creek, he called it. I didn't know it come up this way. The livery fellow said it came down from the Sangre de Santos, then, after a time, disappeared in the ground and came up again south of Spearhead Wells. That's where the town gets its water."

"It should assure Susan plenty water for her stock."

The two men reined their ponies down the bank and

into the flowing stream with its gravelly bottom. The horses stuck their noses deeply into the water, still icy cold after its mountain descent. A few minutes later Humdrum and Johnny turned the mounts back to land and crossed the plank bridge. They passed through a narrow grove of cottonwoods and resumed the trail in more open country once more. The Sangre de Santos Range seemed definitely nearer now, the tall, serrated peaks towering almost overhead, to all appearances, though they were still many miles distant. Another half-hour of travel and Johnny said, "There're the buildings, Humdrum."

They had just topped a low rise of land and, not more than a quarter of a mile farther on, situated in a grove of cottonwoods, they spied the Rocking-A ranch. Details came clearer as they approached. There was a long, one-story ranch house of adobe-and-rock construction, corrals, barns, a bunkhouse and kitchen combined, a blacksmith shop. The fans of a tall windmill whirred steadily and the clanking of the pump came clearly to the ears of the two riders.

Humdrum and Johnny rode past the ranch house and headed their ponies toward the bunkhouse with its adjoining mess shanty, from the chimney of which smoke drifted in the morning air. There were a few horses standing in the nearest corral but no sign of any human about. Just as they reached the bunkhouse a man appeared in the doorway and stood gazing at them with no particular show of pleasure. He reminded Johnny of nothing so much as a length of weathered rawhide, with a pair of unusually keen eyes. His legs in their faded denim overalls were considerably bowed; his long mustaches were sun-bleached to a dry, wispy appearance; his battered old sombrero was shoved back on a head of scrubby, iron-gray hair. He said tersely one word: "Howdy."

Johnny said, "We're looking for Mecate Bowen."

The man in the doorway replied, "You're looking at him."

Johnny and Humdrum slipped down from the ponies. Without a word Johnny handed Bowen the note Susan had given him to deliver. Bowen took the note, looked at Johnny, then at Humdrum; he looked back at Johnny a moment longer, eying Johnny's tall-crowned black sombrero. "Seen you coming right after you crossed that ridge of land yonder. Figured you was a Mex. See different now. Well, them steeple hats ain't always wore by Mexes. I remember, several years back, feller by name of Ogallala Mitchell wore one." There was a distinct purpose behind this talk; Mecate Bowen was employing the time used in conversation to narrowly size up Johnny and Humdrum. "Don't happen to know Mitchell, do you?"

"Might be a good idea to read that note Miss Aldrich sent," Johnny suggested. "Maybe it will answer your question."

Bowen grunted a short "Humph!" and opened the note. He read it through, then glanced again at Johnny and Humdrum. There was a warmer light in his eyes now, and he extended a gnarled hand in their direction. "Shake, Donshawnee and Hartigan. I'm always glad to grip claws with anybody that can stop them Mitchells cold, like Susan says you did." They shook hands and Bowen went on, "There's one question this note don't answer."

"What's that?" Johnny asked.

"I'm wondering why you two are offering to ride for the Rocking-A without salary."

"We got to have some place to sleep, haven't we?" Humdrum drawled lazily.

Bowen looked rather dubiously at Humdrum. Johnny said, "We like the country. Miss Aldrich said that once the Rocking-A got on its feet it would make up the wages due. We're not broke at present, so we can afford to wait a while. Meanwhile, we're tired of loafing around the country and this looked like a good place to light."

Bowen nodded. "I can imagine you being tired of loafing," he said bluntly, "but not him." He jerked a stubby thumb in Humdrum's direction. "Well, put up yore horses. We'll just spend today getting acquainted. I put on some stew when I first sighted you. 'Tain't dinnertime, but we can eat if you like."

"That suits me fine," Humdrum said.

He and Johnny turned their ponies into a corral and returned with their saddles. Bowen led them into a long bunkhouse, with a double tier of bunks along one wall and a table and benches in the center of the room. The kitchen was entered through a doorway at one end of the bunkhouse. Bowen put plates of stew on the table and brought in a pot of coffee. The men seated themselves. The three got acquainted over food. Bowen insisted on Johnny supplying the details of his encounter with the Mitchell brothers. He wasn't surprised when he heard Ogallala claimed Johnny's hat.

"I 'member back, several years, Ogallala had a hat mighty nigh the same as yores. He's shore a cantankerous ol' buzzard. For that matter, I don't like none of them Mitchells—never did. Don't trust 'em!"

"You missing cattle?" Johnny asked directly.

"Ain't many left to miss," Bowen evaded. "We were a spell back though."

Humdrum drawled, "Of course the Mitchells were back of it."

Bowen frowned. "As a matter of fact, we could never get any proof in that direction. To tell the truth the sign pointed directly away from the Spur-Bar. Mebbe you'll see what I mean when you get to riding this range." He broke off suddenly and commenced to stuff tobacco into a smelly old briar pipe. Johnny and Humdrum rolled cigarettes. They didn't pursue the question. Dinner was finished and the dishes cleared away.

"I'll wash the crockery," Bowen said. "I've been chief cook and bottle washer around here. Just got one hand at present, Dave Franklin. He'll come riding in around sundown. Meantime, there's some odds and ends need takin' care of, which same I've been too busy to tend to. Hartigan, you look like a hombre that likes to sit. Suppose you take a *pasear* down to the barn. You'll find some harness that needs mending and everythin' there to do with. Donshawnee, there's a mite of painting and sprucin' up to be done before Susan comes home—"

"Miss Aldrich going to come out here?" Johnny asked in surprise.

"Shore enough. You didn't figure she was roped to that table-waitin' chore, did you? Shucks! She just took that for a spell to raise some money that was needed quick. She'll be turnin' up to run her outfit come two— three days. I'd sort of like to get some fresh paint spread around 'fore she shows up. It's just about a month she's been away. Y'see, she had a note at the bank to meet and it plumb wiped her out of cash. She was just makin' some extra dollars to carry on here."

"Where's your paint and brushes?" Johnny asked. "I'll get busy pronto. However, if Miss Aldrich has been away from her house for a month it might need some

85

cleaning or mopping, unless you've been living in the house—"

"Cripes crickety!" Bowen exclaimed. "Yo're right. I ain't been in thet house in so long I'd plumb forgot it. Yo're right. You redd up the house and we'll let the paintin' ride over for a spell."

At supper, after a day of "reddin' up," as Bowen termed it, Johnny and Humdrum were introduced to Dave Franklin, the Rocking-A cowhand. Franklin was a tall, serious-faced man in his early forties, with a weather beaten countenance and a taciturn manner. Johnny and Humdrum both liked him, though he didn't have a great deal to say. With the dishes cleared away after supper, and tobacco burning evenly, Franklin got a small book out of his bunk and settled himself to read near an oil lamp on the table. Humdrum squirmed around until he could read the title of the book.

"*Merchant of Venison,* eh?" Humdrum commented lazily. "By Bill Shakespeare. Must be about some coot shooting deer out of season."

"Venice, not venison," Franklin reproved mildly and continued reading.

"Dam'd if I can understand how you can keep your eyes open to read a book." Humdrum chuckled. "Me, I'm about ready to turn in now."

An hour later he did turn in, as did the others. Lights were put out and the men, excepting Johnny, were soon snoring. Johnny lay in his bunk, thinking about Susan Aldrich. That the girl was soon to arrive at the Rocking-A was good news.

SHOTS IN THE NIGHT

JOHNNY DIDN'T KNOW EXACTLY WHEN HE SLIPPED OFF to slumber, but there was little doubt regarding his awakening. His eyes opened abruptly; every sense was alert for something. He knew not what. A distinct feeling of uneasiness permeated his whole being. Had his half-dreaming, half-waking consciousness deceived him? He could have sworn the stealthy scratching of a match had penetrated his sleep. Or had he just dreamed that? He listened intently. There wasn't a sound to be heard, beyond the varied snores emanating from three other bunks.

He was about to relax, considering himself mistaken, when a cool draft of fresh air brushed across his face. It appeared to come from the doorway leading to the kitchen. Johnny remembered seeing the kitchen windows closed after supper. Now something else came to him: he sensed rather than actually saw or heard, the presence of some fifth person in the bunkhouse, somewhere in the vicinity of the door. Johnny tensed again. A slight movement, like the withdrawing of a door bolt, caught his ear.

Johnny carefully edged one hand toward the holsters hanging at the head of his bunk and drew himself half erect. His fingers closed about a gun butt, silently drawing the weapon from its scabbard. He was certain now someone was standing near the bunkhouse door. It might, of course, be some friend of Mecate Bowen's. Well, a friend would speak up if challenged. Johnny shifted in his bunk and spoke softly:

"Stand right where you are, hombre."

87

That brought a number of things to the happening point all at once. The door was flung violently open. Bright moonlight poured inside, and against it Johnny saw clearly the silhouette of a moving figure. Johnny caught a quick movement an instant before an abrupt burst of gunfire blossomed in the bunkhouse.

Even as he heard the leaden slug rip into the wooden framework of the bunk, above his head, Johnny fired one quick shot. Events came swiftly after that. The intruder disappeared beyond the moonlight shining through the doorway. Johnny heard his running footsteps across the earth as he took flight. Humdrum, Bowen and Dave Franklin came out of bunks as one man, exclamations bursting from their lips.

Johnny had already dashed past the three. He halted in the bunkhouse doorway, the forty-five in his right fist spitting lances of flame. Even as he pulled trigger he saw his running target stumble and sprawl, face down, on the earth, a few rods distant from the waiting horse he'd been trying to reach.

"I must have got him with my first shot," Johnny said to no one in particular and stepped through the bunkhouse doorway. Mecate Bowen, Humdrum and Franklin were right behind him, asking excited questions. They reached the fallen man almost as soon as Johnny.

The man lay as he had dropped on the earth, both arms stretched toward his waiting pony. One hand held a six-shooter, the other clutched tightly the brim of Johnny's black sombrero. The intruder's own hat had fallen off and lay a few feet away. Bowen, Franklin and Humdrum were all talking at once. Johnny explained:

"I woke up, heard someone moving in the bunkhouse. I got my gun and ordered him to stand. He cut down on

88

me with his iron and I hammered a shot back. He ran and I followed, shook two more shots from my barrel. Figure I missed those two; he went down as I fired. I reckon I must have nailed him with my first shot."

Johnny stooped and turned the man over. He was still alive but breathing with difficulty. A dark blot on his chest attested the accuracy of Johnny's first shot. There weren't any other wounds. The man's eyes were closed and he was unconscious. He wasn't more than nineteen or twenty years old.

Mecate Bowen swore suddenly. "I know this cuss. He's that young Mex, Ramón Vinazo, who wrangles hawsses for Kane Mitchell on the Spur-Bar."

"What do you suppose he came here for?" Franklin said.

Humdrum drawled, "It sure as hell looks like he came for Johnny's black sombrero. Well, it ain't likely he'll want his pony for a spell. I reckon I'll put the horse in the corral." He left the group about the wounded man and started toward the horse. Dave Franklin's face showed lines of perplexity in the bright moonlight, as he digested Humdrum's words about the hat.

Johnny continued his examination of the wounded Vinazo. "He's bad hit," Johnny reported, "but there's a chance we could pull him through and learn something. He's bleeding plenty."

Bowen ordered Franklin to light a lamp in the bunkhouse and spread some blankets. Franklin hurried off to obey. Then, as tenderly as possible, Johnny and Bowen lifted the unconscious man and carried him to the bunkhouse where they placed the limp form in a vacant bunk. After getting into clothing they again turned their attentions to Ramón Vinazo. Bowen produced a flask of whisky and clean bandaging cloths, preparing to do what was possible in the way of first-aid treatment.

While Bowen was working over the wounded Mexican Humdrum entered, bearing a pair of boots. "I found these outside the bunkhouse. I reckon he figured to move softer in his sock feet. Mebbe softer, but not easier. Me, I don't crave to move around much that-a-way." He commenced drawing on his own boots and overalls. "I wonder how he got in here anyway."

Dave Franklin emerged from the kitchen at that moment, bearing a pan of hot water. "There's a window open out there that wasn't open when we went to bed," Franklin said.

"That explains it." Johnny nodded. "I knew I felt a draft across my face. Vinazo probably figured it would be easier leaving by the door than climbing through the window again. Reckon he had to light a match to find my sombrero—"

He broke off suddenly, watching Bowen bathe and cleanse the wound in Vinazo's chest. Vinazo had started an incoherent muttering in which Johnny could discern clearly only a syllable here and there. Once the Mexican said quite plainly, ". . . is not enough, señor. For theese risk . . . twenty pesos . . . not e-nough . . ." Silence for a few minutes, while Bowen worked, then Vinazo spoke again, ". . . no, no, señor. Is not needed that . . . you strike me . . . like that. I weel go . . . and try to . . . get theese sombrero . . ."

"Sounds to me," Johnny said grimly, "as though Vinazo didn't want to come here to get my hat but somebody took a punch at him and—"

"You figure it was Ogallala Mitchell?" Humdrum asked.

"I'm not figuring," Johnny said, hard voice, "but I am
90

doing a heap of guessing. If I ever find out for sure . . ." His voice trailed off, not completing the sentence.

Bowen worked in silence, while the other three stood about watching and handing him things when he asked for them. Dave Franklin had lighted another lamp and placed a fresh pot of coffee on to boil. Finally Bowen lifted his head and said with a sigh, "I can't get that damn blood stopped. I don't reckon there's much can be done until that bullet is dug out. I figured maybe I could fix things up until we could get of Doc Pickett out here, but it's beyond me."

"How long would it take to get the doc here?" Johnny asked.

Bowen shook his head. "Too long, I'm afeared. Vinazo would bleed to death first. The only chance the cus is got is to be taken into town where the doc can work on him. I'm not sure, then, that it would be worth while. Vinazo might jolt to death on the way."

"He'll bleed to death here," Johnny pointed out. "We might as well take the chance. I'll drive him to Spearhead Wells."

Bowen turned to Franklin. "Dave, you go hitch up the buckboard." Franklin nodded and hurried from the bunkhouse. Bowen said to Johnny, "I'll drive to the doc's. You'd better saddle up and come along though. We'll have to report to Sheriff Pritchard and he'll probably want to question you. Not that I think there'll be any trouble, but you being a stranger in this country and all it's best if you tell Pritchard, yoreself, just how it happened."

"You probably know best." Johnny nodded.

Bowen bandaged Vinazo's wound as well as possible, forced a few drops of whisky past the unconscious man's lips and sat down to wait for the buckboard to be drawn up before the bunkhouse. Johnny hurried out to saddle up his horse. Within a few minutes he was back and Franklin, with the buckboard, wasn't far behind him. The moon had dropped nearly from sight by this time and there was a definite chill in the air.

Bowen went to the bunkhouse doorway and squinted at the eastern sky. "Dawn ain't far off," he observed. "We'll have to move slow, but I figure we should reach Doc Pickett's house 'long about seven o'clock—no, Dave"—he turned to answer Franklin's query—"don't bother cookin' up any breakfast. We don't want to wait for that. We'll spill some java down our gullets and get under way. Dave, you carry on today, like you've been doing. Humdrum, you'll find an oilcan hangin' beside the pump. I've noticed that ol' mill creakin' a mite lately. You see can somethin' be done about it. Put in the rest of yore time sort of reddin' up about the place. I'll get back soon's possible."

"Unless you think it's really necessary that you drive the wagon," Johnny commenced, "I can take Vinazo in—"

"I want to go along," Bowen interrupted. "Can't tell, some of them Spur-Bar hombres may be in town and get nasty. My word will back you up with Sheriff Pritchard."

"Just as you say." Johnny nodded and commenced strapping on his gun belts.

He and Bowen swallowed scalding cups of coffee and then warmed blankets to place in the wagon bed. "Don't want Vinazo to get a chill," Bowen said.

Finally all was in readiness. They carried Vinazo out to the wagon and arranged his limp form as comfortably as possible, though it is doubtful if the wounded man now experienced any pain. Johnny climbed to his saddle and Bowen mounted the driver's seat on the wagon. "Well, see you later," he called back to Humdrum and Franklin. He spoke to the team, slapped the lines along their backs and the wagon moved on, with Johnny riding at its side.

The sky overhead was dark now, but already, along the eastern horizon, a faint streak of gray was commencing to show. Bowen drove carefully, so as not to jolt the wagon more than possible. Even so a faint moan escaped Vinazo's pallid lips on three or four occasions. Bowen swore softly. "Maybe that pore cuss tried to do us harm," he said, "but I shore as hell hate to see him hurt when he's in this condition. I don't like to see no human hurt unnecessary. I doubt if he'll live till we reach Doc Pickett's."

"All we can do is try," Johnny replied. "I hate to think of killing a man, but he threw down on me. There was nothing else I could do."

"Pshaw, Johnny! Nobody's blaming you."

It was dawn by the time they reached the Rio Arenoso. The wagon rumbled across the plank bridge, then Bowen pulled the horses to a halt. Johnny soaked a bandanna in the river and sponged Vinazo's face. Bowen twisted around on his driver's seat, asking, "How is he?"

Johnny grimly shook his head. "He's burning with fever."

"Fever always accompanies gunshot wounds."

"I know"—Johnny nodded—"but this seems even worse than usual. Mecate, we've got to take a chance."

"How do you mean?"

"At the rate we're going Vinazo will be dead before we reach Spearhead Wells. If he's to live he's just got to stand for some jolting. We've got to move faster."

Bowen nodded. "That's sense. All right. We'll move faster." He spoke to the horses and they got under way, this time at a speedier gait. Johnny looked anxiously at the wagon a moment, then climbed back into his saddle and touched spurs to his pony.

SIDEWINDERS OR WOLVES

IT WASN'T QUITE SEVEN O'CLOCK WHEN THEY ROLLED into Spearhead Wells. By this time Vinazo's face was a deathly gray, and Johnny and Bowen held out small hope for the man. It was too early for many citizens to be abroad, though a few ponies and wagons were scattered at hitch racks along the main thoroughfare. Bright morning sunlight reflected heat from the tops of buildings. As they passed the combination jail and sheriff's office they saw Sheriff Pritchard just emerging from the doorway. The sheriff's eyes opened a trifle when he saw the wagon. Before he could ask a question Bowen called, "We're headed for Doc Pickett's, Nick. We'll come back and see you."

Pritchard nodded and said, "I hope there's nothing wrong."

"It could be worse," Johnny replied.

The wagon turned from Main Street at the next corner, went on a block and turned right along a tree-lined road known as Latigo Street. Here Bowen pulled the wagon to a halt before a two-story frame house, surrounded by a neat, whitewashed picket fence. "This is Doc's combination home, office and hospital," Mecate commented. "His wife does what nursin' is necessary."

Johnny got down from his pony. At that moment the

94

front door of the house opened and a lean man with white hair and stooped shoulders stepped out. "What you got there, Mecate?" he called.

"Hi-yuh, Doc! Gunshot wound. Didn't know whether you'd be in or not."

"Just got in," the doctor grumbled. He came down the walk leading from his house to the street: "Been up all night at the Jenkins'. Amos' wife has delivered again."

"I hope Missis Jenkins is doin' nicely," Bowen said politely.

"Certain. Babies never bothered Letitia Jenkins to any extent. It's always Amos requires most of my 'tention. The dang idiot won't realize I never yet lost a father in such cases."

"Doc, shake hands with Johnny Donshawnee."

The doctor had reached the wagon by this time. He took Johnny's hand, at the same time looking at the unconscious man in the wagon bed. A dubious look came into his lined features. "Don't know what you brought this to me for, Mecate," he grumbled. "Better turn around and head over to Undertaker Collins' on Main Street."

"Is he dead?" Johnny asked.

"He should be if he isn't," Pickett grunted. "He certain looks dead." Reaching one hand into the wagon, he felt for Vinazo's pulse. After a moment he grunted again. "Humph! Pretty thready. Not much chance, but I'll try." Then, in answer to Johnny's query, "Consciousness? He might come to for a few minutes before he dies. I couldn't say. If he lives he might be this way for days. Well, let's get him into bed."

They carried Vinazo carefully into the house where the doctor's wife was already preparing a bed. Bowen started to tell how the shooting happened, but Dr.

Pickett cut him short, "Get out and don't bother me now. I'll hear about this later. Right now I've got my work cut out. I'll manage to let you know how he gets along. No, no, I won't know anything until nightfall, at best."

Johnny and Mecate headed back toward the street. Outside, Mecate said, "Well, Doc will pull Vinazo through, if anybody can."

"I hope so; I'd like a chance to talk to Vinazo a mite." Johnny got into his saddle and Bowen mounted to the driver's seat of the wagon and turned the team. Johnny said, "Where to now? Don't forget we've got to see the sheriff."

"I'm aimin' to get a bite of breakfast at the hotel. We'll run into Nick someplace. No particular hurry about him."

They returned to Main Street and tied the horses in front of the Cowman's Rest Hotel. As they were about to enter the sheriff approached. They stopped and talked. Mecate Bowen explained what had happened. Pritchard heard him through in silence, then turned to Johnny.

"Johnny," he said slowly, eying Johnny's black sombrero, "that top-piece of yours 'pears to be causing trouble around here. Well, I'm glad to learn you can take care of yourself."

"You don't figure it's necessary to hold Johnny then?" Mecate asked.

Pritchard shook his head. "Don't see any reason for it," he stated. "As I get the story—and your word's good with me—it was a case of self-defense. Vinazo ain't dead yet. If he's dead and there's an inquest held I may have to act, should Kane Mitchell prefer charges, but I don't reckon that will happen. Do you suppose Vinazo

96

really did break into your bunkhouse to steal that hat?"

"It's what he had in his hand when he fell," Johnny said.

"Uh-huh. Well, it seems sorter strange, don't it? On t'other hand, if Vinazo mumbled something that led you to believe that he'd been forced to go to your place after that hat it might put a different complexion on things. Ogallala Mitchell is plumb stubborn—fact is, after the way Johnny and Humdrum treated 'em, night before last, all three Mitchells is prob'ly determined to get that hat. Yep, the Mitchells might be back of the move. I'll be anxious to see how they take it when they hear what's happened."

Johnny nodded. "I've been thinking about that. If the Mitchells did send Vinazo to the Rocking-A they'll be wondering why he doesn't show up. It wouldn't surprise me a bit if they drifted into town to hear what they can hear."

Bowen nodded. "It's likely. I reckon we better stay around town for a spell. Meanwhile let's go eat. Had your breakfast yet, Nick?"

"Quite a spell back." The sheriff nodded. "Well, I'll see you later." He walked off in the direction of his office.

Johnny and Mecate passed through the hotel and into the dining room. Three of the tables were occupied. Susan wasn't in sight. The two men found a table near the entrance to the kitchen and sat down. Johnny's eyes were glued to the kitchen door. Eventually the door opened and a girl Johnny had never before seen came through. The new girl was evidently the waitress, for she was carrying a stack of food-laden dishes to one of the tables. Johnny looked her over and decided she wasn't nearly so pretty as Susan.

"Wonder where Susan is," Mecate observed. "That's a new filly that just come in."

"Just what I was wondering," Johnny said.

At that instant Susan entered from the kitchen. Her blue eyes opened a trifle wider when she spied Johnny and Mecate. She came directly to their table. "Well, this is a surprise. Good morning, gentlemen."

Johnny was on his feet. Mecate looked at him in some surprise, then he rose also. Johnny said, "We were wondering where you were."

"Well, here I am." Susan laughed. "Sit down, both of you. What brings you to town?"

She stood by the table, listening, while Bowen related what had happened. The smile quickly faded from her face. Once or twice she glanced with some trepidation at Johnny. Finally, when Mecate had finished, she said slowly, "I don't like it. I don't like my men running risks—"

"Wait a minute," Johnny broke in. "That had nothing to do with you. Vinazo was after my hat. It would have been the same if I'd been working at some other outfit."

They talked a few minutes longer, then Susan departed to bring their breakfasts. Within a short time she returned, bearing food and hot coffee. "I've been thinking, Mecate," she commenced; "so long as you have the buckboard here, you might as well wait over until tomorrow morning. Today's my last day, you know."

"Pshaw! Is that right?" Bowen said. "I didn't figure you'd be comin' home for two—three days yet. I must have lost track of the time."

"This is the twentieth of the month," Susan said. "I've been helping that new girl get started. I've some things to be taken back to the ranch. My trunk's here and the buckboard will be needed. There's no use of driving home today, then returning with it tomorrow—"

"Seems sensible," Johnny put in, smiling. "I reckon I can find my way back to the Rocking-A, Mecate. If you've got any special work you want done you can give me my orders before I leave."

Mecate nodded. "I was just thinking, Susan, if you're going to be through today why can't we drive back tonight? No use both of us spending the night in town."

"But Guadalupe is due to arrive tomorrow morning—" Susan stopped short. Her face was serious. "It's not going to be pleasant for her to arrive and hear about Ramón."

"Guadalupe Vinazo—Ramón's maw?" Mecate asked.

Susan nodded. "I wanted a woman to stay on the ranch with me, so I wrote to Guadalupe. She's been staying with relatives over at Verdeville. She'll be glad to come back to the Rocking-A. I guess things haven't been too pleasant in Verdeville—"

Bowen interrupted to say to Johnny, "Guadalupe's a Mex, like Ramón. Pretty good old scout too. Her and Ramón used to live on Rocking-A holdings. There's an old adobe house in the foothills. George Aldrich let 'em have the place. Never charged 'em any rent. Then Guadalupe got an idea she wanted to live someplace else for a spell. You know how such folks like to move around. She took Ramón with her when she left, but he came back here a coupla years ago and went to work for the Spur-Bar."

"Just a minute," Johnny said. "It looks like I'd better stay away from the Rockin-A. It won't be pleasant for Guadalupe or me either, in view of the fact I shot her son."

Susan shook her head. "Don't let it worry you, Johnny. Guadalupe won't blame you after I've

99

explained things. She knows Ramón is no paragon of virtue. I think he had to leave Verdeville because of some crooked business he got mixed in. He always has been wild. I think you'll like Guadalupe. She's a peach. I've known her since I was a baby—or she's known me—whichever way you put it."

Breakfast was finished. It was decided that Johnny would return to the Rocking-A, while Mecate Bowen waited over to drive Susan and Guadalupe to the ranch the following morning. Johnny said goodbye and he and Mecate left the hotel. On the street Mecate said, "One thing about waiting over, I can keep in touch with Doc Pickett and learn how Vinazo's getting along. If he gets well enough to talk I'll let you know what's said."

Johnny nodded. "I'll stick around town for a couple of hours before heading back. I'd like to see if the Mitchell brothers put in an appearance."

Mecate agreed. The two men strolled down the shady side of the street. Mecate stopped in two or three stores, trying to get a particular brand of smoking tobacco. He met acquaintances, introduced them to Johnny and stopped to chat. The morning passed quickly and it was nearing noon almost before Johnny realized it. Returning toward the center of town again, Johnny had just about decided to get his pony and head for the Rocking-A, when they encountered Sheriff Pritchard.

Pritchard said without preliminaries, "The Mitchells are in town."

"All three of 'em?" Bowen asked.

The sheriff nodded. "Pat Scudder's with 'em too." He turned to Johnny. "Scudder is the Spur-Bar foreman and a loudmouthed bully, if there ever was one. I reckon he's a good foreman though. He seems to keep the Spur-Bar hands in line and get plenty of work out of

100

'em." He hesitated, then, "I've warned the Mitchells not to start any trouble."

Johnny said quickly, "Have they shown intentions in that direction?"

"They were doing some talking in the Continental Saloon a spell back. It's got around town how you and Humdrum treated 'em night before last. They've had to stand for some joshing, and they don't like it. Howsomever, I don't reckon they'll start anything after my warnin'."

Johnny said, "You say they're in the Continental now?"

Pritchard nodded. "Leastwise Kane and Pat Scudder are. Ogallala and Vink didn't like me warnin' 'em the way I did. They tossed out some ugly talk. I told 'em if they couldn't keep civil tongues in their heads to get out of town. They left the Continental, but a few minutes ago I saw 'em headin into the Mecca bar, so they're taking their time about obeying my order."

Johnny smiled thinly. "I'd like to see if Kane Mitchell has anything to say to me. I reckon I'll head for the Continental."

"I'll go with you," Bowen said promptly.

"Now look here," Pritchard said with some sternness, "I don't want to hear of you starting trouble, Johnny."

Johnny grinned. "All right, I'll try to keep it quiet, Nick."

"You do that," Pritchard ordered, then softened a trifle. "And if you do get jammed up, Johnny, watch yourself. Those Mitchells are wolves when they get started."

Johnny said dryly, "I sort of figured 'em as belonging to the sidewinder family."

Mecate Bowen snorted. "Yo're both correct, I reckon.

Sidewinders or wolves! They're both prompted by the same mean instincts and I don't see much to choose between 'em."

"Maybe," Johnny said quietly, "we'll learn these particular Mitchells are also related to the little animal that has a wide stripe down his back—only in this case I wouldn't be surprised if the stripe wasn't white. Let's go see, Mecate."

He and Bowen started in the direction of the Continental Saloon, leaving the sheriff musing on the sidewalk behind them.

A FAST DRAW

THERE WERE A NUMBER OF MEN STANDING AT THE BAR in the Continental when Johnny and Mecate Bowen entered. A couple of Rafter-N cowpunchers stood at the far end of the long counter discussing beef prices with a TL waddie. Near the front end Kane Mitchell and a hulking brute of a man with small eyes were pouring drinks from a bottle of Old Crow. Corkscrew Jones was talking quietly with a round-bodied, elderly man, with a Teutonic cast of countenance and white hair, near the middle of the bar. The elderly man was sipping beer. Three or four other customers in citizens' clothing were also drinking.

Corkscrew Jones, looking up, saw Johnny and Bowen enter. "Hi-yuh," he called. "How's the day treating you?"

"Not so bad." Johnny smiled. "I haven't any kick so far."

The elderly man turned and a look of pleasure lighted his face. "Mecate Bowen!" he exclaimed. "It is a long time I have not seen you."

"Hello, Henry," Mecate responded, a trifle shortly, Johnny thought.

"For why you do not come and visit sometime?" the man persisted.

"Too busy." Bowen clipped the words and turned to Corkscrew. "I'll take a touch of liquor."

"Nothing for me except a sack of Bull Durham," Johnny said.

Corkscrew placed on the bar a bottle and glass and the tobacco Johnny had ordered. Johnny placed some money on the counter. Corkscrew jerked one thumb toward the elderly man, then, "Johnny Donshawnee, shake hands with Henry Linbauer. Henry owns the Wagon-Wheel, not far from the Rocking-A."

Johnny shook hands. Mecate Bowen frowned. Linbauer smiled warmly. "It is a pleasure to meet you, Mister Donshawnee." His words were thick and held just a trace of German accent.

By this time Kane Mitchell and the man with him had noticed the entrance of Johnny and Bowen, though their backs had been to the two when they entered the saloon. Kane Mitchell said something to his companion. The big man glowered angrily at Johnny and started away from the bar. Kane Mitchell grabbed his arm and pulled him back.

Henry Linbauer was talking to Johnny. Mecate was taking no part in the conversation. Linbauer was laughing now. ". . . and it is all over town"—he chuckled—"about you and your pardner. About how you have made those Spur-Bars back down. That was very funny—"

Corkscrew interrupted to speak hastily to Linbauer and gestured down the bar where Mitchell and his companion stood listening. Linbauer cast a contemptuous glance along the bar. "For why I should lower my voice?" he demanded. "Is this not a free country? Did I not come here from the old country where a man is not free to say what is on his mind?" He laughed and turned back to Johnny. "That hat you wear, that is the one Ogallala Mitchell says is his? He is a liar, of course."

Johnny wished the old German wouldn't talk so loud. He tried to change the subject, but at that moment the big man standing with Kane Mitchell plunged along the bar and shoved a six-shooter against Linbauer's stomach.

"Take it back, Dutchy," the man growled, "or, by Gawd—"

Linbauer looked stolidly at the gun stuck against his middle. "I take back nothing," he growled.

At that moment Kane Mitchell's hand closed down on the gun, his thumb sliding between the drawn-back Hammer and the cartridge. "Cut it, Pat," he said sharply. "Put that gun away."

"But this Dutch fool—" the man commenced angrily.

"I said, 'Cut it!' " Kane Mitchell repeated.

The big man reluctantly placed the gun back in his holster.

Kane Mitchell eyed Linbauer a moment. "This is a free country, like you say, Linbauer, but I don't like to hear people calling any Mitchell a liar: Next time it happens you'd better be ready to back up your statement. Only that you're a heap older than Pat I'd have let you two fight it out."

"I am ready at any time," Linbauer said belligerently.

Kane Mitchell said wearily, "Oh hell," and half turned away. Linbauer ordered another bottle of beer and stood defiantly eyeing the glowering man who had put the gun on him.

Mitchell said pleasantly enough to Johnny, "Mornin', Donshawnee—Bowen. Donshawnee, let me make you acquainted with my foreman, Pat Scudder. Pat's a mite quick-tempered with his shootin' iron, but don't let that scare you."

Johnny smiled and nodded at Scudder. Neither made a move to shake hands. Johnny said, "I haven't seen anything about Scudder to scare me yet."

"That," Scudder rasped, "is because you ain't pushed me too far yet."

"Cut it out, Pat," Kane Mitchell snapped. He turned to Johnny. "That sombrero of yours seems to be causing a heap of trouble, Donshawnee. Me, I'm all for peace."

"Suits me." Johnny nodded coolly. "You've got to admit, Mitchell, that the trouble hasn't been of my starting."

"Possibly there's something in what you say," Mitchell conceded quietly. "There's no dodging the fact that Ogallala tried to ride roughshod over you. On the other hand, he's my brother. I know he's getting a mite cantankerous, but I try to humor him. Whether that's his hat or not I won't try to say. But he wants it. I'm afraid there won't be much peace in these parts until he gets it. Donshawnee, I'll give you thirty dollars for that sombrero."

Johnny shook his head. "This bonnet's not for sale."

Kane Mitchell smiled good-humoredly. "Fact is, I didn't think thirty would tempt you. I'm raising my offer to fifty."

"You still don't tempt me."

"Seventy-five," Mitchell snapped.

Johnny hesitated. There was something queer about

105

this. Thirty dollars would have been more than sufficient for the black sombrero. Kane Mitchell wasn't offering such money just to keep peace and pacify Ogallala. Johnny commenced to feel curious as to just how high Mitchell would raise his offer. Johnny laughed softly. "It's this way, Mitchell. I like this bonnet. Seventy-five dollars might not buy another like it—"

"One hundred dollars!" Mitchell said impatiently.

"*Gott im Himmel!*" Linbauer exclaimed excitedly. "For a Mexican sombrero he would give one hundred dollars!" Others in the barroom, becoming interested, drew nearer. Pat Scudder said eagerly, "That's a dang good price, Donshawnee. You'd better take it before Kane changes his mind."

"If you doubled that offer, Mitchell—" Johnny commenced.

"Two hundred it is," Mitchell snapped.

"—I wouldn't be interested in selling." Johnny grinned. "I just put it that way to see how high you'd go. Now you've got me wondering. If I said three hundred would you go that high?"

A sudden light gleamed in Mitchell's eyes, then died. No, he considered, Donshawnee was just baiting him. He wondered how much Donshawnee knew about the hat. It wouldn't do to display too much eagerness. Mitchell laughed suddenly. "I wouldn't even give you one hundred now," he said "I was foolish to offer that much. It was just that I wanted to please Ogallala."

Johnny smiled thinly. "You were willing to pay two hundred dollars for a secondhand hat to please your brother?" he queried skeptically. "That certainly is brotherly love."

The humor of the situation suddenly struck others in

106

the saloon. Laughter broke out. Kane Mitchell flushed angrily. "Just why are you so anxious to keep that hat?" he demanded.

"I might ask why you're so anxious to get it." Johnny grinned

"I'm not—now," Mitchell snapped. "I don't give a curse in hell about it. Wouldn't take it as a gift!"

"No?" Johnny sounded a bit sarcastic. "You've changed your mind plumb sudden."

"What do you mean?"

"You've tried every way you know to get this sombrero, but it didn't occur to you to pay money for it until after your man had tried to steal it."

Kane Mitchell's eyes narrowed. "Now, I don't know what you're talking about."

"One of your Spur-Bar hands," Johnny went on, "might explain it to you. We caught him last night, just as he was getting away with the hat—"

"That's a blasted lie," Pat Scudder bellowed, unable longer to keep silent, "and you're a liar, Donshawnee!"

Johnny whirled, took two quick steps. His right hand raised and he slapped Scudder twice across the mouth, once with the back of his hand, once with the palm. "I don't like to be called a liar," he said quietly.

Red rage flamed in Scudder's eyes. His face darkened, throwing into bold relief the white marks of Johnny's fingers across his mouth—a mouth that opened and ripped out a savage, choking curse as his right arm plunged down and his fingers closed about a gun butt. The gun cleared holster.

Johnny's gun was out too. He took another quick step and brought his gun barrel down sharply across Scudder's knuckles. Scudder emitted a yelp of pain and his forty-five clattered to the floor.

107

"Now, Scudder," Johnny said grimly, "if you want any more pick up that iron and go to work. Either that or admit that I'm not a liar."

"I—I—I reckon I must have been mistaken," Scudder gulped. He was deathly pale now, as he realized that Johnny could have shot him instead of knocking the gun from his hand. He stooped cautiously, retrieved his gun and shoved it quickly into holster.

A long sigh of relief went up in the Continental. Men who had made haste to get away from the bar now moved slowly back.

"*Donnerwetter!*" Linbauer gasped. "Such a quick draw I have never seen. You could have shot him, Johnny!"

Mecate Bowen nodded with something of approval in his eyes. "You were right about the stripe along the back, son," he said quietly.

Johnny nodded. "That's the way I figured it."

Kane Mitchell hadn't moved from his position at the bar. His eyes were narrowed, studying Johnny closely, as though he had just realized Johnny might prove a more formidable foe than at first expected. Now he spoke cold reproof: "Pat, get out of here. You made a fool move. What's happened should be a lesson to you."

"But, Kane—" Scudder commenced.

"Get out!"

"Have it your way, Kane," Scudder growled. "But I'm not through with Donshawnee by a long shot—"

"You fool!" Kane Mitchell lost his temper. "Get out, before Donshawnee decides he ain't through with you!"

Scudder quailed in the face of Mitchell's rage. "All right, all right," he mumbled thickly. "I'm going. You don't need to get sore—" He paused, gulped at the look in Mitchell's face, then quickly turned and hurried from

108

the Continental.

Mitchell slowly cooled as he watched Scudder leave. "Damned fool," he swore wrathfully, then turned to Johnny. "I'm sorry about that, Donshawnee."

"No need to be." Johnny smiled. "It didn't bother me any."

"It bothered me," Mitchell said frankly. "Pat didn't have any call to put the lie to you that way. What he got he deserved. He should have waited to see what you'd say. Now I'm quite sure you didn't intend us to understand that one of my men had been caught stealing your hat at the Rocking-A."

"That's exactly what I intended," Johnny said shortly. "I woke up when he was making his getaway. When I tried to stop him he threw down on me. There was nothing for me to do but plug him."

"I swear I don't know anything about it," Mitchell said.

Mecate Bowen broke in. "The feller's hawss is in the Rocking-A corral, any time you care to pick it up, Mitchell. It's branded Spur-Bar."

Mitchell looked frankly puzzled. "I tell you, this is all news to me. Who is the hombre?"

"Ramón Vinazo," Bowen put in before Johnny could reply. "He's one of your hands all right, Mitchell. He's down at Doc Pickett's now, in case you feel inclined to pay his doctor bill."

"Vinazo? Oh, him . . ." Mitchell did some quick thinking, then turned to Johnny. "You didn't kill him then?"

Johnny shook his head. "Doc Pickett doesn't figure he has much chance to pull through though."

"Damn Mex!" Mitchell growled. "It'd served him right if you'd blown him clean to hell. By Gawd! If he lives I'm going to have Sheriff Pritchard take him in on a charge of horse stealing."

"I'm afraid the charge won't hold water, Mitchell," Mecate said. "There ain't no law against him ridin' your hawsses so long as you pay him wages."

"Cripes! I don't pay him wages. I fired him two days ago. So you see, Donshawnee, it wasn't a Spur-Bar man you plugged last night."

Johnny smiled. "Uh-huh, I see," he said, unconvinced.

Mitchell frowned. "You don't believe me, do you?"

"What do you think?"

"Look, Donshawnee," Mitchell said testily, "you seem to be on the prod against me. I'll admit we got off on the wrong foot but there's no reason we can't be friends now. If you won't believe me you won't, but I want to make one thing clear—if there's any more trouble between us it won't be of my making."

Johnny nodded. "Suppose we drop the subject, Mitchell. I'm not out anything. We'll consider new troubles when they come up. Right now it's dinnertime, and I want to get a bite to eat before I head back to the Rocking-A. Coming, Mecate? I'll see you later, gents. Glad to have met you, Mr. Linbauer. S'long Corkscrew."

"Drop in again, Johnny," Corkscrew said.

Mecate followed Johnny to the doorway and they passed through the swinging doors in the direction of the street.

"By jiminy!" Linbauer's admiring eyes followed Johnny until he was gone. "That boy looks like a man to me."

Kane Mitchell glared at Linbauer, growled one word of profane disgust and strode wrathfully out of the Continental.

110

"STOP DONSHAWNEE!"

MITCHELL CURSED IN A STEADY MONOTONOUS undertone as he made his way along the street. Crossing at the next intersection, he paused on the corner, angrily looking across toward the Cowman's Rest Hotel. He recognized the Rocking-A buckboard tied there; the horse next to the wagon must belong to Donshawnee. Damn that stranger and his black sombrero! Or Ogallala's black sombrero! Ogallala could be mistaken. "If I thought he wasn't," Mitchell growled, "I'd bump Donshawnee off at the first chance and get that hat. But I'd hate to go to a lot of trouble and find Ogallala had just guessed wrong."

He moved on and turned into the Mecca Saloon. As he had expected he found Vink, Ogallala and Pat Scudder there, with glasses and bottles on the bar before them. There weren't any other customers in the place and the barkeeper dozed on a high stool at the far end of the bar. The man awoke as Kane Mitchell stepped inside.

"Don't get up," Kane said shortly, "I'm not drinking right now."

The bartender nodded and slipped off to sleep again.

Vink, Ogallala and Scudder turned at the sound of Kane's voice. Kane eyed the three disgustedly without saying anything. Ogallala looked away after a moment, a guilty look stealing into his hardened features. Scudder blew softly on the badly skinned knuckles of his right hand, the result of their violent contact with Johnny's gun barrel. Vink refused to be faced down by his brother and said after a minute, "Well?"

"It ain't well at all," Kane snapped. "C'mon outside."

111

Turning he led the way out to the saloon porch, away from the bartender. The others followed, Ogallala somewhat reluctantly. They gathered about Kane, waiting for him to speak. Kane didn't say anything, just stood there, watching the daily activities of the main thoroughfare, bitter thoughts churning in his mind.

Vink finally broke the silence. "I understand from Pat that Donshawnee sort of put the bee on him. What are we going to do about it?"

"Nothing about that," Kane said coldly. "Pat made a damned fool of himself. What he got he had coming. He's just lucky Donshawnee didn't plug him. He could have easy enough."

Scudder didn't say anything as he continued to blow on his wounded knuckles.

"But I don't understand," Vink continued, "this business about one of our men trying to steal that hat at the Rocking-A. I'd have called Donshawnee a liar too. We didn't send anybody —"

"No, you and I didn't," Kane rasped, "but somebody sent Vinazo there. I denied we had anything to do with it, told them I'd fired Vinazo a couple of days ago. Donshawnee plugged the Mex. He's at Doc Pickett's now, not expected to live. Lucky for us, I guess he's not able to talk—"

"Why lucky for us?" Vink asked. "We didn't send him."

"Like I said," Kane resumed, "you and I didn't. I reckon we'd better ask Ogallala about it."

"Me?" Ogallala asked with assumed surprise. He tried to look innocent, but the bluff wouldn't hold water.

"I figure it was you, Ogallala," Kane said angrily. "By Gawd, you're getting worse all the time. Can't Vink and I trust you at all? We're all in this together—

112

or we should be. It's share and share alike, the three of us, when we get that gold."

Vink swore at Ogallala. "Figuring to grab it all for yourself, eh?" he snarled. "Of all the double-crossin'—"

"What's this talk about gold?" Pat Scudder asked, eyes widening. "I reckon something's going on I don't know about."

"I reckon there is," Kane said coldly. "You'll hear about it in time and be cut for a share, if you learn to mind your own business. Right now, Pat, I figure it's time you headed back for the Spur-Bar."

"Just as you say, Kane." Pat Scudder nodded and stepped down from the porch. He got into his saddle and without another word turned his pony and headed out of town.

Kane turned back to Ogallala. "When you learn to obey orders like that," he said grimly, "you'll be some use to me. But none of us will ever get any place so long as you keep trying to pull these underhanded tricks. The sooner you stop trying to use your head, Ogallala, and leave the thinking to me the better off we'll be."

The words stung Ogallala to speech. "I'll swear you got me wrong, Kane," he said earnestly. "Yes, I'll admit it was me sent Vinazo to try to get that hat. I told him I'd give him twenty pesos—Mex pesos, y'understand— if he'd get it for me—us. I just figured that might be the easiest way—"

"From now on," Kane said hotly, "don't do any more figuring. I'm sick of this sort of business. One more move of this kind from you, Ogallala, and I'll take action—the sort of action you won't like. Don't forget, the El Paso authorities are still looking for the murderer of George Aldrich. A word from me as to who owned that gun and—"

"My Gawd, Kane! You don't know what you're saying—"

"I know what I'm saying, Ogallala," he rasped. "You're a Mitchell, yes, but between your skin and mine, I'm most concerned about mine. You can pull as many fool stunts as you like, so long as you don't endanger my plans—but the minute that happens—well, like I say, I'll take action."

He fell silent, angrily rolling a cigarette. Ogallala scratched a match and held it for his brother. The older man's hand trembled. Vink swore a couple of times and the atmosphere cooled. Kane said suddenly, "All right, there's no need crying over spilt milk. There's plenty more cows on the range. Just don't let it happen again."

"I'm plumb sorry, Kane," Ogallala said humbly. "From now on I'll move plumb careful. What do we do next?"

"We've got to stop Donshawnee and get that hat—someway," Kane said calmly.

"I've been thinking about something," Vink put in. "Ogallala says he saw Tony Aldrich give George Aldrich that black sombrero. Somebody was in that hotel room the night George Aldrich was killed, Donshawnee shows up here with the sombrero. Do you suppose Donshawnee was the man in Aldrich's room that night?"

Ogallala said, "It might be that way."

Kane considered a moment, then said slowly, "According to the newspapers the man in the room was named Donne—John Donne. He's the one suspected of the murder—"

"John Donne—John Donshawnee," Vink said quickly. "The names sound something alike. It could be the same man. By cripes! I'll bet he's the same—"

114

"Don't go running off at the head, Vink," Kane cut in. "You might be right, but at the same time we mustn't forget that Donshawnee came here with a law officer. We all saw Hartigan's badge that night he dropped it. It's not likely that Donshawnee would be traveling with the law if he's wanted for murder. Maybe he knew Aldrich and got the hat before Aldrich was killed."

"What we could do," Ogallala said eagerly, "is drop a hint into Sheriff Pritchard's ear to the effect that George Aldrich had a black sombrero before he was killed. Then the sheriff could run it down."

"And just how," Kane asked coldly, "are *we* supposed to know that Aldrich had that black sombrero? Are you going to explain to Pritchard how you learned that fact, Ogallala?"

"We-ell"—Ogallala looked sheepishly at his brother—"I hadn't thought of that part. Nope, I reckon we'd better not say anything."

Kane eyed his elder brother contemptuously. "Didn't I just get through telling you not to try to use your head?"

"But what are we going to do?" Vink insisted.

Kane moodily shook his head. "Right now I can't say. Just wait until luck breaks our way, I reckon. If we'll be patient and not try to force our luck something is bound to happen—" He broke off suddenly and moved back into the shadow of the Mecca Saloon porch roof, drawing his two brothers back with him. "Something is bound to happen," he said softly, a triumphant smile. curving his thin lips. "Look yonderly, over there toward the Cowman Rest."

Vink and Ogallala glanced diagonally across the street to the next corner, where the Cowman's Rest Hotel was located, and saw Johnny just getting on his horse. Near the horse's head, talking to Johnny, stood Mecate Bowen. Bowen wasn't making any move to mount to the driver's seat of the buckboard as he should have been doing if he expected to leave with Johnny.

"It looks," Kane Mitchell said softly, "as though Donshawnee is riding alone back to the Rocking-A."

"It shore does," Ogallala said hoarsely, his voice dropping to a whisper.

"Sometimes," Vink said tensely, "it's not safe for fellers to ride alone. They might lose their hat—or something."

Kane nodded. "I was just thinking that," he said. He laughed suddenly. "It might be a good idea to meet him on the road, just to see he doesn't come to any harm."

"There's a short cut running from the Spur-Bar trail," Ogallala said. "If Vink and me was to leave for home now we might be able to cut over to the Rocking-A trail in time to meet Mister Donshawnee. Once we were out of Spearhead Wells we'd have to ride hard to get there in time, but I think we could make it."

"Exactly the way my thoughts were running." Kane nodded. By this time Johnny had turned his horse away from the hotel and was heading out of town at an easy lope. Bowen looked after him a minute, then crossed the street to the Continental bar. Kane Mitchell continued, "I think you two had better be getting along to the ranch and see how things are going. No use wasting any more time here."

By now Johnny was out of sight. Vink turned to Ogallala. "C'mon, we've got to get traveling."

Ogallala nodded and followed Vink out to the tie rail where they got into saddles. No further words were spoken by Kane Mitchell. He stood watching them until they passed beyond view at a turn in the roadway

116

leading to the Spur-Bar. Then, with a deep sigh of satisfaction, he moved into the saloon.

"Now I feel like I can stand a drink," he told himself. "The pendulum's swung back; luck's coming our way for a change."

While the three Mitchell brothers had been discussing him on the porch of the Mecca Saloon, Johnny had been enjoying his dinner with Mecate Bowen, though it is possible he might have eaten more if he hadn't spent so much time watching Susan Aldrich, as she moved about the hotel dining room. He rose reluctantly and said goodbye to the girl when Mecate hinted it was time for him to be starting back to the Rocking-A. Bowen followed him out to hitch rack and watched Johnny climb into his saddle.

"There ain't much about the work Franklin can't tell you," Bowen said. "I'll leave it to you to find what jobs need doin'. Susan and me will be seeing you early tomorrow mornin', as I reckon it. Right now I'm aimin' to drift over to the Continental for my after dinner drink."

"You mentioning the Continental," Johnny said, looking down from his saddle, "reminds me of something. Mecate, I sort of got the impression this morning that you don't take to Henry Linbauer. He seemed like a nice old coot to me. What you got against him?"

Bowen frowned. "I didn't say I had anything against him."

"Maybe I'm mistaken," Johnny replied, not convinced. "The Wagon-Wheel and the Rocking-A haven't had any trouble, eh?"

Bowen shook his head after a moment. "Not yet," he said cryptically.

Johnny smiled and said, "When?"

"*Quién sabe?*" Bowen shrugged his shoulders. "You'd better be getting along, Johnny."

"Right you are." Johnny smiled and turned his pony out to the road. "I'll see you in the morning, Mecate. *Adios!*"

"*Adios!*"

Johnny put spurs to his pony and loped quickly out of town. At the end of Main Street, where the trail forked, he turned his mount in a northwesterly direction. Within the space of five minutes' time he had left the last house to his rear and was moving easily across the range.

The trail wound like a long brown snake over the rolling grass country with its scattered clumps of yucca, sage and prickly pear. Occasionally Johnny spied low-growing mesquite trees. After a time outcroppings of granite commenced to appear here and there. He wasn't pressing the pony hard; the sun overhead was sending down waves of heat, causing hills and vegetation to quiver and undulate in the distance.

"I wonder," Johnny mused, "just what Mecate has against old Henry Linbauer. He wouldn't admit it, but there's something wrong there. I sort of liked Linbauer. The old cuss has nerve. He didn't back an inch when Scudder jabbed that gun in his middle. There's something funny in that direction. Kane Mitchell is sure anxious to get this sombrero of mine. That's dang queer too. I really believe Mitchell would have paid me three hundred dollars for this bonnet if he'd thought I'd take it. I should have stalled him along more, just to see how far he would go. Well, if the hat's worth that much to him it's worth more to me—though I'm danged if I know why—yet." He smiled and touched spurs to his pony's ribs.

118

The horse was approaching an incline in the trail where it lifted to swing in a wide arc between two hills, the sides of which were dotted with brush and huge broken slabs of rock. Ahead, just around the turn, a mighty boulder jutted from the hillside, preventing view of what lay beyond. The opposite side of the hill was clustered thickly with great rambling clumps of high-growing prickly pear. The hillsides were steep at this point; it was probably the narrowest spot in the whole length of the trail.

Johnny spurred up the slight incline, the pony's hoofs striking sparks from the stony roadbed. Reaching the top of the rise, he pulled the pony to an easier gait to swing it around the huge boulder obstructing his view of the trail ahead. And then, just as he made the turn, he brought the pony to a quick halt.

There, barring his path, were two riders with drawn guns. One of the riders was Ogallala Mitchell; the other, his brother Vink. The two men tilted their guns a trifle as Johnny's horse carried him into view.

"Raise 'em and raise 'em high, Donshawnee!" Ogallala snapped. "We've got you covered!"

"Keep your hands away from your guns," Vink rasped. "Quick! Up with 'em!"

CORNERED

"UP WITH 'EM—FAST!" OGALLALA REPEATED IN UGLY tones, spurring his horse nearer. Vink Mitchell, too, moved his mount in closer. They sat their ponies on either side of Johnny, the heads of the three horses almost touching. Johnny hesitated a second, then raised his arms and locked his hands in back of his head.

"They're up," he said coolly. "What's on your mind?"

"You know what we got on our minds," Ogallala rasped. "We want that black sombrero yo're wearin'— my sombrero!"

"That point is open to discussion," Johnny replied.

"No, it ain't," Vink said flatly. "We're tired of discussing that hat. We're taking it now, hombre."

Johnny laughed softly. The situation looked bad, no doubt, on that score. Apparently the Mitchell brothers had him where they wanted him. He glanced to the left and saw Vink's gun barrel tilt a trifle. On his right, above the leveled six-shooter, Ogallala's hard, merciless eyes bored into his own. Johnny laughed again, stalling for time.

"What's so damn funny?" Vink snapped.

"You," Johnny replied. "You and your brother."

Ogallala whipped out a sudden curse. "What's so blasted funny about me?"

"I was thinking," Johnny replied, "what a joke it would have been on you two if you'd come out here to wait for me and I hadn't showed up."

"We knew you'd be comin' all right," Ogallala growled. "We saw you pull out of Spearhead Wells—"

"Shut up, Ogallala," Vink said.

Johnny nodded. "That explains it."

"Explains what?" Vink asked suspiciously.

"How you happened to be here." Johnny laughed. "Cripes! Don't you even know what we're talking about?"

"Get down to business, Vink," Ogallala growled.

Johnny's smile widened. "Any business you were in you'd have to get down to. It'd be just that low."

Ogallala cursed. "By Gawd, you—"

"Let be, Ogallala," Vink cut in. "No use losing your temper. We hold all the best cards. This hombre is cornered, and he knows it. He's just stalling for time. But that ain't going to do him no good neither. Hand over that hat, hombre!"

Johnny made no move to obey. "You know," he said quietly, "you're going at this wrong. If you got to shooting somebody might get hurt—"

"That's not worrying us." Ogallala laughed harshly.

"—and," Johnny concluded, "I'm right certain it wouldn't be me. Now if you'd come to me straight off and made a decent offer for this black sombrero of mine—"

"Kane made you an offer," Vink interrupted. "He told me—"

"That!" Johnny snorted contemptuously. "Sure, he offered me money, but he didn't go about it right. Now if he'd had something to trade he and I might have done business. I had money in my pocket at the time. If Kane Mitchell could have showed me something I didn't have maybe we'd made a deal."

"What do you mean?" Vink frowned. Despite himself, he had relaxed his vigilance a bit under the spell of Johnny's remarks. His gun barrel had lowered a trifle. Ogallala sat his pony, frowning, intent on the discussion between Johnny and Vink.

"What do you mean?" Vink said again.

Johnny touched his pony lightly with his spur. The pony shifted slightly to one side, scarcely enough to be noticeable. Now the pony's head was a little more toward Vink. Johnny went on, "What do I mean? Well, I've been noticing that turquoise ring you're wearing, Mitchell. It's not a bad piece of Navajo work."

"Not a bad piece?" Vink snorted. "Cripes! it's dang nigh perfect. I paid good money for this ring—sa-ay, do you mean you'd trade your sombrero for this ring?"

"I didn't say that," Johnny smiled. "I was just considering a mite. You got two rings there."

"Give him the rings and take the hat, Vink," Ogallala broke in impatiently.

"Not so fast," Johnny protested. "I didn't say I'd trade for the two rings."

"By Gawd," Ogallala snapped, "one way or the other we're goin' to get that hat."

"Yeah?" Johnny said coolly. "Suppose I let you have the hat, what then?"

"You're free to leave the country," Ogallala said promptly, "without no hurt being done to you. You got to get out though."

"Uh-huh." Johnny looked thoughtful. Apparently he was considering the matter. Finally he asked, "And suppose I don't see fit to let you have this hat?"

"Try it and see." Vink laughed nastily. "What do you think we got guns for?"

"Yeah, I see what you mean." Johnny appeared to ponder the situation. "It looks like you got me in a tight situation."

"Yo're lucky you can see reason," Ogallala grunted.

"Yep, it's a tight situation." Johnny nodded, half as though talking to himself. He unclasped his fingers and meditatively scratched his chin. "On the one hand I have to trade my hat for a turquoise ring." He dropped his right hand carelessly to saddle horn, the movement going unnoticed, so sure were the two Mitchells that they had Johnny just where they wanted him—cornered tightly. "On the other hand," Johnny went on, "if I don't let you have the hat I'm likely to find myself plugged with lead. Somehow I don't relish the idea."

"Now you're getting sense, Donshawnee. Hand over the hat and we won't have any more trouble," Vink said.

"That might be the sensible thing to do," Johnny nodded. "I don't like trouble, and it seems there should be some way out of this difficulty. I tell you, we might look at it this way—"

The words weren't completed, as Johnny suddenly plunged his spurs sharply into his roan pony. Startled, the pony emitted a snort of righteous indignation mingled with pain and, rearing abruptly to hind legs, struck at Vink's horse with its fore hoofs.

Vink's horse shied violently to one side, unsettling Vink's aim as he fired, the bullet passing above Johnny's back. Johnny had crouched low behind his pony's head as it reared, both hands reaching to holsters. He thumbed one swift shot under the pony's neck and saw dust puff out from Ogallala's vest, even as the bullet from Ogallala's gun breezed past his face.

Through a blue haze of powder smoke Johnny saw Ogallala clutch at his heart and plunge from the saddle. Vink's horse had taken to bucking and the shots its rider was firing recklessly at Johnny were flying far wide of their aim. Johnny spun the roan toward Vink. A stream of fire ran lance-like from his left hand, accompanying

123

the roar of the heavy forty-five.

A sudden yelp of pain was torn from Vink Mitchell's lips. The gun went flying from his grip and as his pony leaped swiftly to one side Vink lurched out of the saddle and struck the earth where he lay quiet. The echoing shots died away in the hills as Johnny quieted his roan and stepped down from his horse's back.

"That," Johnny said to no one in particular, "was fast and furious for a few moments. I reckon I'm lucky."

He cast a glance at Ogallala who lay as he had fallen. There wasn't any doubt about Ogallala. The man's horse stood quietly by. Vink's horse had run back the road for a short distance and now stood watching. After a moment it commenced to crop grass at the side of the road.

Johnny crossed to look at Vink. Vink was sprawled on his face, one hand still clutching his gun. As Johnny approached Vink groaned and made struggling movements. Johnny quickly kicked the gun from his grasp, then, stooping, turned him over. Vink's eyes were open, but held a shocked, dazed expression. There was a bloody gash across his forehead and more blood coming from the back of his right hand. Vink was mumbling something incoherently, but Johnny couldn't make out what it was. He looked at the wound on Vink's forehead, then examined the furrow that ran diagonally across Vink's hand.

Vink commenced muttering again. Finally he groaned, "Water—I'm—I'm dying. Don't—don't shoot—again—"

"Quit bellyaching and stand up," Johnny said disgustedly. "You're lucky and don't know it. Your horse was pitching so my bullet just scratched the back of your hand, without even touching bone or cutting

124

nerves. When your horse threw you you hit your head on a rock. You were just stunned for a minute. You got a better break than you deserved."

Johnny picked up Vink's gun, then grasped the man's arm and yanked him upright. Vink swayed a moment, but held his balance. His eyes were clearer now. "You—you didn't need to do this, Donshawnee. We were only figuring to josh you a mite—" He broke off suddenly as his gaze fell on Ogallala's lifeless body. "Ogallala—"

"Is dead," Johnny said coldly. "You both had first shots and you couldn't make 'em count—"

"Dead? Ogallala dead?" Vink gasped unbelievingly. Fury blazed in his eyes. "By God! you'll pay for this. Wait until Kane hears what's happened. He'll blast you wide open!"

"Shut up, Mitchell," Johnny snapped. "I don't figure Kane will be any tougher than you two. There's your horse. Go catch him up and come back here. We're going back to Spearhead Wells. And once you're in saddle don't try to run. My roan could catch you before you went a quarter mile. And don't forget, I've got your gun."

Vink's nerve was too shaken for him to refuse to obey. He walked rockily down the road to get his horse. The horse shied as he came up to it, but Vink caught the dangling reins and hoisted himself up to the saddle. Then he rode slowly back where Johnny waited beside Ogallala's dead body.

By this time Johnny had retrieved Ogallala's six-shooter and stuck it into the waistband of his overalls beside Vink's weapon. Vink drew to a halt in the middle of the road and watched dully while Ogallala's body was lifted to the saddle of its dead owner and lashed in place. Johnny completed tying the final knot in the dead man's lariat, then handed the reins of the horse to Vink.

"You lead your brother's horse, Mitchell. Get going. I'll be close behind."

Vink didn't say anything. He accepted the reins and, touching spurs to his pony, started back in the direction of Spearhead Wells. Johnny gazed grimly after him a moment, then climbed to the back of his roan and fell in behind.

***

The sun was edging toward the peaks of the Sangre de Santos Range and reflecting redly from the roofs of houses by the time Johnny herded his captive and dead brother back to Spearhead Wells. Vink Mitchell hadn't uttered a word during the journey, and Johnny hadn't attempted to make conversation. Two or three excited yells sounded at the edge of town when the dead man was first sighted. As they progressed a crowd gathered and fell in behind the horses. Someone darted ahead to inform the sheriff of what was coming.

The sheriff was just emerging from the door of his office when Johnny drew to a halt before the building. The sheriff's jaw dropped as he caught sight of the three-horse procession, and he put up one hand to catch the bridle of Vink's pony. He looked at the dead man on the horse Vink was leading, then from Vink to Johnny.

"Cripes a'mighty" Pritchard exclaimed. "What happened now?"

Vink said sullenly, "Aw, let him tell it. But he'll lie to you. I'll tell my story later when Kane is here. Is he still in town?"

Somebody in the crowd of assembled men said that Kane had been sent for, down to the Mecca Saloon.

"What about it, Johnny?" Sheriff Pritchard asked

126

shortly.

"There isn't much to tell," Johnny said calmly. "Vink and Ogallala held me up on the road to the Rocking-A. They insisted on getting my hat. I didn't see it that way. There were some shots fired and I come off lucky."

"You stopped 'em both?" Pritchard gasped. "Did you pull first?"

"They had their guns on me before I saw 'em."

A murmur of surprise ran through the crowd.

"I'm damned if I know how you did it." The sheriff looked puzzled. "Is this correct?" turning to Vink Mitchell.

"I warned you he'd lie about it," Vink snarled.

At that moment Kane Mitchell came plowing through the crowd. "What's this I hear—" he commenced, then stopped short, gaze glued on the body of his dead brother. His eyes flashed toward Johnny, then, like a flash, one hand whipped to his gun butt.

Johnny's hand dropped at the same moment, but he didn't draw. Mecate Bowen had come up behind Kane Mitchell and seized the man's hand. "Hold it, Mitchell!" he snapped.

"Good work, Mecate." Sheriff Pritchard nodded. "Mitchell, you keep that gun in your holster. That applies to you, too, Johnny. We've had enough shooting for one day. Now let's get to the bottom of this. Johnny, you tell that story again."

Once more Johnny told briefly what had happened. The sheriff shook his head. Kane Mitchell stood staring at Johnny, hate blazing from his eyes. He turned to Vink. "Is that the way it was, Vink? It don't sound reasonable to me."

" 'Tain't reasonable," Vink growled. "I knew he'd lie about it. We was ridin' along, mindin' our own business, when sudden he comes tearing up behind and plugs Ogallala. The shot scared my horse which took to pitchin'. Otherwise I could have done some shooting myself, but I was thrun before I could help myself, knocked unconscious. Before I could recover Donshawnee had the drop on me—"

"Sheriff," Kane Mitchell said hotly, "arrest Donshawnee for the murder of my brother!"

"Just a minute, Mitchell," Johnny said grimly. "You all heard Vink say he'd have done some shooting if his horse hadn't thrown him. Well, when he landed he hit his head on a rock. I reckon he must have forgotten he did do some shooting before his horse threw him." Johnny withdrew the guns of the Mitchell brothers from his waistband and handed them to the sheriff. "There's Vink's gun and Ogallala's. Examine 'em and you'll see they both threw plenty of lead. Furthermore, examine Ogallala's wound. You'll see he was shot from the front, so I couldn't have attacked from the rear like Vink Mitchell says. You can take my word for it, he's a liar!"

Sheriff Pritchard gave orders and two men unlashed Ogallala's body and lowered it to the earth. Meanwhile the sheriff examined the cylinders of the two guns Johnny had turned over to him.

"And I might add," Johnny continued, "that the fact the Mitchell's were on the Rocking-A trail, instead of the road to their own ranch, makes the whole thing look very premeditated."

Vink Mitchell bit his lip, realizing that his story wasn't holding water. Kane Mitchell stood glowering at Johnny but not saying anything. The sheriff was examining Ogallala's wound now. Finally he rose to his feet and gave his verdict:

"Both those guns have been fired. Ogallala was shot from the front. It's the type of wound that wouldn't let him do any shooting *after* he was hit, so I reckon he had his chance—"

"I'm still insisting," Kane Mitchell said wrathfully, "that you arrest Donshawnee for my brother's murder."

Pritchard snapped, "Insist and be damned, Mitchell. The evidence shows Johnny fired in self-defense."

An angry muttering ran through the crowd, directed at Vink and Kane Mitchell. Vink paled. Kane tensed and glared around him. Finally he said, "We can't get a square deal right now, Vink. Let's take Ogallala down to the undertaker's and—"

"Just a minute," the sheriff said sharply. "Johnny, do you want to prefer charges against Vink? To me it looks like he ought to be put behind bars."

Johnny shook his head, said grimly, "I don't want him behind bars. Let him get his hand fixed up and some court plaster for that cut on his head. No, leave him free, so he can finish what he's started if he has the nerve. I'm just warning him—and you, too, Kane Mitchell—that I'm not figuring to be pushed around any. Next time you come after me you'd better come with your guns smoking. And, incidentally, Sheriff, you might as well turn Vink's gun back to him. I wouldn't want him handicapped in any way, should he get an urge to carry on this scrap."

Kane Mitchell pushed through the crowd to the side of Johnny's horse. Johnny looked down at him, his eyes hard against the hate blazing from Mitchell's eyes. Mitchell said tensely, "This game isn't finished yet, Donshawnee. Maybe you've won a hand, but next time we meet it'll be my deal. Don't forget that!"

Johnny nodded. "Suits me, Mitchell. Deal 'em when

you're ready. I'm ready any time!"

"Cut it, you two," the sheriff broke in sharply. "Mitchell, you and Vink better get Ogallala along to the undertaker's. There'll be no more trouble here."

Johnny reined his pony through the crowd. Mecate Bowen followed him to one side. "You must have been fast on your draw, boy. Tell me just how it happened."

Johnny told his story. "I wasn't so fast, maybe, as I was lucky," he concluded.

Bowen sighed. "We haven't heard the last of this. Howsomever, I'm glad to know you can take care of yourself."

They talked a few minutes longer, then Johnny once more started for the Rocking-A, with Bowen's, "We'll be seein' you tomorrow," echoing in his ears. That meant he'd be seeing Susan too. The thought brought a lift to his heart as he loped out of Spearhead Wells.

SUSAN'S STORY

SUPPER WAS BEING HELD LATE AND JOHNNY WAS greeted anxiously by Humdrum and Dave Franklin when he arrived at the Rocking-A that night. "Cripes," Humdrum drawled, "we figured you'd be back early this afternoon. Where's Mecate?"

"Did you get Vinazo there alive?" Dave Franklin asked.

Johnny nodded. "Maybe Doc Pickett will pull him through. He couldn't talk though."

"What held you up?" Humdrum asked. "You must have been sleeping along the way someplace."

Johnny smiled. "Not sleeping, pard. So far as I know your disease isn't contagious."

"Aw, you go to hell," Humdrum said good-naturedly. "Dave and I were sort of worried though."

"I'll tell you about it in a minute," Johnny replied. "Wait until I put this pony in the corral."

Over a supper of beans, potatoes and coffee Johnny told Humdrum and Franklin of his encounter with Vink and Ogallala Mitchell. The words brought exclamations of surprise and Johnny was forced to go into minute details of the fight. When he had finally concluded Humdrum said admiringly, "You must have been moving—and thinking—fast. You're sure lucky, cowboy."

Franklin looked serious. "I reckon we'll all have to oil our irons for those Spur-Bar coyotes one of these days soon. Between them and the Wagon-Wheel we're sure having our troubles." He paused suddenly.

"What's the trouble with the Wagon-Wheel?" Johnny asked quickly.

Franklin's face reddened. "I was supposed to keep my mouth shut about that," he confessed. It just slipped out. Anyhow, Henry Linbauer has been blotting our brands."

"You're sure of that?" Johnny asked.

"I don't know of anybody else who would make a Wagon-Wheel out of a Rocking-A," Franklin returned.

"What's been done about it?" Humdrum asked.

"Not one solitary thing," Franklin said resentfully. "George Aldrich—you know, Susan's paw that was murdered in El Paso a spell back—he refused to take action. Why, I don't know. But, like I say, I was supposed to keep my mouth shut. Maybe we'd better not talk about it."

Johnny and Humdrum didn't press the subject. Supper was finished and the dishes cleared away and washed. There was little more conversation that evening

131

before the lamps were extinguished and the three men took to their bunks.

They were up with the dawn the following morning to prepare the place for Susan's arrival. Franklin hadn't saddled up but was devoting his time to building up one of the water tanks, preparatory to the coming of winter rains. Even Humdrum had showed more activity than usual in working at the ranch house: he had made beds for Susan and the Mexican woman who was coming with her and laid mesquite roots and firewood in the big fireplace in the main room of the ranch house. Water buckets had been filled and all the kitchen range needed was a lighted match to start it going. Humdrum showed so much ability, in fact, that Johnny remarked, "Danged if you wouldn't make a good wife for some man, if you could keep awake," which had elicited from Humdrum the advice that Johnny might just as well keep his mouth closed as, "I'm not open to proposals at present."

The bunkhouse and mess shanty had to be cleaned up, and this job Johnny took over. Rummaging through the kitchen, he found some canned corned beef and decided to make hash for dinner. Potatoes were peeled, and by the time dinner was well on the way to being prepared it was nearly noon.

Shortly before twelve o'clock Mecate Bowen tooled the buckboard into the ranch yard. Johnny relaxed a trifle when he saw Susan seated on the driver's seat beside him. In the bed of the wagon were a large trunk and a smaller one, also a large stock of supplies. Seated on one of the trunks was a gray-haired Mexican woman of plump form, with sharp brown eyes, whom Johnny judged was Ramon Vinazo's mother. Johnny emerged from the bunkhouse as the wagon rolled to a stop.

"Hello, Johnny," Susan greeted, stepping down from

the wagon before he could get there. "Oh, it's good to be home again!" Her face became serious for a moment. "Mecate tells me you had some trouble with two of the Mitchells yesterday afternoon."

"I reckon it wasn't anything to talk about," Johnny replied. "Not now, leastwise."

Humdrum and Franklin appeared and received greetings. They started unloading the buckboard. Johnny helped the old Mexican woman down from the wagon, feeling particularly conscious as he did so that he had shot her son.

"Johnny," Susan said, "this is Guadalupe Vinazo—Ramón's mother. Oh yes, Doctor Pickett says Ramón will recover, but he is unable to see anyone yet. Guadalupe and I were there this morning."

The old woman's sharp brown eyes studied Johnny. Johnny met the close scrutiny without turning away. "I'm sorry, Guadalupe," he said simply in Spanish. "It was by accident, you might say."

The old woman sadly shook her head. "Not by accident, señor. It was God's will it should be that way. None of the fault is yours, I know my Ramón. Always he was very wild. But at heart he is not a bad boy—only wild, señor," She stretched out one hand and Johnny took it, liking her firm, sincere clasp.

"Well, I'm glad he is going to get better," Johnny said in English.

As though proud of her accomplishment Guadalupe employed the same language. "*Si, si*, he weel get bettair. The doctaire tells me I should have none of fear. Maybe theese time he teach heemself the lesson."

The wagon was finally unloaded and Dave Franklin drove it to the barn, where he unhitched the horses and put them into a corral. Johnny gave a long sigh of relief as he watched Susan and Guadalupe head for the ranch house. "That's over," he told himself. "I didn't know but what she might take after me with a knife. She took it like a gamester. I reckon Guadalupe and me will be friends." He raised his voice to call to Susan: "There's hash for dinner, and coffee. Also biscuits, if you can stand my cooking."

"Put it on, Johnny. We'll be right back," Susan replied.

Johnny took considerable joshing regarding his cooking when they sat down to dinner. Mecate and Humdrum both claimed the biscuits must have been mixed with cement. Susan took Johnny's part: "Don't you believe a word they say, Johnny. These biscuits are light as a feather."

Mecate Bowen said dryly, "What was the name of that bird with the scaly feathers, back in prehistoric times?"

"Mecate!" Susan exclaimed "that was cruel. Johnny, don't pay any attention to them. You cooked a delicious dinner, considering the few things you had to do with."

"Yep," Humdrum drawled, "I figure Johnny would make a good wife for some man. You open to proposals, Johnny?"

Johnny said boldly, looking at Susan, "Yes, from the right person."

Susan met his eyes for a moment, then suddenly glanced away and said, "Tonight I'll cook the supper. I really felt I should celebrate my homecoming. We'll eat up at the house and I've got some ideas about making pies. We bought supplies in town. I imagine Mecate is pretty weary of doing the cooking here. From now on I'll take over."

The afternoon passed swiftly. Most of the time

134

Mecate Bowen spent at the ranch house, talking to Susan. Franklin, Johnny and Humdrum busied themselves about the place, doing odd jobs.

That night, as Susan had promised, there were two fat pies for supper and other good edibles. There was even a bottle of wine and cigars for the men. Susan smiled wryly. "You'd never dream the Rocking-A was practically on the rocks, would you? But I just had to celebrate a little bit."

"I've been wondering," Johnny said, "just what has put the outfit in such a situation. I don't want to appear curious about something that's none of my business but—"

"I figure it is your business, Johnny," Susan cut in. "You and Humdrum are working here without wages. I figure you're entitled to know. Let's go in the other room."

Dave Franklin was invited to stay, but he said he had business at the bunkhouse and departed. Guadalupe commenced to clear off the table and get ready to wash dishes. Johnny, Mecate and Humdrum followed Susan into the big main room of the ranch house where the cheerful fire of mesquite roots was staving off the chill of the evening. It was a comfortable room in which to sit, with many animal skins and Indian rugs about. The chairs were easy and an oil lamp burned brightly on an oak table. The three men lighted cigars.

"I think all the trouble started," Susan commenced finally, "about the time my father's brother, Tony, came to live with us. He was quite a bit younger than Dad and always did have a wild streak in him. He'd been living in California quite happily with his wife. Then his wife died. After that Tony didn't appear to care what happened to him. He wouldn't work steadily and he

135

took to drinking. Finally Dad got him out here, thinking we could straighten him out. However, it didn't do much good. He still liked drinking better than working."

"Sometimes," Johnny put in, "when a man's had a streak of tough luck you can't blame him too much."

Susan smiled. "Also, nearly every family has its black sheep. No matter what they said about Tony I still like him. I wish I knew where he was though; somehow, since Father's death, I fear Tony, too, is dead."

"I wish we could get proof of that, one way or t'other," Mecate put in. "It might clear up a heap of things."

"Anyway," Susan continued, "it's something over seven years ago that Tony came here to live. As luck would have it he and Ogallala Mitchell became quite chummy. The two put in their time around Spearhead Wells, drinking and carousing. Nothing much that Father said seemed to have much effect, though Tony was always promising to turn over a new leaf and straighten up. Now what happened next we learned from various people. To cut a long story short, Tony Aldrich and Ogallala Mitchell went over into Montaldo County, the other side of the Sangre de Santos, west of here, and held up a payroll stage, consigned to the Little Bonanza Mine."

"And that," Mecate Bowen growled, "just about broke George Aldrich's heart. He was wrapped up in Tony, particular after yore ma died, Susan."

Susan nodded. "Tony and Ogallala Mitchell got away with a strongbox containing thirty thousand dollars in gold. A posse was organized to follow them. The posse caught up and there was a pitched gun battle. Ogallala Mitchell was badly wounded, but Tony managed to make an escape with both Ogallala and the gold. The

136

posse again got on their trail, but they managed to cut through Coyotero Pass in the Sangre de Santos and get back to Rocking-A holdings, where they holed up in an old adobe house not many miles from here. For the moment they had eluded the posse. They didn't dare go to Spearhead Wells or the Spur-Bar. But Ogallala Mitchell required rest. He was badly wounded."

Mecate cut in on the story to say, "This Guadalupe Vinazo you met today was living in the old adobe house at the time—her and her boy, Ramón. George Aldrich let them live there free of rent, her being a widow."

Susan continued: "Guadalupe didn't know what had happened when they came to the house, but she saw Ogallala Mitchell was badly wounded and that Tony's extra horse had a strongbox lashed to its back. She had suspicions but, seeing them in an ugly mood, wisely refrained from asking questions. Tony ordered her to another room in the house. She obeyed, taking Ramon, who was just a boy at the time, with her. She heard Tony step outside and, through a window, saw that he had a shovel. He was gone quite a long time. Later, when he returned, he asked Guadalupe for a needle. Apparently be was trying to close the wound in Ogallala's side. The man was bleeding badly—"

Johnny cut in: "When Guadalupe saw him with the shovel he was preparing to bury the stolen gold, of course."

"That's what everybody thinks," Susan replied, "but where, nobody seems to have learned, so far as we can discover, though a good many people have come sneaking up to that old adobe house at various times and dug all around it. But to get back to Tony and Ogallala: toward morning the posse again got on their trail and surrounded the adobe house. They captured Ogallala, but Tony managed to escape. Ogallala was brought to trial when his wound healed and sent to prison. On Tony's account Dad tried to settle matters out of court. He went to the owners of the Little Bonanza Mine and offered to repay the thirty thousand dollars if they'd drop prosecution proceedings. They agreed. Dad borrowed the thirty thousand on the Rocking-A and paid over the money."

"That helped some," Mecate said, "but not much. The law authorities of Montaldo County were determined to prosecute, and they went through with Ogallala's trial. He probably got a lighter sentence than he would have otherwise, but that wasn't what George Aldrich expected. There's a warrant still out for Tony Aldrich."

"Gosh," Humdrum said, "wasn't the buried gold ever found?"

Susan shook her head. "Not so far as we know. Ogallala claimed that Tony didn't tell him where it was buried. I've a feeling that is so. Father caught Ogallala digging over near Ghost Rock a couple of times—that's after Ogallala got out of prison, of course, a few months back."

"Where's Ghost Rock?" Johnny asked.

"Not far from the old adobe where Guadalupe lived when the posse captured Ogallala. Another time when Father was digging, trying to find the gold himself, somebody shot at him. He always figured Ogallala did the shooting, but he had no proof. But I'd sure like to know where that gold is buried."

"It would belong to you, naturally," Johnny said, "so long as your father made good the loss of the Little Bonanza Mine."

"That's the way we always figured it." Susan nodded.

"And you never learned what became of Tony

Aldrich?"

"Father had a letter from him down in Mexico about the time of Ogallala's trial. Later another letter came from the Argentine country. With the law still on his trail Tony was staying far away from this part of the country. He told Dad, in his letters, that when he could get an opportunity to return safely he'd tell him where the gold was buried. After that he dropped from sight completely."

"Now's a good time to bring in the Wagon-Wheel business," Mecate prompted. "Johnny and Humdrum might as well hear about that. It ties in."

Susan nodded. "With the interest on the thirty-thousand loan to keep up things were bad enough. Then, suddenly, our cows commenced to disappear and it looked as though we might lose everything. At first we blamed the Spur-Bar outfit. Kane Mitchell knew we were in difficulties. He'd like to own the Rocking-A as there isn't sufficient water on the Spur-Bar. Dad figured perhaps Mitchell was working to put us in a hole, where we'd lose our ranch to the bank. Then Mitchell could buy it in cheap."

That sounds like something Mitchell would do," Johnny said.

"It wasn't the Spur-Bar though. One day Mecate found a Wagon-Wheel cow in one of our herds. He examined the brand closely and discovered the Wagon-Wheel had been blotted from a Rocking-A. From time to time after that more such evidence of brand-blotting was turned up. Mecate wanted to declare war on Henry Linbauer right then, but Dad vetoed the proposition, saying he didn't want a range war breaking out in the Spearhead country."

"It'd been the only way to handle it," Mecate

139

growled. "Only for George shushin' me, I'd have plenty to say to Linbauer."

"Dad was more hurt than angry," Susan went on. "He thought Linbauer was a good friend. He'd helped him out of a bad hole one time. Anyway, rather than accuse Linbauer himself, he thought the accusation should come from someone connected with the law. In short, Dad decided to call in the help of some good detective who knew range work to help him on the rustling problem and to also see if something couldn't be done about finding that buried gold. Dad wanted a man who wasn't afraid of danger and who would be willing to gamble his chances of finding the gold for his compensation."

The story was making things clearer to Johnny now. Now he realized why George Aldrich had inserted such a strange advertisement in the El Paso *Banner-Independent.*

Susan continued: "Dad finally decided to consult an old friend and have him suggest a man for such a job. The old friend was Steve Sharples, head of the Border Rangers. Maybe you've heard of him." Both Johnny and Humdrum nodded. Johnny was unable to speak. Susan resumed: "Dad left here to go to Austin to consult Mr. Sharples. Several days passed, then I had a letter from Dad, written in El Paso. Dad wrote that Mr. Sharples had recommended an ex-Ranger named Donne, whom Dad expected to meet in El Paso within a few days."

It was becoming more difficult now for Susan to go on as she approached the part telling of her father's death. Once her voice broke and she fell silent. The occupants of the room sat waiting for her to continue. The mesquite roots cracked and blazed in the fireplace. Finally Susan resumed:

"The most important things in Dad's letter he left to the last. He wrote that he had passed his brother, Tony, on one of El Paso's streets. Tony recognized him but passed on, refusing to speak. Dad returned, perplexed, to his hotel, but within a short time a boy came with a note from Tony, asking Dad to meet him outside of town where they wouldn't be seen. With the law still after him Tony was afraid to be seen in El Paso, especially in Dad's company, for fear of being recognized. Dad's letter closed with the word that he was just leaving to meet Tony and that he'd write further particulars after he had talked to him." Susan paused, finding difficulty in continuing.

Mecate Bowen took up the story. "We waited days for that next letter from George, but it never came. The next news we got was that George had been killed in his hotel room. The last man known to have visited him was a feller named Donne. Donne, the ex-Ranger! The police are still looking for Donne. Susan and I both went to El Paso. We couldn't learn anything."

Humdrum put in, "Maybe this Donne wasn't guilty—"

"Where is he then?" Mecate snapped. "He disappeared. We learned that Donne was suspected of another murder, too, while he was with the Rangers. By God, if I ever meet up with him—"

"Hush, Mecate, hush," Susan protested. "We've been through all that before—"

Johnny interrupted to change the subject. "You've never heard anything from Tony Aldrich?"

"Not a word." Susan shook her head. "Somehow I feel he must be dead. The man who killed Father may have killed him too. I don't even know if Dad met him that day. We did learn that Dad was already wounded seriously, in bed at his hotel, at the time he was killed, but we couldn't uncover any details regarding that. Well, Johnny, you've wondered what put the Rocking-A on the rocks. You've got the story. There were expenses to meet after Dad's death, interest on the loan—it required practically all our ready cash. I took that job at the hotel to get money for necessary supplies. I've arranged to sell some of our blooded stock to Jake Norris of the Rafter-N. Jake wants to improve his strain. The money will keep us going until something else turns up—but I'm sure I don't know what." The girl sounded hopelessly weary, tired of the whole uneven struggle.

Mingled emotions surged through Johnny, pity and a sudden love for the girl, prompting him to say earnestly, "Believe me, something will turn up—we'll make it turn up. Bad luck can't continue forever."

"Thanks, Johnny. It's helped already having you here—you and Humdrum," she added hastily. "At the same time I don't know what we're going to do."

"Somehow," Johnny said determinedly, "we're going to learn where that gold is buried. It should be yours and it's going to be!"

He sensed that Susan didn't want to talk further about her father's death so didn't press any more questions. A short time later he and Humdrum said good night and followed Mecate down to the bunkhouse.

GHOST ROCK

FOR THE NEXT TEN DAYS AFFAIRS MOVED PEACEFULLY enough on the Rocking-A. Nothing more was heard from the Mitchells and, though Johnny had been to Spearhead Wells twice, he saw no sign of any of the Spur-Bar crew. On the Rocking-A things were getting slowly back to normal, with Susan and Guadalupe doing the cooking for the outfit, thus releasing all four men for the necessary labor out on the range as well as about the ranch buildings.

Some time had been spent gathering the cattle the Rafter-N outfit were buying from Susan. With the cattle delivered and the purchase price in her hand Susan commenced to breathe a bit more freely, though she realized if she were going to make a going proposition of her ranch she'd have to restore her range as soon as possible. This, until she raised more money somewhere, somehow, was impossible. But at least she now had the money for supplies and her crew was willing to work to the utmost to keep the Rocking-A on an even keel with what cattle remained under her brand.

Sheriff Pritchard arrived early one morning shortly after breakfast. He refused coffee and got down to the reason for his visit, without dismounting from his horse. Susan, Guadalupe and the men stood outside, listening.

"It's just this," Pritchard explained, "Doc Pickett allowed me to talk to Ramón Vinazo last night for about a minute. He wouldn't let Ramón say much, but Ramón did admit that Ogallala Mitchell hired him to come here and steal your black hat, Johnny."

Johnny nodded. "We suspected that much—at least,

143

we suspected the Mitchells were back of it, despite Kane Mitchell's denials. What else did Ramón say?"

Pritchard shook his head. "Nothing. Doc Pickett wouldn't let him talk any longer. He's pretty weak, you know, and Doc didn't want to take chances."

"It's good news that Ramón is going to recover anyway," Johnny said, glancing at Guadalupe. "Thanks for letting us know, Sheriff."

"What I came out to ask," Pritchard said, "do you want to take any sort of action against the Mitchells?"

Johnny hesitated. Susan said, "It's up to you, Johnny." More and more the problems of the Rocking-A seemed to be left to Johnny's decisions; even Mecate seemed ready to follow his leadership. Mecate echoed, "It's up to you, Johnny."

Johnny replied, "The hat belongs to me, but, after all, the attempted theft took place on Rocking-A property."

"We'll still leave it to you." Susan smiled.

"In that case—" Johnny turned to Sheriff Pritchard— "I figure we'd better let the matter drop. Ogallala's dead, so we can't proceed against him. There's no need, I can see, for taking action against Ramón. Kane Mitchell will deny all knowledge of a hand in the affair and it might be difficult to prove otherwise. Let's forget it."

The sheriff nodded with satisfaction. "Exactly my sentiments, but I didn't know how you'd feel about it." He wheeled his horse. "Well, I've got to be getting back to town, folks. *Adios!*"

With the sheriff on his way Mecate commenced giving orders for the day: "Dave—" to Dave Franklin— "I wish you'd ride over in them brushy foothills south of here. You might be able to scare a few strays out of them mesquite thickets. Humdrum, you saddle up and

144

throw a rig on a bronc for me at the same time. There's a quicksand at one spot down along Arenoso Creek that's needed fencin' for a right long spell. I'll go along and help. The fence and posts are there. We'll just have to right 'em and stretch the wire—"

"Shucks!" Humdrum drawled indolently, "you're always finding tasks for me. I'd sort of figured to just sit around and loaf all day."

"You got another think comin'." Mecate chuckled. "Howsomever, by the time we ride there and back we won't be able to put in only around a half day's work."

Humdrum brightened a trifle. "Oh well, I reckon half a loaf is better than none."

"Poor Humdrum—" Susan laughed—"you are abused. Never mind, cowboy. If the Rocking-A ever gets on its feet I'll pay you good wages and a bonus. Or we might even find that buried gold soon—" She broke off, then, "Mecate, if you haven't any particular job picked out for Johnny I'd like him to make a ride with me."

Johnny glowed with pleasure. "That's the sort of job I crave."

Mecate Bowen eyed the girl. "Where you figuring to ride?"

"Over near Ghost Rock. I'd like Johnny to see that country around there. He might pick out a likely spot where gold would be buried."

Humdrum grumbled lazily. "Some folks have all the luck. I have to stretch wire while Johnny goes looking for gold—and he rides in plumb pleasant company too."

Mecate Bowen looked dubious. "Maybe it's worth trying. I don't know though. Your paw done plenty of digging around there. And I know he ordered Ogallala Mitchell off, on two occasions, when Ogallala was prospectin' around. Lord only knows how many folks have shoveled up earth—"

Susan interrupted: "At least Johnny should know the layout. Besides, I want to climb into a saddle again. Do you realize I haven't been on a horse's back for weeks and weeks? My pony's getting positively butterfat, eating his head off in the corral."

"Like I say"—Mecate nodded—"it might be worth trying. Go ahead." He strode off, followed by Franklin and Humdrum.

"Saddle up for me, Johnny," Susan said, her eyes sparkling. "I'll be out as soon as I can get into some riding things."

The girl emerged from the house twenty minutes later, clad in soft leather high-heeled riding boots, faded, well-worn overalls and a mannish woolen shirt, open at the throat. A blue bandanna, matching her dark-lashed eyes, was tied about her neck; the hair of pale gold was tucked neatly beneath the brim of an old gray Stetson. A cartridge belt encircled her waist from which was slung a holstered Colt's .38 six-shooter.

From his saddle Johnny eyed the girl with frank admiration, the steady scrutiny causing the color to rise in her cheeks. She said uncertainly, "Well, cowboy, what are you staring at?"

Johnny drew a long breath, saying fervently, "You asked for it, lady. What am I staring at? Just about the prettiest sight I've laid eyes on in all my long life." He started down from his saddle to help her up.

Susan's flush deepened; she glanced away. "You're sure covering a lot of territory, mister . . . No, I don't need help, Johnny. Stay on your horse."

She vaulted lightly into the saddle of her plump mouse-gray pony and picked up the reins. The horses started off.

Johnny was still gazing at her. "Darned if I know," he said at last.

"Darned if you know what?" Susan queried.

"Whether I like you best in dresses or overalls."

"Pants, cowboy—" Susan smiled—"are a heap more comfortable in which to get around—especially when riding. I never used to wear anything else around the ranch. You see, Mother died when I was quite young and Father brought me up as he would a boy."

"Your dad certainly did one elegant job," Johnny said fervently.

"Thank you. And now let's ride." Susan touched spurs to her pony and darted ahead.

Bright morning sun bathed the rangeland in golden light. The horses loped easily along, sometimes through lush grass as high as the ponies stirrups, heading in a northwesterly direction over the rolling grazing country. Now and then small bunches of Rocking-A cows were seen. Ahead, towering majestically against the turquoise sky, rose the serrated peaks of the Sangre de Santos Range, the deep ravines and draws etched sharply in the clear, sunlit air.

Susan and Johnny didn't talk a great deal. The girl kept her pony slightly in advance of Johnny's roan, and the swift rush of wind past the riders swept words away. An hour's steady loping brought them to a narrow, gravelly creek, where they paused to water the horses, then forded the stream to continue up a long rising stretch of land.

"That's the Rio Arenoso," Susan said, jerking her head toward the creek. "It heads up in the Sangre de Santos."

"Figured this must be it," Johnny replied. "It sure

widens out when it gets farther along on your holdings."

Reaching the crest of the long rise, Susan slowed her pony to a walk. Johnny reined in alongside the girl. Ahead lay more ridges of grassy land. They were getting into the foothills now. Susan lifted one arm and pointed. "There it is."

Johnny's gaze followed the direction of her pointing finger. "There what is?" he commenced, then stopped short as he saw what the girl indicated.

Three or four miles farther on a huge rock reared itself steeply from the surrounding country. Strangely, the rock appeared white as contrasted with the reddish granite of the Sangre de Santos Mountains. An abrupt exclamation parted Johnny's lips. The big rock had the appearance of a human figure.

"Why, it's shaped like a man," Johnny said, "a man with a long robe on. You can make out the head and shoulders. You don't have to tell me that's Ghost Rock."

Susan nodded. "We're approaching it from the end. It's really a long ridge of rock-light gray granite. But coming from this direction, it really does look like the huge figure of a man. You should see it at night sometime, under moonlight. It really does look ghostly then." She gave a mock shudder.

Johnny studied the rock a moment. "It's queer to find that light gray granite here, when all the other rock I've seen had a reddish color."

"The Indians used to have a story about that. They always said Ghost Rock was haunted, you know. I talked to an old Indian one time who claimed the rock was once red like the other rock hereabouts. And then one night a great shaking came over the land—as he told it. I presume it was an earthquake. After the shaking had ended the long rock had a great crack through the center. The Indians claimed all the blood had run out of the rock. It was they who named it Ghost Rock, because from that time on the rock looked white instead of red. So far as concerns the end of the rock being shaped like a man, I imagine countless centuries of erosion are responsible for that. But the Indians, and many Mexicans, too, are mighty superstitious about that gray-white rock."

Johnny nodded. "I can well believe it. Indians go for that kind of stuff."

Now, Susan said, "cast your eyes along the highest peaks of the Sangre de Santos. Do you see that one peak, shaped something like an arrowhead?" Johnny nodded. Susan went on: "The Indians named that Superstition Peak. They maintained that when Ghost Rock cracked open it not only let out the blood of the Great Spirit who had inhabited it but the soul as well. And the soul was supposed to have gone to dwell on Superstition Peak. I believe the peak was supposed to have stayed white all that summer. Probably the snows didn't melt."

"It's a nice story anyway."

"Isn't it?"

They rode on, veering more to the right now. As they traveled Johnny kept his eyes on Ghost Rock, and before many minutes the manlike appearance of the rock had changed and he realized that it was, indeed, nothing more nor less than a long hogback of gray granite, jutting up from the plain.

The horses dipped down a long, rock-littered incline, but just before they commenced the descent Johnny had caught a glimpse of a flat-roofed adobe building. He mentioned this to Susan. Susan nodded. "That's where

Guadalupe used to live. The house where Ogallala Mitchell and Tony Aldrich holed up that night the posse was after them."

"Somewhere around there you think the gold is buried?"

"Somewhere—" Susan smiled—"I think it is. You'll be able to see the building complete by the time we top the next rise."

The girl pressed spurs to her pony and raced down the long slope, then started up the next incline. Johnny jammed his black sombrero tighter to his head and sped after her. Abruptly a premonition of impending trouble had come over him. He didn't know what caused such feeling, but he was determined not to let the girl approach the adobe house until he had reconnoitered the vicinity. He gave his pony the spurs, rapidly overhauling Susan's mount. Closing in, he reached down and grasped the girl's bridle just before reaching the next crest of land. Gripping the bridle firmly, he brought the pony to a firm stop.

"Why, Johnny—" Susan commenced her blue eyes wide, strands of pale gold hair whipping about her face.

Johnny said, "Wait!" Already he had caught the picture in one swift glance: the long grassy slope down to the adobe house; the house itself, situated in the shadow of Ghost Rock; the clump of cottonwoods growing not far from the house and the saddled horses tethered beneath the trees. Quickly Johnny backed Susan's pony down below the top of the ridge.

"Johnny! what's wrong?"

"There's somebody down at that adobe. I don't like it! You wait here while I drift down to investigate."

"Johnny, I'll go with you—"

"You wait here." Grimly Johnny ignored the girl's

protestations and rode quickly over the top of the slope to disappear from view. Susan started to follow, then checked her pony as Johnny had requested. Some minutes slowly passed. After a time Susan reined her pony cautiously to the top of the incline. From there she could see the old adobe and horses standing beneath the cottonwood trees. There weren't any men in sight, not even Johnny, though she could see Johnny's pony standing before the ancient building. She thought she could hear voices now, though the distance was too great to be certain. Focusing her gaze on the earth before the house, she thought she saw what looked like a fresh trench dug around the building.

"Why, I wonder—" she commenced in perplexity and then caught her breath. From the vicinity of the adobe house had come the heavy roar of a forty-five six-shooter!

BLACKIE FALCON

AT APPROXIMATELY THE SAME MOMENT SUSAN AND Johnny were first sighting Ghost Rock, Kane Mitchell was sitting at a table in the barroom of the Mecca Saloon. It was hot outside; within the Mecca the air seemed cool, almost damp, and Kane was enjoying a bottle of beer while he waited.

There weren't any other customers in the saloon. The beetle-browed bartender behind the long counter had tried to make conversation but without much success. "You waitin' for somebody, Kane?" he asked finally.

"Supposing I am?" Kane said coldly. "Is it any of your business?"

"None at all," the barkeep replied promptly. "I was

151

just wondering. Not that I care. Only I haven't seen much of you Spur-Bar hombres the last ten days—except that day you buried Ogallala. It was a shame he had to die—"

"Do you have to talk all the time?" Kane demanded wrathfully.

"Excuse me," the bartender said. "Like I say, it's none of my business, only it seems queer not seeing even Vink. He used to come in here every day reg'lar, even if none of the rest of you got to town."

"Vink's been keeping busy at home," Kane growled. "I'm keeping him busy, that is."

The barkeep nodded. "Young fellers like him should be kept to work reg'lar. Must be he's takin' a new interest in the ranch."

A cold smile crossed Kane's lips, as though something had amused him. "Yep—" he nodded—"he's certain taking an interest in our business. Right now I'll bet he's diggin' in, in real earnest."

"Well, that's fine."

Kane sipped his beer meditatively. A shadow darkened the entrance and Sheriff Pritchard came in. He looked about the saloon and nodded to Mitchell: "H'are you, Kane?"

"Tol'able, Nick," Mitchell returned pleasantly. "You looking for somebody?"

The sheriff shook his head. "Just making my first round of the day before dinnertime. I always like to check up first, before I sit down to my fodder, just to make sure there's no scraps bein' started."

"It's all quiet here," the barkeep said. Pritchard nodded and withdrew. Kane looked after him a moment, then slowly got to his feet and went to the door. He glanced east along Main Street and saw the sheriff just

152

stepping into another saloon. Mitchell frowned thoughtfully, then withdrew from an inner pocket of his vest a small leather-covered notebook, filled with blue-lined paper. He found a stub of lead pencil and wrote rapidly on a page in the notebook, then tore out the written words and folded the paper. Leaving the saloon doorway, he proceeded quickly west along Main Street.

Five minutes later he re-entered the saloon and resumed his seat at the table. The barkeep said, "Where'd you go?"

Mitchell gazed at him, level-eyed. "Where'd I go? I didn't go anyplace. I was right out in front, standing on the sidewalk."

"You were?" Disbelief showed in the barkeep's eyes. "Cripes! I could have swore I heard your footsteps hurrying along the sidewalk—and they were really hurrying."

Kane laughed heartily. "You must have heard that feller I saw running past."

"Mebbe—that's it. What was he running for? Who was it? Was anything wrong?"

Kane carelessly shook his head. "One of those TL cowhands. His horse had got away. He caught him— Cripes a'mighty! Don't you do anything but ask questions?"

"Nope." the barkeep grinned. "How about another bottle of suds?"

"That's one question that can be answered with a yes."

The fresh bottle of beer was placed on Kane's table and he again sat back to meditate. His beer was nearly gone when a shadow darkened the door and a man entered, pausing a moment just inside the doorway to accustom his gaze to the interior light after the sun glare

153

of the street. He was of medium height with sharp black eyes, a long stubbly jaw and jet hair, worn rather long, beneath his roll-brim sombrero. In the hatband of the sombrero was stuck a long eagle feather. He wore black corduroys, a flannel shirt, cowman boots and a stringy vest. About his neck was a red bandanna, and a pair of beaded Indian sleeve bands encircled his arms above the elbows. His mouth was a thin slit in his swarthy features, from one corner of which hung a brown-paper cigarette. A pair of walnut-butted forty-fives hung low at his thighs; he was stamped with all the earmarks of the professional gunman.

Kane Mitchell studied the man a moment, then raised his voice: "Hi-yuh, Blackie! Long time no see you."

"Kane Mitchell, you old son of a bustard!" He crossed the floor with quick light steps. The two men shook hands.

"You got my letter?" Kane said.

The other nodded. "Certain. What did you think brought me here? You said it was urgent. I took a train most of the way, then bought me a bronc and—well, here I am. When do I get a drink?"

Mitchell signaled the barkeep who quickly approached with a bottle of bourbon and two glasses which were placed on the table. Mitchell said to the barkeeper, "Jogger, this is my friend, Blackie Falcon. Give him anything he asks for."

"Blackie Falcon!" The bartender looked nervous.

Falcon laughed softly. "Heard of me, eh, Jogger? Well, I'd be insulted if you hadn't. I been advertised plenty through the Southwest country. Prob'ly heard my gun butts were notched like washboards, didn't you? Well, it's a lie. I never notch." He paused to let that sink in, then added, "I'd wear out too many guns if I did."

154

He suddenly burst into cruel, mirthless laughter.

"That'll be all," Kane told the barkeep. "Blackie and me want to talk. Keep away from us for a spell and we'll like you a heap better. Why don't you go set on your porch and watch folks go past? We'll call if we need you. Blackie is figurin' to buy some cows from me, and what price he pays is nobody's business. It's sort of a secret deal, see?"

The barkeep nodded, "I reckon I will go set outside for a spell." He rounded the bar, his face darkening, and started toward the doorway. On the porch he snorted skeptically. "Geez! Going to buy cattle! Any time Blackie Falcon is imported into a town it's not for the purpose of buying cattle. I've heard enough about that gun-slingin' hombre to know somethin' is up. But it ain't none o' my business."

Within the saloon Kane Mitchell was tilting the bottle above glasses. They gulped down their drinks, then Blackie Falcon asked, "How much you paying?"

"Three hundred."

Falcon shook his head. "No dice! My price has gone up since you used to know me. I've put a minimum of five hundred on my jobs—and that's five hundred each. Sometimes it's higher, dependin' on who it is—"

"Look, Blackie," Kane protested, "I can't afford five hundred dollars—"

"Cut it out, Kane," Falcon said coldly. "If you sent for me the job's worth five hundred. You wouldn't go to so much trouble—not considerin' the way you can handle a hawg leg. As I remember you used to be nigh as fast as me."

"I figure I'm faster now," Mitchell said.

"I doubt that, but, for the sake of argument, we'll say you are. Why don't you do this job yourself?"

155

Mitchell shook his head. "Don't get me wrong. It's not fear, Blackie. I could do it myself." Mitchell sounded confident enough to impress Falcon. "It's just that I've a position to maintain hereabouts. I'm going to be a big stock raiser someday. Ten years from now I don't want folks pointing a finger in my direction and remembering that I was a gun fighter."

Falcon sneered. "Gone respectable, have you?"

Mitchell looked uncomfortable. "Call it that if you like. Howsomever, that's neither here nor there. If it wasn't for us respectable hombres hiring men like you you'd be punchin' cows for your beans and biscuits."

"There's something in what you say," Falcon admitted. "But that's not changing my price. Five hundred spot cash."

They dickered a few minutes. Finally Mitchell gave in. "Two-fifty now, two-fifty when the job's done," he suggested.

Falcon nodded quickly. "That second two-fifty is as good as in my pocket now. Shell out."

Mitchell produced a roll of bills from his pocket and peeled off two hundred and fifty dollars which he passed across the table. Carelessly Blackie Falcon stuffed the money into his overalls. "Call that a consultin' fee." He smiled thinly. "Who's the patient, Doctor?"

"Hombre named Donshawnee. They call him Johnny."

Falcon nodded. "Guess he won't have any trouble taking my prescription, the same being a lead pill guaranteed to work on the proper organs. I've never heard of him."

"I reckon nobody else ever did until he hit this town," Mitchell grumbled. "He runs around with a sleepy-eyed cowhand pard. Once Donshawnee is out of the way I might make it worth your while to prescribe for him, too—but I wouldn't pay any five hundred. He ain't worth it."

"What you got against this Donshawnee?"

"He killed my brother Ogallala and wounded Vink slightly. They had Donshawnee cornered, out on the range, but something slipped up."

Falcon's beady eyes narrowed. "I never knew your brother Vink very well, but Ogallala used to sling a gun right handy before he went to the pen. And they both had this Donshawnee cornered? Hmmm! And something slipped up? I'm commencing to think, Kane, that five hundred is too cheap. This Donshawnee might prove to be a troublesome patient—"

"You named your price," Mitchell reminded testily.

"I did that," Falcon said promptly. "The price stands. I've had a heap of things said against me, but nobody ever could say Blackie Falcon broke his word . . . What was the trouble between your brothers and this Donshawnee?"

"It didn't amount to much," Mitchell evaded. "Donshawnee wears a hat that Ogallala claimed was his. Donshawnee wouldn't give it up. Ogallala and Vink tried to take it away. They didn't have any luck."

Falcon eyed Mitchell with a cold, steady gaze. "You're not coming clean with me, Kane," he stated in chilly accents. "I never yet saw the hat that was worth that much trouble. What's back of all this?"

Mitchell said, "Falcon, I'm paying you the price you named. I want a rebate if you insist on hearing any more than I've told you. You can take the story or leave it, just as you like."

"In other words," Falcon said coolly, "it's none of my

business. Right, we'll let it ride that way. I had a hunch there must be something afoot when you refused to risk your own skin. Well, let's forget it. Where do I find this Donshawnee?"

"He comes to town off and on. You'll just have to wait your chance. Unless you want to ride out to the Rocking-A, where he's working, and do the job there."

Falcon shook his head. "That'd look too much like I was looking for trouble. I'd sooner pick my quarrel here, spontaneous like, so nobody will have suspicions."

"That's better. Just how do you expect to do it?"

"Pick a quarrel, as I just said, then invite Donshawnee to go for his iron. It's simple. Anyway, what do you care how I do it, so long as it gets done?"

"So long as it gets done," Mitchell echoed with satisfaction. "Now you're talking. Let's have a drink." Once more he lifted the bottle above the two glasses.

Falcon lifted his drink to the light, his beady eyes seeming to see something deeply satisfying in the whiskey's amber depths. "Here's to a quick prescription and a successful operation"—he smiled cruelly—"successful, that is, for the doctor in attendance—never for the patient!"

SUCKERS CAUGHT WITHOUT BAIT

AS JOHNNY LOPED HIS PONY DOWN THE LONG SLOPE toward the old adobe house he glanced back over his shoulder, half expecting to see Susan following behind. "I'm glad she did what I told her," he muttered. "I don't know what's ahead and I don't want a girl messing up

158

things."

He was nearer to the adobe house now—near enough to count eight saddled ponies standing under the cottonwood trees. Still there were no men in sight. He pulled the pony to a walk, hoping its moving hoofs wouldn't strike a rock and warn whoever was at the adobe house of his approach. His eyes were alert for the first sign of movement about the place. Now he saw that a long earthen trench had been excavated before the house, which was about thirty feet long with a wooden porch running along its width. The walls were cracked and old. Two windows in the front wall had once held glass but were now paneless. A wide oaken door hung, half open, by one hinge.

To the left of the house, some short distance, rose the gray, precipitous side of Ghost Rock, towering fifty-odd feet above the house. To the right of the house were the cottonwood trees with the horses beneath lazily switching at flies. Johnny could hear voices now and the sounds of metal striking against earth. He pulled his pony to a halt and stepped down from the saddle. Then he proceeded on foot, leading the pony behind.

The voices he heard were coming from the rear of the adobe building. Johnny approached cautiously and when he'd reached the front of the house he stopped his pony, leaving the reins to dangle on the earth. Moving on tiptoe, he first approached the house and peered in through the doorway, past the loosely hanging door. The house was empty within, so far as his gaze penetrated. Slipping down from the porch; he made his way toward one end. The earthen trench turned the corner of the house. Apparently someone was digging completely around the building.

Abruptly Johnny paused as a man's voice reached his

ears:

" . . . and it's damn hot digging, if you ask me," a grumbling tone carried through the words. "I don't get the sense of this. I think we should scatter out and—"

"What you think doesn't matter," cold tones cut in on the complaint. "You should be glad me and Kane let you in on this. You'll be well paid if we find it—better than you'd make punching cows for the Spur-Bar. You were ready enough to come out here and start in, but now that the work's tough you're commencing to get ideas."

To Johnny the second speaker sounded like Vink Mitchell. The men were trying to find the buried gold!

"This digging all around the house looks plumb cuckoo to me," another voice broke in. Grunts, the sounds of metal striking on rock and gravelly earth punctuated the remarks. "We've dug clear to hard-pan now."

"You'll dig clear to hell if I say so!" That sounded like Pat Scudder's voice.

And then another complaint: "It's all right for you and Vink to talk. You're not doing the work—"

A sudden curse from Scudder and the sound of a clenched fist landing against bone and flesh. A scraping, stumbling sound was heard, then a body struck the earth.

"Now get up and I'll give you another," came Scudder's wrathful tones. "Either that or get to work."

The sounds of picks and shovels were resumed. Vink Mitchell spoke again, as though trying to excuse Scudder's violence: "I don't figure Pat hit hard enough to hurt you, Scopey. You know, we're just following Kane's orders. He said to dig all around the house first. We'll spread our operations later if we don't find it

160

here—Huh? What's that?" Vink swore. "Sure, I know you could come and dig by yourself, but you might run afoul of the Rocking-A. This way, if we find it, we all get a share. If trouble comes you've got the Spur-Bar to back you. That's why Pat and me aren't handling tools. We keep watch, in case any Rocking-A hombres come messing around—"

"Aw, they never come 'way over here," a new voice cut in. "Folks have dug all around these parts, too, and never found anything. I'll bet that gold was dug up long ago—"

"You'll keep digging anyway," Scudder cut in harshly, "so long as you're on the Spur-Bar payroll."

Johnny softly rounded the corner of the house and stopped, several yards away. There, standing side by side to oversee the work, were Scudder and Vink Mitchell, while half-a-dozen cowhands toiled industriously with picks and shovels. Scudder was angrily puffing on a stinking briar pipe. A strip of court plaster ran across Vink's forehead; another strip diagonaled the back of his right hand. A few feet away was piled a collection of guns and belts, the property of the toiling cowhands. Only Vink and Pat Scudder were armed.

Johnny queried coolly, "Looking for something, hombres?"

As though by magic faces jerked in his direction, digging operations ceased. Scudder ripped out an oath, the pipe nearly dropping from his mouth, as he swung about to see Johnny, thumbs hooked in gun belts, calmly and amusedly surveying the scene. Vink swore in amazement, then his face clouded as one hand swung down.

Like a flash Johnny's guns were out, the cedar butts

161

cradled ominously in his fists. "Don't touch 'em!" he warned.

Vink's hands flew in the air. The cowhands threw down their tools and quickly elevated their arms. Pat Scudder cursed again and half swung away, one hand going in the air while the right arm started toward his hip.

Johnny thumbed one quick shot. Scudder's hands had been too occupied to remove the briar pipe from his mouth. Johnny's shot saved him that trouble, the bullet tearing the pipe savagely from between Scudder's teeth. Scudder emitted a yelp of fright and shot both hands in the air.

Johnny laughed at the expression on Scudder's face. "That shot was plumb lucky." He grinned. "Maybe I'm better than I think I am."

"You're a damn sight worse off than you think you are," Vink growled sullenly. "We ain't done nothing to you—"

"You're on Rocking-A property," Johnny stated crisply. "Ogallala was warned off by George Aldrich. You knew dang well the order covered all you Spur-Bar coyotes. If there is any gold hereabouts it belongs to the Rocking-A—"

"If!" Vink sneered. "As if you didn't know—" He stopped suddenly.

Johnny hesitated. "Just what do you mean by that, Mitchell?" he asked.

"Never mind what I mean," Vink growled sullenly. He changed the subject. "All right, Donshawnee, you got the drop on us. We know when we're covered. Right now you got us licked, but you ain't heard the last of this. We'll be getting out now—"

"Not so fast," Johnny interrupted. "You're not

leaving yet. You"—speaking to the cowhand nearest him—"unbuckle Scudder's and Mitchell's gun belts and put their hardware with that pile of other weapons there."

The man started to obey. Vink swore at him. "Don't you do it, Larry!"

"Get busy, Larry," Johnny snapped.

"Cripes a'mighty, Vink, I got to," the man said apologetically.

Vink didn't say anything more but stood glowering at Johnny, while the man known as Larry quickly removed his and Scudder's six-shooters and dropped them on the pile of weapons near by. That done, the men stood, hands still in air, awaiting Johnny's next move. Baffled resentment, rage, cold anger, showed in their features, but none dared make a move in the face of Johnny's leveled six-shooters.

Hoof beats drummed suddenly beyond the adobe house. Hopefully the Spur-Bar men lifted their faces in the direction from which the sound was coming. It might be Kane Mitchell or some other comrade. Then their faces fell as Susan came riding around the corner of the house, her drawn .38 in hand. She stopped her pony so suddenly at the scene before her eyes that the little beast went to rear haunches in a scattering of dust and gravel.

"Johnny! whatever—" she exclaimed. Then, seeing he had the situation well in hand, she shoved her gun back into holster.

"Hello, Susan." Johnny grinned. "You're just in time to see the fun."

"But—but what—" Susan commenced.

"The Spur-Bar," Johnny explained gravely, "suddenly got a desire to do some fishing in Arenoso Creek. They

163

came over here to dig worms."

"I presume"—Susan nodded coldly—"they'd also feel entitled to any gold they turned up while seeking worms."

Scudder cursed under his breath. The cowhands remained silent. Vink Mitchell, with a smirk, removed his hat, saying, "Miss Aldrich, we admit we're in the wrong, trespassin' here. We're willing to leave, but Donshawnee won't let us. I protest such unneighborly treatment—"

"Unneighborly!" Susan sniffed contemptuously. "At any rate, Mr. Donshawnee speaks for the Rocking-A. I'll leave the decision to him."

"I demand to know why we ain't allowed to leave," Scudder bellowed hotly.

"Because," Johnny explained succinctly, "you've thrown up earth halfway around this house, something you had no right to do. I figure the dirt should be replaced and tamped down before you leave."

"Fair enough," Susan nodded, suppressing a smile.

A howl of protest arose. At first the men refused.

"We won't do it!" Scudder snarled. "You can shoot and be damned to you, Donshawnee. You can't make us—"

"True enough, I can't," Johnny concluded gravely. "But I could take you all before the sheriff, *tied into your saddles,* and prefer trespassing charges. You'd go to jail, at the very least. In the end you'd have to make things right. It's up to you."

The very thought was humiliating. The men looked anxiously at Vink Mitchell. Vink started to plead and was augmented by Scudder. Adamant, Johnny cut short their begging. "You can leave here," he told them coldly, "only when all earth has been replaced and

164

tamped down. Scudder, you and Mitchell can throw dirt with your hands, if there aren't enough tools to go round. Now make up your mind!"

Scudder was so angry he trembled. Vink Mitchell's eyes were boiling cauldrons of hate. Johnny stifled all further protests. In the face of his attitude—and guns— the Spur-Bar men finally gave in. Reluctantly they set to their task. Then, as they worked, anxious to be finished, anger lent a spur to their efforts. Dirt flew and settled in the trenches. Dust rose in clouds about the perspiring men. Sweat coursed channels down Mitchell's and Scudder's features as they cursed angrily to themselves.

Johnny had Susan bring his horse around the house. He climbed into the saddle and sat by the girl's side, amusedly watching the shovel-swinging toilers. Johnny's gaze settled on Pat Scudder who had commenced to shirk on the job: the man's shovel carried but a small particle of earth at each scoop he made. Johnny grinned, tilted his left gun a trifle and triggered one shot. The bullet struck the shovel with a resounding clang, nearly tearing the tool from Scudder's hands.

Scudder jumped as though he were the one shot. He turned white. His voice shook: "You'll be hurting somebody, Donshawnee. That bullet ricocheted!"

"That's too bad," Johnny said unfeelingly. "The next one won't."

Scudder gulped and bent to his shovel with renewed vigor. All the men redoubled their efforts. At the end of an hour and a half all earth had been replaced and tamped down to Johnny's satisfaction. The men straightened wearily from their task and faced Johnny.

Vink Mitchell, his face covered with dirt and sweat, panted heavily. "I reckon we can go now, eh?"

Johnny nodded. "Get your horses and slope. And don't put a foot on Rocking-A holdings again—not ever!" The men threw down their tools and started toward the pile of guns. This was the moment for which Scudder had been waiting. He walked wearily toward the pile of weapons. Now he'd have a chance to square with this blasted Donshawnee—"

"Never mind that hardware," Johnny interrupted Scudder's thoughts. "Just get your horses and drift out of here. No, you can't take those guns. You might as well leave those picks and shovels too. I might want to dig for worms myself some day—though I sure caught a mess of suckers today without bait."

He hushed the sudden storm of protest that arose by tilting his guns a trifle. A sterner light came into his eyes. His voice went cold. "I said 'get out!' and I meant just that. I don't figure to be ambushed by those guns on the way back. Drift, you scuts! Slope, ride, *vamos* pronto! I'm losing patience and this hardware is likely to start talking about it any minute!"

They faced his guns for a moment, eight angry men, then turned toward horses and climbed into saddles. Only Mitchell hesitated after he had reached his pony's back. He turned in the saddle, shaking his right fist. "Wait until Kane hears about this, Donshawnee," he threatened. "Your life won't be worth a plugged peso!"

"I hope you tell him soon," Johnny snapped. "You can add that I wish he'd been here. I'd like to watch him swing a shovel."

Mitchell cursed, then jabbed spurs into his mount to overtake his men. Within a short time the Spur-Bar men had disappeared over the first rise of land, riding hard.

Johnny turned back to Susan. The girl gave a long sigh of relief as the smile faded from her face. She looked worried now. "Oh, Johnny, it was funny for a time, but I'm afraid for you—deathly afraid. Making them work like that was a worse humiliation that if you'd shot one of them. They won't forget it. The Mitchells won't readily overlook this—"

Johnny's careless laugh interrupted the words. "I'm not worrying, Susan. You shouldn't."

"But I am."

Johnny said directly, "Why?"

Susan met his ardent gaze for a moment, then glanced away, color stealing into her cheeks. For a moment Johnny was tempted to say the words that had been on the tip of his tongue for so long, then he paused. After all, he was Johnny Donne, suspected of Susan's father's murder. Abruptly he swung down from his pony, saying shortly, "I'm going to collect those Spur-Bar guns, then we'd better be getting along home."

Somewhat surprised, Susan reined her pony around after him. Neither spoke while he collected the pile of belts and guns and distributed them between the two to hang on the saddle horns. Within a short time they were riding across the range at a smart clip, heading toward the Rocking-A. Susan rode in silence, still wondering why Johnny's manner had so abruptly changed.

They were within a few miles of the Rocking-A when Johnny spied a rider approaching them from the south. He spoke to Susan and the two drew their ponies to a slower gait until they could learn the man's identity. Not knowing what to expect, Johnny shifted his right holster a trifle nearer the front.

Suddenly Susan said, "It looks like Dave Franklin. I wonder if anything has turned up. Ordinarily he wouldn't be heading for the ranch for a couple of hours yet."

The rider was Franklin. Ten minutes later he drew to a stop and greeted them with some surprise as his gaze noted the belts and guns they were carrying on saddles. "You two look like a pair of traveling arsenals," he chuckled. "Where did you collect all the hardware?"

"The Spur-Bar donated." Johnny grinned and told the story.

When he had finished Franklin laughed uproariously. "That is good!" he exclaimed. "Those Spur-Bar hombres have always considered themselves right tough too. Making them work that-a-way was sure rubbing it in. At that you were taking chances. They might have rushed you. You'd never have got all of them—"

"The fact remains they didn't," Johnny said dryly. "Every man was waiting for the other fellow to start something, which same worked to my advantage. They never did get started."

Susan changed the subject. "Did you find any strays, Dave?"

"Not many. I scared a few out of the brush and turned 'em over toward the Arenoso. I figure they'll stay near the stream for a spell now. I did find this though." He indicated a rolled section of cowhide tied to his saddle horn. He untied the roll and handed Johnny a freshly skinned-out oblong of hide, approximately eighteen by twenty inches in size.

Susan leaned near while Johnny studied the Wagon-Wheel brand burned on the hide. The Wagon-Wheel design stood out sharply on the hairy side of the skin. Suddenly an exclamation burst from Johnny's lips, and he turned the hide over, studying the wet, fleshy side. "Cripes!" Johnny snapped. "This Wagon Wheel has been blotted over a Rocking-A brand. You can see where certain lines are superimposed. It's plainer than ever from the underside. The crossbar of the A has been used to form part of the hub of the Wagon-Wheel—why, why—this is mighty clumsy work!"

He looked at Susan and Franklin. Susan didn't appear surprised. She said wearily, "Another one, eh, Dave?"

Franklin nodded grimly. "We've found quite a few animals branded that-a-way, Johnny. Today I was riding over near the Spur-Bar holdings and I saw a bunch of buzzards hovering. I came near and found a dead cow with this brand. Somebody had shot it, just over the property dividing line. Oh, it was on our holdings all right. The coyotes had been at the carcass, and the hide was pretty well chewed. Luckily this brand hadn't been touched, so I skinned it out for evidence. Damn that Linbauer!"

Johnny didn't say anything. His eyes were fixed meditatively on the distant horizon. Finally he spoke, "Somehow I can't feel that Henry Linbauer is responsible for this. From what I saw of the man he looked honest. Dave, you take these Spur-Bar guns and accompany Susan back to the Rocking-A."

"But what are you going to do?" Susan asked.

"I'm going to show this to Linbauer," Johnny replied. "He's been under suspicion for a long spell now. I figure it's time he learned what's what. By heading for the Wagon-Wheel now, I'll get there in time for supper. I want to look over his crew—"

"But, Johnny," Susan protested, "if Linbauer is guilty you'll be taking a risk."

Johnny shook his head. "I don't figure it that way, Susan. I know what I'm doing. I won't mention this piece of hide until I've got everything in hand."

Somewhat dubiously, Susan finally consented to his making the trip to the Wagon-Wheel. The guns were transferred from his saddle to Franklin's, then, lifting his hat, he turned his pony across the range, heading toward the northeast.

AN ANONYMOUS CLUE

IT WAS NEARING TEN O'CLOCK THAT NIGHT BY THE time Johnny sighted the lights of the Rocking-A buildings. A lamp gleamed in the ranch house. The bunkhouse, however, was dark. Johnny turned his pony into the ranch yard and headed down toward the corral. As he neared the enclosure a man's form loomed up before him and a cigarette butt described a short arc through the darkness to land on the earth where a booted toe extinguished the sparks.

"Johnny, that you?" It was Humdrum's voice, sounding a shade more alert than usual.

"It's me, Humdrum. What's up?"

Humdrum talked while Johnny stripped off his saddle and turned the pony into the corral.

"You didn't have any trouble at the Wagon-Wheel?" Humdrum asked.

Johnny shook his head. "I'll tell it later, when Susan and Mecate can hear. Where's Franklin?"

"In his bunk. He turned in early. Susan and Mecate are waiting for you at the house. Susan's a mite worried: I felt certain you wouldn't have any trouble with Linbauer. I figured you knew what you were doing—"

"How come you're waiting here to meet me?"

"I wanted to warn you."

"Of what, Humdrum?"

"Sheriff Pritchard was here this afternoon, just a while before supper. He wanted to see you."

"Now what's up?"

"Plenty. You're in a tight place, Johnny—or you were, until I talked to Pritchard. But you'll have to fix up some sort of story for Mecate and Susan. They're wondering plenty, especially Mecate—"

"What in the devil are you talking about?" Johnny demanded.

"It's this way. Sometime around noon today—leastwise Pritchard found it on his desk when he returned from dinner—some anonymous skunk left a note for the sheriff."

"What sort of a note?"

Humdrum reached into his pocket, paper rustled, then he scratched a match. Written in a bold backhand, on a sheet torn from a notebook, Johnny read:

Make Donshawnee tell where he got that black sombrero. George Aldrich had it shortly before he was murdered.

There was no signature. The match flared and then went out. There came a rustle of paper again as Humdrum folded the note and put it away. Various emotions surged through Johnny. He held his voice steady and said, "That's dynamite if Susan sees it, or Mecate."

Humdrum said lazily, "They've seen it. Luckily I was able to fix things up. At least to some extent. You'll have—"

"I'd like to know how," Johnny said bitterly. "With George Aldrich's murderer still at large a clue like this won't be overlooked. I never will be able to do what I came here to do."

Humdrum went on, "As soon as Sheriff Pritchard saw

171

this note he headed for the Rocking-A, figuring to talk to you. You weren't here, of course. He showed me the note and then after Mecate had seen it waited for Susan to get here. I lied like a trooper and swore that I knew the man who had given you the hat. I pointed out that it was probably one of the Mitchells, just trying to make trouble, who had written the note—"

"That's the way it looks to me. Incidentally, I wonder what the Mitchells know about George Aldrich's murder, seeing they know so much about this bonnet of mine. There's a thought, Humdrum."

"That idea's not original with you."

"What did Susan and Mecate have to say?"

"Susan doesn't know what to think. Mecate is feeling right ugly, though he's somewhat up in the air too. The sheriff waited until after supper, then he had to get back to town. I came to the corral with him and talked him into letting me have this note."

"You must have talked powerful persuasive."

"I showed him my badge." Humdrum chuckled. "Told him we were both members of the Border Rangers and that we were here secretly on the Aldrich murder case. You could have knocked him over with a feather when he heard that. He's promised to be mighty secretive about the whole business and not mention it to a soul. Oh, I persuaded Pritchard all right—"

"Just a minute." Johnny frowned. "Do you mean to tell me you fooled the sheriff with that tin badge of yours?"

"What do you mean, fooled him with my badge?" Humdrum said with mock indignation. "Ain't I a full-fledged law enforcer?"

Johnny swore disgustedly. "By cripes! Sheriff Pritchard is a bigger idiot than I dreamed he could be . . . Come on, let's go up to the house."

Humdrum fell in alongside Johnny as he strode toward the ranch house. "Remember, Johnny, I swore that I knew the man who gave you that sombrero. Fix up your story so it will tally with mine."

"Did you tell Susan and Mecate that you—and I— were Border Rangers?"

"No, I didn't figure that was necessary."

They reached the house and entered by the rear door. Guadalupe was kneading a mass of bread dough to rise overnight. She smiled at Johnny when he passed and wondered why he had no cheerful word for her as usual. Mecate and Susan were waiting in the big main room. A fire was burning in the fireplace. Susan looked relieved when Johnny entered. Mecate shot him a puzzled angry glance and said, "We've been hearing things about that hat of yours, Donshawnee. I want an explanation—"

"Mecate!" Susan said, "I feel sure Johnny will explain everything. You know, Humdrum said—"

"Sure," Humdrum drawled, "no use getting excited. I knew the hombre gave Johnny that hat. He'll tell you about it." Apparently unable to stand any longer, Humdrum sank wearily, carelessly, into an easy chair, his eyes half closed.

Johnny didn't sit down. He went over to the fireplace and stood with his back against the mantel. His voice was steady when he started to speak. "I'll get to that hat business in a minute," he commenced. "But first I want to tell you what I learned at the Wagon-Wheel—"

"T 'hell with the Wagon-Wheel," Mecate burst out bluntly. "What we want to know is where you got that hat. I'm commencing to think you knew that murderin' buzzard, Donne, who killed George. Come down to cases, Donshawnee—"

173

"Yes. I knew him, Mecate," Johnny said, wincing at the name he had been called, "but if I am to tell what I know I've got to do it in my own way."

"Please, Mecate," Susan said wearily, "let Johnny talk."

Mecate sank back in his chair, wrathful gaze fixed on Johnny.

"I had my supper at the Wagon-Wheel," Johnny commenced steadily, "and met all but two of Linbauer's hands. They seem like a right-square crew to me. I'd stake my life they don't know about the rustling. If the two hands who were missing—they were up on Linbauer's north range someplace and didn't arrive while I was there—if they know anything about changing our—that is, the Rocking-A brand, I can't say. Linbauer himself doesn't know much about them, except that they're good workers."

"Did you mention that piece of hide to Linbauer?" Humdrum asked.

Johnny nodded. "I talked to him alone after supper. He's pretty much upset about the whole business. He swears he knows nothing about it. I believe him. He's square as a die."

"How do you account for the brand changing then?" Mecate growled, becoming interested in spite of himself.

"I figure the Spur-Bar is doing it."

"The Spur-Bar?" Susan said. "But why should they burn a Wagon-Wheel brand?"

"To make trouble between your two outfits," Johnny said promptly. "If Mitchell could get a range war started between the Rocking-A and Wagon-Wheel both outfits would be so busy fighting that Mitchell could come in and rustle cattle to his heart's content. The Rocking-A could go broke a heap sooner under such conditions. Here's something else to think about. I talked enough to Linbauer to learn that he's a topnotch cowman. He'd never allow such clumsy brand-blotting. He's capable of doing a far better job. I tell you, the man who ordered that branding done wanted you to learn that the Wagon-Wheel had been burned over the Rocking-A brand, so you'd start a fracas with the Wagon-Wheel."

"I wonder if that could be so," Susan said thoughtfully.

"I've a hunch it is." Johnny nodded. "You say that you've found cattle branded that way before—that it's been going on a long time. What happens? Apparently you've taken no notice of it. Mitchell—we'll say Mitchell is responsible—gets impatient. He orders a cow shot where you'll be sure to see it—as Franklin saw it today. Here's another point: The Wagon-Wheel is northeast of here. The Spur-Bar lies south of the Rocking-A. *If* Linbauer was doing that brand-blotting would he come away over south of here to do it? No, he'd do the dirty work near his own holdings. That's logical. I'm saying that Linbauer's innocent. I'd stake my life the Spur-Bar is responsible for the brand-blotting."

Mecate Bowen looked thoughtful. "You got proof of this?"

Johnny shook his head. "No more proof than I have that one of the Mitchells left that note, regarding my hat, in the sheriff's office today. I'm just following a hunch. Regarding what that note said, well, I reckon it's time I explained a few things, Susan—"

"Johnny!" Humdrum said swiftly, sensing what was coming, "it's not necessary for you—"

"I reckon it is, Humdrum," Johnny said quietly. "I've

175

sailed under false colors long enough. Mecate, you spoke of a certain Donne as being a murderous buzzard. You're plenty mistaken on that score—"

"How do you know?" Bowen demanded savagely.

"Because, Johnny admitted, "I happen to be the Donne you mentioned—now wait a minute!"

Mecate was on his feet, one hand dropping to the gun he hadn't removed that evening. Susan went white, started from her chair and then slumped back. "Johnny!" she wailed.

Moving surprisingly fast, Humdrum had leaped up and thrown one arm around Mecate, forcing him back in his chair, while his other hand seized Mecate's gun wrist. "Take it easy, Mecate," Humdrum advised. He loosened his hold and placed one hand in his pocket. Mecate's angry gaze widened as it focused on the badge Humdrum held before his eyes.

"You—you're a detective?" Mecate blurted out.

"Border Ranger," Humdrum said promptly. "But that information isn't to leave this room—"

"Humdrum," Johnny started a weary protest, "why do—"

"It's all right, Johnny," Humdrum drawled brazenly. "Mecate and Susan won't tell anybody."

Johnny shrugged hopeless shoulders. At any rate, Humdrum's maneuver had calmed Mecate so the story could be told. Things quieted down after a few minutes and Johnny was able to speak.

"It's true, Susan," he commenced, his eyes meeting the girl's without faltering. "I'm Johnny Donne, suspected of being responsible for your dad's death. I never intended to take that Donshawnee name. The day we arrived here Humdrum introduced me to Corkscrew Jones as Don Johnny—a name folks called me some time back. Jones misunderstood and called me Donshawnee. One thing led to another, so I let the name ride as it was. I didn't figure it made any difference at that time—"

"What do you know about George's death?" Mecate broke in.

"I don't know who killed him, but I was there when it happened," Johnny said, wincing inwardly at the thought of hurting Susan. However, the story had to be told sometime. From that point on he related frankly all that had happened, from the time he went to Aldrich's hotel room until he caught the freight train out of El Paso. By the time the story was concluded there was no doubting his word. Neither Susan nor Mecate could deny the open honesty shining in his gray eyes.

Susan crossed the room, one hand outstretched. Her eyes looked moist. "I believe you, Johnny. I know you couldn't have been the one who—"

"Sorry I flew off the handle the way I did, Johnny," Mecate interrupted. "Sure, it's all right. We believe you."

Johnny said thanks in a relieved voice. He felt better now. Mecate and Susan resumed their seats. Johnny found a chair near Susan. "I'm still wondering," Mecate continued, "if you didn't make a mistake in running away like that. It might have been better to stay and face the police."

Johnny shook his head. "I didn't see it that-a-way. Circumstantial evidence would have been against me. I was up against that sort of thing once before. You see, when I was with the Rangers a man was murdered and robbed. Someone planted part of the stolen money on me. I was accused and tried for murder. I was acquitted, but public opinion was against me. That's why I resigned from the Rangers. I'll give you the details sometime. But getting back to the night I left George Aldrich's hotel room—well, I had only one thought in mind. To keep free of the police so I could carry out a job George Aldrich had hired me to do. Six weeks later, on my way here, I ran into Humdrum. We came on together and promptly got mixed into an argument with the Mitchells—"

"And so," Susan said, "you really did get that black sombrero from Dad. I wonder where he got it. Perhaps he did meet Tony and Tony gave it to him. But why? I wonder if the hat ever did belong to Ogallala Mitchell."

"I can't answer those questions," Johnny said, "but I do think that note the sheriff had left on his desk may furnish a clue that will help clear up the whole problem. I've no proof, of course, but it seems to me one of the Mitchells must have written that note. They'd like to get the Rocking-A. In the face of what we've learned so far, that note makes me wonder just what, if anything, the Mitchells had to do with George Aldrich's death. One of them must have known your dad had this hat before he was killed."

"That sounds logical." Mecate nodded. "I'd like to compare that note to Kane and Vink Mitchell's handwriting."

"Probably wouldn't do any good," Humdrum put in lazily. "Like's not the handwriting is disguised."

Mecate turned to Humdrum. "You were sent here to work on this case, eh?"

Eyes half closed, Humdrum nodded listlessly. "I figure a Border Ranger can clear it up if anybody can."

Johnny was about to expose Humdrum as an impostor. Then he paused and remained silent. After all, if Susan and Mecate felt better thinking a regularly constituted law enforcer was on the job why disillusion them?

"Well, what's the next move?" Mecate asked, frowning.

"I figure," Humdrum grunted indolently, "that we'd better keep Johnny's identity a secret. Let him wear that Donshawnee moniker for a spell longer—that is, if he don't get a rush of conscience to the head."

Johnny smiled sheepishly. "It's all right with me, now that Mecate and Susan know who I am. I felt pretty uncomfortable before . . . As to the next move, well, I figure to take those Spur-Bar guns in to Sheriff Pritchard tomorrow and tell him to warn the Spur-Bar we don't want any more trespassing. Maybe if Mitchell gets mad enough he'll tip his hand and we'll learn something to work on."

They talked a few minutes longer, then the three men rose and headed for the bunkhouse. It required some time for Johnny to get to sleep that night but his mind was more at ease than it had been since he first saw Susan Aldrich.

HUMDRUM DISAPPEARS

IT WAS SHORTLY AFTER NINE O'CLOCK THE FOLLOWING morning when Johnny and Humdrum drew rein before the sheriff's office and stepped inside, carrying the belts and six-shooters captured from the Spur-Bar men the previous day. Sheriff Pritchard was seated at his desk, talking to a hatchet-faced man with bushy eyebrows whom he introduced as his deputy, Ed Hunter. The men shook hands, Hunter saying, with a genial smile, "I've been hearing about you fellers. Looks like you've had the Mitchells on the run a mite."

"Ed's been up in Montany, visitin' his folks," Pritchard explained. "Just got in this morning. I'm right glad to have him back on the job again—Say, what's all them guns for?"

"They belong to the Spur-Bar crew," Johnny said. "I had to take 'em away from 'em yesterday."

"Oh, sure." Pritchard commenced to laugh. "Susan told me about that happenin' when I was out to the Rocking-A last evening. You'd gone to the Wagon-Wheel for something. Did you see that note?"

Johnny nodded carelessly. "Just somebody trying to make trouble. I figure it's one of the Mitchells, but there's no proof, so we might as well forget it."

The sheriff nodded agreement. "I talked things over with Humdrum," he said meaningfully. "I know how things are."

Humdrum said languidly, "Sure, Johnny, I made things clear to the sheriff."

Ed Hunter looked a bit puzzled but didn't ask any questions.

The sheriff went on. "What do you want me to do with these guns?"

"Give 'em back to the Spur-Bar hombres and warn 'em not to trespass on Rocking-A holdings again," Johnny replied.

"I'll be glad to warn 'em"—Pritchard frowned—"but I'd sure like to withhold these weapons. It wouldn't do no good though. They'd just buy new ones. Incidentally, they'll all be in town today. This is the Spur-Bar payday and the whole passel of 'em come in and raise hell. I sure wish I knew some way to keep 'em disarmed."

"Cripes!" Ed Hunter growled, "let them have their hawg laigs. I don't like to take advantage of an unarmed

180

man, and I sure know I'm going to have to gun-whup one or two of those coyotes when they get their hides full of liquor."

"Do you mean to say," Humdrum asked, "that the whole outfit comes to town on payday? Don't they leave nobody on the Spur-Bar?"

"Not generally," Pritchard said. "Mostly they get slicked up in their best bandannas and come roarin' into Spearhead Wells to drink up their wages. Like Ed says, we generally have to throw a couple of 'em in the clink. No. Kane Mitchell doesn't bother his head over a little thing like that. He pays their fines and we let 'em go next morning. I reckon Kane realizes the type hands he hires has to go on a bust at reg'lar intervals."

"I'll see you later," Humdrum drawled and passed through the doorway.

"Where you going?" Johnny asked, but Humdrum was out of sight and no reply came back. Johnny didn't think anything about Humdrum's leaving at the moment. Undoubtedly he wouldn't be far away.

"What's all this about you taking the guns away from the Spur-Bar crew?" Ed Hunter asked. "I haven't heard that story yet."

Pritchard laughed. "Tell him about how you caught the Spur-Bar gang trespassing, Johnny. It's downright comical, when I think how you made 'em shovel back that dirt."

Johnny told the story. Ed Hunter laughed when it was finished. "That's probably the first honest work them coyotes ever did, if the truth was known—"

A great hooting and yelling was heard at the edge of town, mingled with the drumming of horses' hoofs. The sheriff swore. "There's those Spur-Bars coming now." Grabbing up the belts and guns, he went out to meet the approaching riders. Johnny and Ed Hunter followed close on his heels.

The riders came loping along Main Street, yelping like mad coyotes. There were nine men altogether, with Scudder riding near the front. Apparently all the Spur-Bar crew hadn't been taken on the digging expedition the previous day. Neither of the Mitchells were with the men, some of whom had already procured six-shooters. As their eyes fell on Johnny, standing with the sheriff and the deputy, the riders suddenly pulled their lathered, panting ponies to a swift halt.

"There he is now!" a cowpuncher shouted. "There's the hombre that took our guns—"

"You hush your mouth," the sheriff said sternly. "Donshawnee isn't holding any grudge. He's asked me to return your irons to you. But don't put foot on Rocking-A holdings again."

Some of the men, realizing the humor in the situation, laughed. Others glowered sullenly at Johnny and the law officers. Pat Scudder swore, saying, "Donshawnee, there's a score to be settled between you and me."

"I'm ready any time you are," Johnny snapped.

"My time will come," Scudder promised evilly.

The sheriff handed up the guns and belts. There was a mocking something in the eyes of the Spur-Bar men that Johnny didn't understand. According to all the rules, there should have been much more resentment shown. Johnny commenced to wonder just what was being cooked up for his particular benefit; he knew the Spur-Bar wouldn't overlook readily the humiliation put on them the previous day. And Pat Scudder had appeared too cocksure of himself. It was Johnny's guess that Kane Mitchell had ordered his men to leave Johnny alone. But if that were so what reason lay behind the move? Johnny shook his head and decided he'd have to be on his guard.

The Spur-Bar men prodded their ponies into action again and headed for the nearest saloon. Pritchard looked puzzled. "They sure took it tame," he commented. "I half expected one or two of those hombres to start a fight with you, Johnny. And Pat Scudder acted mighty cocky."

"Maybe Johnny's got 'em buffaloed," Ed Hunter suggested. "I wish I could put the Injun sign on 'em like that. They'll be orderly enough for the next two—three hours, I expect, but long about this afternoon I'm going to have my work cut out for me, I'm thinking."

"You and me both." The sheriff nodded.

"Looks like Vink and Kane Mitchell stayed at their ranch," Johnny commented. "I didn't see them."

"They're both in town," Pritchard said. "They rode in about an hour before you got here. By the way, there's a feller named Blackie Falcon in town. He seems to be right chummy with Mitchell—"

"Blackie Falcon!" Johnny echoed unbelievingly. More than one stout heart had quailed at mention of the killer's name.

"You've heard of him, eh?" Pritchard said.

"Who hasn't heard of that professional assassin?" Ed Hunter said moodily. "I just hope he stays peaceful while he's here. I'd hate to face his guns. Falcon is heap bad medicine!"

"Yes, I've heard of him," Johnny said slowly, "but never anything good. They say he's greased lightning with his six guns—just a natural born killer."

Things were coming clearer for Johnny now; he was commencing to realize why the Spur-Bar crew hadn't started any trouble; they'd probably been ordered to

183

leave matters in Falcon's hands. It explained Scudder's cockiness too; Scudder was certain he'd never have to face Johnny's guns. Johnny drew a long breath. So Mitchell had imported Blackie Falcon to do a job of killing. The cards were down for certain this time. It looked very bad.

"We might," Ed Hunter suggested, "order Falcon to leave town—tell him we don't want him here. If he and Mitchell got chummy there's no telling what might happen."

"You can't order him to leave town so long as he behaves himself," Johnny said dully, "and doesn't break the law."

"If we wait for that," Hunter said grimly, "it will be too late. I don't like the setup."

Pritchard was struck with a sudden idea. "Look Johnny, maybe Mitchell imported him to make trouble for you. You'd better slope back to the Rocking-A, until he decides to leave Spearhead Wells."

There was no use arguing the matter with Pritchard. Johnny nodded. "Maybe it's a good idea at that, Nick. I reckon I'll go find Humdrum, then we'll pull out. I figure his appetite has got the best of him and he's to be found in the Cowman's Rest dining room. At any rate, he can't be far away. I'll see you later."

Doggedly, he jammed the black sombrero more firmly on his head and started off along Main Street. No use postponing this sort of thing. Sooner or later he'd have to face Blackie Falcon's guns. It might as well be now as any time. It would be good if he could find Humdrum first though. There were things he wanted to tell Humdrum—just in case . . .

"COME WITH YOUR GUNS SMOKING!"

BRIGHT SUNSHINE BEAT ALONG MAIN STREET. FLIES buzzed and droned about the horses tethered at hitch racks on the thoroughfare. Occasionally a man in high-heeled boots clumped along the sidewalk, but for the most part people were staying out of the broiling heat. Vink and Kane Mitchell and Blackie Falcon were no exception to this rule. They lounged on chairs, tilted against the front wall, on the shaded porch of the Mecca Saloon.

Vink said, "I think I heard our crew hit town a spell back. They prob'ly stopped at the Steerhorn Bar first off to get primed for the day."

Kane laughed. "It'll take them until noon to work down this far. Then back on the other side of the street. I'm in favor of men drinking, but dam'd if I see any sense in spending a month's wages the way those waddies do. There'll be a lot of aching heads tomorrow—and a few to bail out of the hoosegow, I expect. I gave orders not to start anything with Donshawnee in case he comes to town today. I wanted to make sure he's saved for you, Blackie."

"That's right kind of you," Falcon replied with silky irony. "I hope he does put in an appearance today. I want to get this job finished so I can get out of Spearhead Wells."

"Don't you like our town?" Vink asked.

Falcon smiled coldly. "The town's all right, only I'd like to get back to Fort Worth. There's a yellow-haired gal waiting for me. I promised to bring her a ring this time—"

185

"Blackie!" Kane interrupted, "you're going to get your hope. Yonderly goes Donshawnee, just going into the Cowman's Rest. Today's your day!"

"Good!" Falcon exclaimed and shifted his gaze diagonally across Main Street. Abruptly his lean form stiffened and he stared until Johnny had passed out of sight in the hotel doorway.

"Looks right easy to you, eh?" Vink commented.

"Easy?" Falcon snarled. He jerked around, facing Kane Mitchell. "What sort of game you putting up on me?" he demanded.

"What's the matter with you?" Kane frowned.

Falcon laughed ironically. "All right, you win. I passed my word to do it for five hundred. The price stands. But if I'd known who the patient was I wouldn't have taken the job for three times five hundred—"

"What's the matter with you?" Kane snapped. "What do you know about Donshawnee?"

"Donshawnee, hell!" Falcon said bitterly. "Don Johnny, you mean. That's Johnny Donne! Don't tell me you didn't know it."

"Johnny Donne!" Vink and Kane exclaimed in unison.

"Yes, Johnny Donne! Ex-Ranger Donne. Best man on the force until he resigned. That hombre's hell on wheels when he unlimbers his irons. By God!" Blackie Falcon laughed weakly, mirthlessly. "The joke's on me. For five hundred dollars I go up against Johnny Donne! That's like asking me to—"

"You afraid of him?" Mitchell snapped. "Johnny Donne, or Donshawnee, what difference does it make? You stated your price and by cripes a'mighty! you're going to—"

"Cut it short!" Falcon's cold tones broke in on Kane.

"Did I say I was afraid of him? Hell, no! I'll take him like—" He broke off angrily. "Afraid of him? Oh, blast it to hell, Kane, why should I be afraid of Donne? I know I'm faster than he is. There's nobody can match my speed. I've shot rings around men nearly as good as Don Johnny. Why should I fear him?"

"You sort of talked that way," Vink pointed out.

"You got me wrong," Falcon said earnestly. "I only said I'd have asked a better price. Donne's good! Cripes! I'm running chances that he might even wound me. That's what I meant. But there's no doubt about me taking him. Get that idea out of your mind."

"You're going through with it then?" Kane asked uncertainly.

"Of course I am," Falcon stated in chilly accents. "You know my word's good." He laughed shortly. "I reckon you didn't know who he was, or you'd never have offered me five hundred to get rid of him. You know, don't you, he's wanted now for the murder of a man named George Aldrich? Say, come to think of it, Aldrich came from Spearhead Wells—"

"Yes, we know all that." Kane nodded. "But I don't see—"

"You wouldn't," Falcon said contemptuously. "I'm just pointing out that you could have turned Donne up to the law. In that way you'd have got rid of him—and collected a reward besides."

Kane appeared to consider the matter.

"It's still not too late to handle it that way," Falcon pointed out.

"By geez! I believe you are afraid of him," Vink said.

Falcon turned his cold black eyes on Vink. "One more crack like that out of you," he said viciously, "and I'll be doing a job for no pay at all—except a certain satisfaction."

Vink shrank back and didn't say anything.

Kane said heavily, "Let be, Vink." He turned to Falcon, a crafty light in his eyes. "I'd sooner have him dead, Blackie. Then, just in case you fail, I'll still have an ace in the hole." If he expected Falcon to become angry he was mistaken.

Falcon nodded. "I figured you'd decide that way."

"There he goes again," Vink broke in.

They glanced toward the Cowman's Rest and saw Johnny cutting across the street toward the Continental Saloon. Kane's being swelled with wrath as his gaze fell on Johnny's black sombrero. Vink also kept looking at the sombrero until Johnny had passed from view.

Vink said suddenly, "One thing about wiping him out here, Kane. We can watch a chance to grab that hat. If we turned him over to the law officers he might take the hat with him and—"

"Shut your mouth, Vink," Kane said angrily.

Falcon looked curiously from one brother to the other. "I'm dam'd if I understand all this talk about a hat."

"I don't see as it's necessary you should," Kane said coldly. "You come here to do a job. Are you going to do it or ain't you?"

"I don't know any reason why not," Falcon replied, smiling thinly. "Now that I think it over, it seems no more than right I should be the man to do it. I helped him out of the Rangers and I might as well complete the job."

"What do you mean you helped him out of the Rangers?" Vink asked curiously.

"Ever been in Ox-Bow City?" Falcon asked.

Kane nodded. "I spent a couple of days there one

time." He sneered. "It's what is known as a nice moral town."

Falcon laughed shortly. "Known that way—yes. You don't know the place. They make crime pay by keeping it under cover. That's the sort of leading citizens and Bible-backs that run Ox-Bow City. It used to be wide open, wild like a maverick. Things got right bad, some folks thought. I didn't mind conditions. Anyway, the so-called good folks asked for aid in clamping on the lid. The Border Rangers sent Johnny Donne to do the job— and I've got to admit he got off to a running start. He sure made things hum for a spell, closing saloons and gambling houses—as the so-called better citizens had requested. Then he went too far."

Kane was interested. "In what way?"

"Johnny Donne thought the leading citizens meant what they said when they imported him to enforce the law. But all they wanted was the cheaper houses closed. When Johnny commenced closing honky-tonks, fancy houses and gambling parlors that were in reality owned by the leading citizens—that hurt. I imagine Johnny enjoyed himself showing up some of those dirty old hypocrites. They tried to call him off, but he continued to enforce the law. Next day they tried bribery, but Johnny skinned his knuckles on three different men who came offering bribes. When that happened there was just one thing left to do."

"What was that?" Vink asked.

"They framed him," Falcon explained. "There was a little Frenchman in Ox-Bow City, named Marcel Domergue, who had been loaning money at less interest than the two local banks demanded. Domergue wasn't popular with the bankers, of course. They wanted him out of the way. One day he drew some money from one

189

of the banks. The bills he received were marked. That night Marcel Domergue was murdered in his bed. Promptly the town marshal, who was in the pay of the bankers, arrested Johnny Donne for the murder. Some of the marked bills had been planted in his room. Johnny was brought to trial. Three men perjured themselves, swearing that they had seen Johnny enter Domergue's house the night of the murder. Luckily for him his reputation was clean and an honest jury acquitted him. However, Ox-Bow City's popular opinion, voiced by the leading citizens, claimed he was a murderer. To cut a long story short, Johnny Donne resigned from the Border Rangers."

"And they never found this Marcel Domergue's murderer?" Kane asked.

Falcon shook his head. "They never tried. With Donne gone, Ox-Bow City was satisfied to forget the matter."

"You seem to know a hell of a lot about it," Vink said slyly.

Falcon laughed mirthlessly. "Well, I admit I had all the marked bills that weren't found in Donne's room at the time."

"Meaning you killed Domergue," Kane stated.

"I didn't say that," Falcon snapped. "And don't you go repeating it or I'll get you, sure as hell. I could tell you who killed Domergue—but I won't."

Kane said, "What I'm most interested in is who's going to rub out Johnny Donne. You figuring to start pretty soon?"

"There's no time like the present," Falcon said, getting to his feet.

Kane and Vink also rose. "We'll go with you," Vink proposed. "We'll sort of help things along, should you have trouble picking a quarrel with Donshawnee—Donne—I mean—"

"Donshawnee stands," Kane said quickly. "Let's not spill that Donne name—yet. You ready, Blackie?"

"I'm ready, but you're staying here. When you know as much about Johnny—Donshawnee—" he smiled coldly—"as I do, you'll realize I won't have any trouble arranging matters."

"I reckon we'll go with you," Kane said stubbornly.

"I reckon you'll stay here and let me run this my own way," Falcon snapped. "Your part is just paying the price, I'll see you later."

Reluctantly Kane and Vink resumed their chairs. Falcon slapped his hat on one side of his head and strolled down the steps to the sidewalk. Here he turned left and sauntered carelessly along Main Street, until he arrived before the Continental Saloon. He walked to the entrance and pushed through the swinging doors.

Within the Continental, Johnny stood at the bar, with Deputy Ed Hunter, talking to Corkscrew Jones. He had already asked Corkscrew if he'd seen Humdrum and received a reply in the negative. A half-dozen other customers were strung along the bar, exchanging idle gossip and sipping drinks. Ed Hunter was laughing and telling Johnny of some ridiculous error Sheriff Pritchard had made in his monthly expense account.

"Nick's been working all morning, trying to get it straightened out," Hunter grinned. "They're sure as hell strict about such things up at the county seat."

Johnny was only half listening, as he leaned against the bar, his eyes intent on the mirror above the backbar, where he could see reflected anyone who entered the Continental. Corkscrew Jones put in a word now and then. Johnny didn't hear him either. One thing was

191

certain in Johnny's mind: eventually Blackie Falcon would search him out, so he might as well wait here and let Falcon do the walking around. Cool nerves often depended on a man conserving every ounce of his energy.

The swinging doors parted and Blackie Falcon stepped inside. Falcon paused but a moment, to look about, then started straight toward Johnny. Johnny swung easily around at the gunman's approach and stood waiting. At Johnny's right an abrupt bit of profanity left Ed Hunter's lips. "Johnny!" he exclaimed.

"I know," Johnny said quickly. He didn't turn away from Falcon.

Falcon stopped a few feet away from Johnny.

Johnny said quietly, "Howdy, Falcon."

Blackie Falcon smiled mirthlessly. "It's a long time since our trails crossed—Mister Donshawnee."

"I reckon it is—not since Ox-Bow City days."

Falcon nodded reminiscently. "I always figured you got a raw deal in that direction, Johnny."

Johnny's eyes narrowed a trifle. "Maybe you'd know something about that too."

"Just maybe," Falcon said warily, and his lips twitched a trifle.

By this time the others in the Continental sensed something unusual afoot between the two men. Corkscrew was watching them with a puzzled expression. Other men had drawn a bit away and had ceased talking. Ed Hunter, standing behind Johnny, fumbled at his gun butt and swallowed hard. Just what it was, was difficult to put into words. Neither Johnny nor Falcon had raised their voices above normal; there was nothing defiant, challenging, nor belligerent in their tones. It seemed to go deeper than that. An understanding appeared to have grown instantly between the two men—something deathly, inexorable, final. No preliminary spark of hate had flamed. Rather, it was as though an age-long feud, burning along a slow-creeping time fuse, had at last reached the point of touching off the explosion, the crisis.

Suddenly Ed Hunter said hoarsely, "We don't want your kind here, Falcon. You'd better get out of town."

Blackie Falcon smiled thinly. "I'll be going tonight, feller. I won't bother you long—providing you let me be."

Johnny said wearily, "Let be, Ed. You can't do anything about this. It's between Falcon and me."

Blackie Falcon nodded his appreciation. "Thanks—Donshawnee. You understand how it is then?"

"I understand." Johnny nodded quietly.

"It's just a job I have to do," Falcon said earnestly.

"It's just a job." Johnny smiled easily.

"Nothing personal, you understand?" Falcon persisted.

Johnny nodded. "It's all clear, Falcon."

Blackie Falcon looked relieved. "I'm glad you're taking it like this. I always did hate these hypocritical skirmishes to get a man worked up."

"We're wasting time, Falcon. Let's get down to business. How do you want it?"

Falcon wasn't to be outdone in courtesy. "I'd rather you'd call it," he said. "I don't like anybody to think I take advantage of a man."

Johnny forced a smile of confidence he didn't feel. "Go on, name the place," he urged. "Any way suits you suits me."

A grudging look of admiration appeared on Falcon's swarthy features. "By God," he said, "you're taking it a heap gamer than most men in your position. All right, I'll call it. You know where the Mecca Saloon is?"

"Certain. Want me to come down there?"

Falcon shook his head. "I'll leave there in ten minutes, headed this way. You leave here and head toward the Mecca at the same time. That'll make it about right. The sun will be overhead. I don't reckon there'll be a light advantage either way."

"Suits me. When do we start shooting?"

Blackie Falcon shrugged his slim shoulders. "It's up to you, Johnny—Donshawnee. You can start throwing your lead the instant you leave here for all I care. Just come with your guns smoking."

"In ten minutes." Johnny nodded. "I won't keep you waiting." Falcon made a cold, short bow, ignored the others in the room and turned toward the street. As he left the Continental a draught of chill, dank air seemed to sweep along with him. Slowly the swinging doors came to a stop after his departure.

ROARING FORTY-FIVES

FOR A FULL MINUTE AFTER BLACKIE FALCON HAD LEFT the Continental no one spoke. Then everybody closed in on Johnny, all speaking at once, asking questions. A man said, "I still can't believe my ears, but it sounded like you were making arrangements to fight that feller."

Johnny smiled. "I reckon that's what we were doing."

"My grief a-Goshen!" another said. "That was a cold-blooded business."

"That Falcon is one cold-blooded hombre, if you ask me," a third put in. "What's the fight about?"

Johnny declined to answer. Men commenced to shift

194

through the swinging doors, anxious to tell their friends of the coming gun duel. The word spread quickly along the street. Within another minute or so no one except Johnny, Deputy Hunter and Corkscrew Jones were left in the saloon.

"Look here," Hunter said nervously, "there's no need you going into this. That man will kill you. You haven't a chance, Johnny. You know his reputation—"

"I know his reputation," Johnny said wearily, "probably better than you do, Ed."

"But look," the deputy persisted, "suppose I arrest him for disturbing the peace? We'll stop this fight—"

"He hasn't disturbed the peace yet," Johnny pointed out. "He's done no more than I have. He offered to fight. I accepted. To be fair, you'd have to arrest me too. No, Ed, it won't do." He smiled wistfully. "Queerly enough, I don't mind this as much as you may think. Blackie Falcon stands for defiance of the law and civilization and—and everything that makes life worth while. I'm on the other side of the fence. It's up to me to fight to the last ditch anything that threatens the ideals I believe in—"

"Damn it," Hunter swore wrathfully, "you talk like a blasted crusader—"

"I didn't mean it that way," Johnny said simply. "Falcon has a job to do. Well, maybe I see a job for me too. We'll both take it on to the best of our ability. Just lay off, Ed and don't interfere. That's all I ask. The throw has been made. It's too late to stop us now."

"Do you know anything about Falcon?" Corkscrew asked.

Johnny nodded. "A little. I saw him in action a couple of times. That was a number of years ago."

Corkscrew said one word: "Fast?"

"Forked lightning," Johnny replied. "Steel nerves. He'll let his opponent get right on top of him and then beat the fellow to the draw—" Johnny paused suddenly, thinking of something else. His mind strayed to Susan and how she'd take the news . . .

The swinging doors burst violently apart and Sheriff Nick Pritchard came barging in. "My Gawd Johnny!" he exclaimed, "what's this I hear about you fighting Blackie Falcon?"

"I don't know what you heard," Johnny interrupted, "but it's true. In ten minutes—no, in about five minutes now."

The sheriff swung angrily on Deputy Ed Hunter. "Damn it, Ed! Where's your head? Why didn't you stop this?"

"Stop it!" Hunter exclaimed. "Hell, there's nothing to stop yet. Falcon and Johnny just made arrangements to fight, quiet as you please. There wasn't any fuss. I've tried to persuade Johnny not to go into this fight, but he got some crazy idea about crusading for civilization in his head—"

"Don't jump on Ed," Johnny said. "He's done his best, Nick. And I'm asking you not to interfere either. This is my problem. It's not a matter of crusading to save civilization exactly. I—well, I don't know just what it is, except that this is something for me to handle. Men like Falcon have to be stopped—just as you'd stop a mad dog. I figure I've got the right to try anyway. If I can drop him"—and Johnny smiled wryly—"we're just that nearer to peace—"

"But, Johnny, you can't," Pritchard said earnestly. "You can't match his guns—nobody can!"

"In that case," Johnny said quietly, "you'll have your excuse to arrest him for disturbing the peace, or whatever it is Ed has in mind."

"Rats!" Pritchard said angrily. "You know we can't hold him very long on a charge of that sort. He'd claim self-defense. The thing for you to do is get out of Spearhead Wells, just as fast as your bronc will carry you."

Stubbornly Johnny shook his head. "Quit trying, Nick," he requested soberly. "My mind's made up. I've been hoping Humdrum would come in. I don't know where he's gone to. While I'm waiting for him"—and Johnny smiled gravely—"I might just as well put in the time studying Falcon's gun work. Just in case I become too deeply involved in said study—well, tell Humdrum I said 'So long' and—and—shucks! he'll know what I meant. I reckon I'd better be starting."

He turned away from the bar, lifted his guns from their holsters, one after the other, to see that the mechanism was in proper working order, then replaced them and passed through the swinging doors. The men in the saloon gazed hopelessly after him, then reluctantly started toward the street.

Main Street looked strangely empty when Johnny stepped into the sun glare of outdoors. Word of the fight had coursed like wildfire through the town, but there weren't many men in view. The sidewalks along either side were deserted, though here and there faces could be seen peering around the corners of buildings. A large number of ponies had been removed from hitch racks along the way.

Johnny crossed the sidewalk in front of the Continental and stepped out to the middle of the dusty, unpaved roadway, moving at a slow, deliberate gait toward the Mecca Saloon, more than the length of a city block away. Almost at the same instant he saw Blackie

Falcon leave the Mecca and move out toward the center of the street, heading in his direction. Falcon sauntered carelessly along, arms swinging at his side, every line of his lithe-moving form bespeaking extreme confidence.

Johnny felt a small shiver course his spine. The hair at the back of his neck ruffled slightly. His legs carried him along mechanically; his knees felt strangely weak. He wondered, almost idly, if this were the end. He knew now how other men felt when they'd faced the relentless guns of Blackie Falcon. Something about Falcon's confident attitude robbed a man of all his courage. Various thoughts coursed swiftly through Johnny's mind. He'd heard once how many successful gun duels of this kind Falcon had fought. Was it eighteen? Nineteen? Something like that. It was probably more by this time.

Johnny remembered seeing two of those fights years before. He'd seen Falcon fight a man named Dyer. Dyer was a good man too. He'd held his fire until almost on top of Falcon. Falcon had refused to draw first. And then Dyer had gone for his guns. Johnny had never forgotten how Falcon's hand had abruptly burst into flame, even before Dyer's gun barrels cleared leather. To this day Johnny remembered the savage laugh that left Falcon's lips as Dyer pitched forward.

Falcon's fight with Trigger Malone had produced an almost identical situation. Johnny remembered Malone's eagerness to get in close where he could make his first shot count and Falcon's delayed draw, giving Malone first chance. But it had been Malone who went down that day too. And there'd been that same savage laugh of Falcon's as Malone struck the earth.

Something stirred in Johnny's brain. Always the men who fought Blackie Falcon had worked to get in close.

Maybe that was the wrong way. No one had ever proved it right. Johnny shook his head as though to shake from a blurred vision the sight of those other fights. His eyes focused more clearly along the street now. Blackie Falcon had approached definitely nearer by this time. Johnny could see the sunlight shining on the eagle feather in Falcon's hat.

At the pace the two were going they'd come within normal fighting range at the next street corner. That wasn't much farther on. That was where Falcon would be expecting Johnny to make his draw. "Maybe—maybe," Johnny was telling himself, "I won't wait that long. Maybe that's my only chance."

He strode slowly along, arms swinging, finger tips just brushing the butts of his twin guns as he moved. Passing a building he heard awed whispers. He didn't look around. Someone spoke hoarsely, "Good luck, feller."

From the corner of his mouth Johnny said, "Thanks," without taking his eyes from the grim, relentless figure of his opponent drawing nearer and nearer every second. Johnny wasn't more than fifty feet from the street corner now. "I reckon I'd better commence," he told himself in a dull, lifeless whisper.

His arms moved automatically as he reached for his guns. And then he knew he'd taken Falcon by surprise by the strange look that crossed Falcon's features. He saw Falcon's lips move in some amazed exclamation, as though shooting from such distance was unheard of. And all at the same time he saw Falcon's fingers stab down with the speed of striking sidewinders.

Johnny's right gun was just coming up, his left was clearing holster, when savage streams of white fire spurted from Falcon's hands. A slug whined past

199

Johnny's cheek, another kicked up dust at his feet, a third sped wildly to the left, even before Johnny thumbed his first shot and followed with a second.

And then, incredibly, he saw Blackie Falcon spin half around from the impact of the heavy slug. At the same instant Johnny's left gun roared, then his right again and his left. Blackie Falcon was down, floundering in the dust, but still firing, the leaden missiles flying far wide of their aim.

Johnny stopped, steadied himself; he had that dusty figure in the road lined with his sight now. His right-hand gun spoke and he followed it swiftly with a shot from his left. Through a swirling haze of powder smoke he saw Falcon half lifted from the earth by the heavy jolts. Then the man clumped down and lay still, outstretched hands still gripping his silent six-shooters.

Johnny leaped into a run. A savage laugh jarred on his ears. With something of a shock he realized the sound had burst from his own lips. He got a hold on himself, forced himself to walk steadily toward his fallen opponent. "I—I shouldn't laugh at a man that's down," he told himself unsteadily.

A wild cheer burst along the street. Men poured into the roadway from all sides. Someone clapped Johnny on the back. He saw it was Ed Hunter. Hunter was grinning as was Sheriff Pritchard, close behind him. They said something about good work, but Johnny didn't make out the exact words.

A crowd had surrounded the fallen Falcon by this time. Johnny pushed through the throng. Someone had turned Falcon on his back and had his shoulders propped up. Someone else was holding a whiskey flask.

". . . Yep," Falcon was saying unsteadily, "my ol' eagle feather . . . sure trailed the dust . . . for the first time." His shirt front was a sodden crimson mess, with bits of gravel sticking to the wet cloth. He looked up as Johnny bent over him and a look of grudging admiration slipped into his glassy eyes. "That was good work . . . Johnny. You . . . outfoxed me. . . . I never could shoot accurate . . . at a distance . . . You decoyed me . . . into shooting . . . too soon . . . You made your shots count . . . every one of 'em."

"Nothing personal, you understand," Johnny said quietly. "I had a job to do."

A faint smile twitched at Falcon's lips. "It should . . . have been . . . personal." He spoke with difficulty. "You . . . didn't know though . . . Oh hell, I had to . . . get mine someday. I reckon . . . I'm glad it was you . . . done it. That sort of . . . squares matters . . ."

He could scarcely speak now. Someone placed the flask of liquor to his lips. A momentary spark entered his dull gaze, and his words came stronger: "You see, Johnny . . . I killed . . . Marcel Domergue . . ."

Johnny said, "My God!" and swung about to see Ed Hunter and Sheriff Pritchard standing near. "Did you hear that?" he demanded. He swung back to Falcon. There was no life in the man's eyes now, though a mocking smile still hovered about his lips. Johnny started to speak to Falcon again, then he saw it was no use. Blackie Falcon was beyond hearing.

Johnny rose stiffly and faced Hunter and Pritchard. "Did you hear that?" he demanded again.

Pritchard nodded. "It sounded like he was confessing to killing somebody named Domergue—Marcel Domergue."

"I heard him too." Ed Hunter nodded.

"Good." Relief showed in Johnny's eyes. "Remember it. Don't forget that name. Marcel Domergue! I'll need you two as witnesses someday."

"Who is Marcel Domergue?" Pritchard asked puzzledly.

"He was murdered quite a spell back over in Ox-Bow City," Johnny said evasively. "His murderer never was caught. Just remember that name. It means a heap to me. I'll tell you about it another time." He commenced to reload his six-shooters.

The crowd had grown thicker about the dead Falcon. Johnny started to push through to escape the many men who wanted to shake hands and congratulate him on his victory. On the outside of the throng he almost bumped into Vink and Kane Mitchell. The two stood with gloomy faces, apparently shocked by the defeat of Blackie Falcon, with their backs to Johnny.

"We've got to get away and decide what's to be done now," Kane Mitchell said angrily. "I never thought that bustard would let us down."

A grim laugh left Johnny's lips. His right hand dropped on Kane Mitchell's shoulder, whirling the bigger man around to face him. "At that, Mitchell," he said grimly, "Falcon was a better man than you'll ever be. He was honest according to his own code. And if you're going to decide what's to be done next you'd better think fast, because I'm on your trail hard from now on!" His steely gray eyes beat down Mitchell's wavering gaze.

"You're trying to make trouble," Kane Mitchell said angrily.

"Sure I am," Johnny snapped. "Let's start some now."

Mitchell slowly shook his head and backed away. "I'll handle things in my own time," he evaded. "C'mon, Vink, let's go get a drink."

The two strode quickly away, followed by Johnny's

contemptuous laugh. In a moment they had passed from sight in the rapidly growing crowd that jammed Main Street.

NOT SO SLEEPY

SHERIFF PRITCHARD SAT AT HIS DESK, STUDYING HIS monthly expense account. Now and then he'd put down a penciled figure, but for the most part he found it difficult to concentrate on the report. His mind was too full of that day's fight between Johnny and Blackie Falcon. An oil lamp burned with a steady flame on the sheriff's desk, only one of the many lights that shone out along Main Street. Now and then from down the roadway came a loud cowboy yell. The Spur-Bar hands were again whooping it up, after recovering from the shock of seeing Blackie Falcon go down to defeat. Where Kane and Vink Mitchell were Sheriff Pritchard had no idea, though he judged they were still someplace in town.

Well, the sheriff thought, he hoped today had taught those Mitchells a lesson. From now on they'd think twice before they tried to ride roughshod over Johnny and the Rocking-A. That Johnny was a fighting fool once he got started. The sheriff shook his head in silent admiration and again concentrated on his expense report. Let's see, meals for Deputy Hunter came to— just how many dollars was it, anyway? "Cripes!" Disgustedly, Pritchard tossed down his pencil. "I'll have to talk to Ed and see how many—yep, that's what's wrong with me tonight, the reason I can't think. It's too soon after my supper. A man should never try to think on a full stomach—"

His reveries were interrupted by the sound of a rider outside. Somebody was stopping, it sounded like. The sheriff shielded his gaze from the reflection of the oil lamp and glanced toward the open doorway.

"Howdy, Nick," came an indolent drawl and Humdrum edged lazily into the sheriff's office. As though worn with sheer exhaustion he dropped into a chair across the desk from Pritchard.

"Where in time you been?" Pritchard demanded.

Humdrum languidly waved one paw. "Oh, here and around and some other place. Where's Johnny?"

"You're a fine one to ask that," Pritchard snorted. "He left for the Rocking-A a short spell back. Finally got tired of waiting for you to show up. He decided you must have gone home. He was plumb puzzled."

"Hope he wasn't worried," Humdrum grunted.

"Worried!" Pritchard snapped. "You're the one should be worried. Hell of a time for you to disappear—"

"What happened?" Humdrum straightened out of his slouch. "Did Johnny need me?"

"Need you?" indignantly. Then, "No, he didn't—but for a time there it sure looked like he might."

Humdrum displayed a certain sleepy-eyed interest. "Well, tell me about it."

"Johnny killed Blackie Falcon this afternoon."

"Blackie Falcon! Did you say Blackie Falcon?"

"You heard me the first time."

Humdrum's listless attitude had vanished, "Judas priest! I didn't even know Falcon was in this neck of the range. What did he come here for?"

"I don't rightly know, but I figure Kane Mitchell imported him to kill Johnny. I've questioned Mitchell, though, and he denies that."

"He lies, of course." Humdrum resumed his indolent

204

manner.

"Crackey!" Pritchard said testily. "You don't act surprised that Johnny downed Falcon."

"I'm not. I'd bet on Johnny against Falcon any time."

The sheriff spat disgustedly. "Johnny himself didn't feel that way before the fight. I could read it in his face."

"Just the same I'd have known. I know Johnny—and his guns."

Pritchard looked nettled. "Falcon was faster. He emptied three shots before Johnny shook the first lead out 'n his barrel."

"Ah, but Johnny has brains." Humdrum grinned sleepily. "I'll bet his shots went where he sent 'em. But get busy and tell the story. I'm mighty interested."

"That's plumb surprisin'," Pritchard said sarcastically. He went on and told Humdrum what had happened. When he had finished Humdrum nodded placidly.

"Just the way I'd figure Johnny would work." Humdrum yawned. "He's plenty smart."

"Dam'd if you ain't a know-it-all," Pritchard growled.

"I admit it. Anyway, I know more than I did this morning."

"Mebbe then you can tell me who Marcel Domergue is. Falcon confessed murderin' him before he died."

"Marcel Domergue! That is news, Nick. I'm glad to hear it."

"Huh? Woke you up, didn't I?"

"Just stirred me a mite," Humdrum said complacently. "I'll tell you about Domergue some time. Where's your deputy?"

"Ed's around town someplace, keeping an eye on those Spur-Bar cow hands. I'm surprised he ain't had to haul a couple of 'em into the hoosegow by this time. Must be Johnny's fight has quieted 'em down a mite and they ain't drinkin' natural. Where the devil did you disappear to this morning?"

"I took a little ride out to the Spur-Bar."

"You went where?" The sheriff could scarcely believe his ears. "You don't mean the Spur-Bar."

"I said the Spur-Bar, didn't I?" Humdrum grunted. "The Mitchell outfit, if that suits you better."

"T 'hell you say!" Pritchard's jaw dropped.

"Don't you think it was a good idea?"

"Well, by the seven bald steers of Goshen! How come you did that? What was the idea?"

"It was a sudden idea just come to me this morning." Humdrum chuckled. "When I heard you say it was the Spur-Bar payday and that the whole gang came in to get drunk I just couldn't resist riding out there and giving a look around."

"You blamed fool," Pritchard snorted. "What do you think would have happened to you if the Mitchells had decided to go home? They'd found you and—"

"The fact remains that they didn't."

"But what did you expect to find?"

Humdrum shrugged indolent shoulders. "I didn't exactly know when I left here. But it looked like too good a chance to pass up. A man can often discover a lot of things by doing a mite of intelligent snooping."

"Intelligent? Bah! No matter how intelligent a man is he has to stay awake. You ain't going to try to tell me you discovered anything important?"

Humdrum smiled sleepily and took from his pocket the anonymous note, concerning Johnny's black sombrero, that Pritchard had found on his desk the previous day. This note Humdrum tossed across the desk.

"Hey"—Pritchard frowned—"this is the note that was left on my desk yesterday while I was out of my office. I gave this note to you last night."

"Hold your horses!" Humdrum chuckled. "I just wanted you to identify the note as being the same one. Now here"—he produced a small leather-covered notebook filled with blue lined paper—"is something that should convince you my day wasn't wasted."

Humdrum flipped through the pages of the notebook. About two thirds of the way through he reached a place where a ragged, uneven edge attested that a page had been torn out. "Now," Humdrum said, "just match up that note to what's left of the page in this notebook." Pritchard did as advised. "See," Humdrum said, "how the two edges match? The page on which that note was written came out of this notebook."

"Gee willikens! Where'd you get that?"

"Out to the Spur-Bar. That notebook has Kane Mitchell's name written in it. I found it in an inner pocket of a vest hanging in the Spur-Bar bunkhouse. I reckon Mitchell figured it was too hot for a vest today. Maybe he forgot to transfer the notebook to his pants pocket, or maybe he figured it would be safe where it was."

"Well I'll be damned!" Pritchard's eyes gleamed. "Does the writing in the notebook compare with the hand on the note?"

"Pretty much." Humdrum nodded. "Mitchell made an attempt to disguise the writing in his unsigned note, but there are certain similarities that are too plain to be denied. I've looked all through the notebook. There's a record of sales of cattle, wages paid to certain men— incidentally, Mitchell pays higher wages than most cowhands receive. I imagine there's a reason for that."

"Meaning what?"

"Rustling brings better pay than ordinary cow punching. Certain items in the notebook, under cattle sales, are marked 'Velvet.' I've a hunch the word stands for sales of rustled cattle that have been sold over in the next county. There are other items in the book, too—interest to be paid on notes, reminders of money loaned, some addresses, among them Blackie Falcon's—"

"But nothing real incriminating, eh?" disappointedly.

"One thing." Humdrum nodded. "Here, let me show you." He fished from a small pocket in the front cover of the notebook a number of miscellaneous slips of paper and commenced to sort them out. "These are old receipts, feed bills and so on—with one exception. The single exception is a list of guns, with their numbers, that Mitchell has owned over a long period of time. It makes quite a list—there's eighteen or twenty six-shooters, Colts and other makes; half-a-dozen Winchesters; three shotguns; even a Derringer and an old Sharps gun. This list goes back a number of years—"

"A man has to own guns," Pritchard pointed out. "There's nothing incriminating in keeping a record of the factory numbers of the guns he owns. He might need the numbers in sending away for repair parts—"

"Listen to me, will you?" Humdrum leaned across the desk and spread the list of gun numbers before Pritchard's gaze. One finger ran down the list and stopped at the number of a Colt's six-shooter. "Do you see the number of that gun?"

"Certain," Pritchard said blankly. "It's one-three-two —"

"Cripes!" Humdrum cut in impatiently. "Doesn't that number mean anything to you?"

Pritchard frowned, studied the number again, then shook his head. "Not a thing," he admitted.

"Well, maybe it wouldn't to you—but it would to the El Paso police. That's the number of the gun that was found in George Aldrich's room after he'd been murdered—"

"Sufferin' Hanner!" Pritchard exploded. "Humdrum! We've got the goods on Mitchell—"

"I reckon." Humdrum had again slumped back in his chair. "With that gun number and the anonymous note we've got real evidence. You see, I happen to know that Aldrich did once possess that black sombrero of Johnny's. We'll show this notebook evidence to Kane Mitchell and ask him how he happened to know that fact. He can't very well deny writing the note."

"Humdrum, you've done a good afternoon's work."

"I had to do a lot of drinking too," Humdrum said sleepily.

"Drinking?"

Humdrum nodded drowsily. "Yeah, you told me the Spur-Bar would be deserted, but the cook was still there—a little bit of a scrawny hombre with a red nose—"

"Oh, you saw him, eh? That's Snuffy Ben."

"So I learned. Well, Snuffy Ben was right peeved because Pat Scudder wouldn't let him come to town with the rest of the crew. Howsomever, he was prepared for such difficulties. He had himself a jug of corn likker there and was half drunk when I arrived. He didn't know who I was and didn't care. He'd got to where he wanted company to talk to. So I had to spend the afternoon drinking with him until such time as he passed out, leaving me free to my snooping around."

"By Cripes! You must have the constitution of a

horse if you drank Snuffy Ben under the table."

"I'm commencing to think so myself. We both took a powerful lot of punishment. The more Snuffy Ben drank the talkier he became. He doesn't know much that's going on at the Spur-Bar, but he does know the Mitchells have been stealing stock from both the Wagon-Wheel and the Rocking-A. Snuffy Ben is getting scared for fear he'll be pulled in, if anything happens, and is preparing to quit his job—"

"For the love of Hanner! Rustling, eh? Well I'll be damned!"

"You probably will." Humdrum yawned. "Anyway, it looks like we've got enough evidence to stop the Mitchells now."

"It sure does. Say"—Pritchard hesitated—"I suppose you being a Border Ranger, you'll want to make the arrests."

Humdrum shook his head. "I've been figuring to let you do it, Nick. You're sheriff here. Maybe it will help you at the next election—"

"That's mighty decent of you." Pritchard looked pleased.

"Not at all. Us Rangers don't like too much publicity. I would like you to hold off making the arrests, though, until Johnny can be with us. He might want to tell you a few things you don't yet know. Suppose we plan to put the bee on the Mitchells tomorrow morning?"

"That suits me fine."

Humdrum lumbered up out of his chair and gathered the notebook and other papers. "I'll take these along to show Johnny. We'll be seeing you in the morning."

"Good. I'll be waiting for you. So long!"

"*Adios!*" Humdrum turned and left the office.

The sheriff rose and followed him to the door. He

watched Humdrum mount and ride off down the street. "By damn!" Pritchard muttered. "That hombre ain't so sleepy as he looks. He's plenty smart." He stood there, while the hoof beats of Humdrum's pony faded in the distance, then closed the door, shutting out the myriad noises along Main Street. Happening to notice the expense account on his desk, he sighed heavily and resumed his seat.

MITCHELL STRIKES HARD

FIFTEEN MINUTES PASSED WHILE THE SHERIFF struggled over his accounts. Once he glanced at the old clock ticking monotonously on one wall. "Only ten after seven," he grunted. "Cripes! Enough has happened today to make it seem like it should be midnight." Reluctantly he resumed his figuring.

Abruptly the door of his office opened and Kane Mitchell stepped in, closing the door behind him. "Howdy, Nick." Mitchell smiled thinly.

Pritchard glanced up at his visitor, stiffening a trifle. "Didn't anybody ever tell you it was polite to knock?" he asked sourly.

"Didn't think it was necessary, Nick."

"What do you want?" The sheriff's attitude was cold, uncompromising.

"Nick, I've come to demand that you arrest Donshawnee for murder."

"Arrest Johnny? You're crazy! He killed Blackie Falcon in a fair fight."

"I'm not denying that, though I think he was lucky."

"Sure he was, if having brains is lucky."

"I didn't come here to argue that. Nick, I'll make a

211

bargain with you." Mitchell came across the office and stood near the desk.

"I doubt I want any truck with you," Pritchard said shortly, "but what's on your mind?"

Mitchell spoke slowly, choosing his words with care: "I've just learned that the man you call Donshawnee is in reality named Donne—the same Donne who's wanted for the murder of George Aldrich."

"T'hell you say! Do you expect me to believe that?" Pritchard said contemptuously. "Mitchell, you're just trying to make trouble for Johnny—"

"I'm giving it to you straight," Mitchell said earnestly. "There's a reward to be collected on Aldrich's murderer. I could turn Donne over to the authorities myself and claim all the reward, but I'm willing to split it with you, on one condition, if you'll make the arrest."

The sheriff was curious in spite of himself. "What's your condition?" he asked warily.

"When you arrest Donne I want to make sure of getting that black sombrero he wears."

Pritchard frowned. "What in hell do you want that hat so bad for?"

Mitchell forced a sheepish smile. "I know you'll think it's funny, but maybe I'm sort of sentimental about that hat. You see, Ogallala wanted it and I thought a heap of my brother."

"Bosh! I don't trust you, Mitchell."

"You've got me wrong. I'm trying to do my duty as a citizen in bringing George Aldrich's murderer to justice. Will you ride out and arrest Donshawnee—I mean Donne—or won't you?"

"I certainly won't," Pritchard said wrathfully. "And when you claim Johnny killed Aldrich you're crazy!"

212

For a moment the sheriff was tempted to tell Mitchell what Humdrum had discovered that day, but he desisted. "I don't believe a word you say."

"Why don't you?"

"My reasons," Pritchard stated coldly, "are my own business."

Mitchell's eyes gleamed. He had hoped Pritchard would refuse to take action. "I figured you might act this way, Nick," he said coldly. "Will you deputize me to arrest him?"

The sheriff laughed contemptuously. "You know better than to ask me that."

Mitchell nodded, shrugged his shoulders. "I've been fair with you. Now you leave me just one course of action."

"Meaning just what?" Pritchard rose to his feet.

"Nick, it's the duty of every honest citizen to make an arrest when the legally empowered authorities refuse to act. It's not only the duty, but the right—"

"Do you mean you'd go over my head?" Pritchard snapped.

"You're forcing it on me. I've given you your chance to arrest a murderer and you've refused. I'll take a couple of my men out and apprehend Donne, and when the authorities of this state learn how you've shirked your duty—"

"You fool!" Pritchard said hotly. "You can't do a thing like this. I won't let you. I'm the law here. You arrest Johnny? I'd like to see you try it. I thought you had more sense than that—"

"You can't stop me!"

"I'll show you whether I can stop you or not. Mitchell, I intended to hold off until tomorrow, but you've forced my hand. I'm arresting you right now for

213

the murder of George Aldrich! You owned the gun that killed him. It was you left that note on my desk telling me to investigate that hat of Johnny's. You've rustled cattle right and left. Kane Mitchell, you're under arrest. We've got that notebook of yours and—"

"You're insane." Mitchell had suddenly gone pale and backed away. One hand went quickly to his breast, then he realized he had left his vest and the notebook at home. He was still backing toward the door, trying to collect his scattered wits and overcome the shock Pritchard's words had given him. His lips moved to form swift denials but words wouldn't come.

"You going to come quiet," Pritchard snapped, "or have I got to put the cuffs on you? Stop! Stand where you are!"

Mitchell had started to reach for the doorknob, when he saw the sheriff leap across the room to get his holstered gun hanging on a peg on the wall. For an instant Mitchell saw red. He was cornered and couldn't think. The sheriff was drawing out his gun now. Abruptly Mitchell lost his head. Involuntarily his right hand darted to six-shooter and came up spitting fire.

Powder smoke spread hazily through the room, as the noise of the explosion brought Mitchell to his senses. He saw a strange baffled expression slowly form on the sheriff's features. Pritchard's mouth dropped open. His hands scratched futilely at the wall as he tried to prevent himself from falling. Then, quite suddenly, his body jackknifed and he struck the floor, face down.

"My God," Kane whispered hoarsely, "I didn't mean to do that. I don't know what came over me."

His trembling hand replaced the six-shooter in his holster and he knelt by the silent form of the old sheriff. Mitchell's frame shook violently as he turned the body

214

on its back. It wasn't any use. Sheriff Pritchard was already dead.

The door at Mitchell's back opened suddenly and Deputy Ed Hunter appeared. For just an instant Hunter paused there in the doorway, a look of mingled surprise and anger twisting his features. Then, like a flash, his gun leaped from its holster.

"My God! You've killed Nick!" he burst out. "Put 'em up, you devil, before I blast you clean to hell!"

"I didn't! I swear I didn't!" Mitchell got to his feet, hands high in the air. "I came here to see Nick—I found him here —like this. I was trying to revive him and—"

"Don't lie to me, you dirty, murderin' bustard," Hunter rasped savagely. "I'm going to shoot you down like a dog—"

"Don't, don't!" Mitchell stumbled back against the wall, one arm shielding his fright-contorted features, all courage driven from his body by the terrible fires burning in Ed Hunter's blazing eyes. "My God! You wouldn't kill me like this—"

"I'll take pleasure in doing it," Hunter snarled.

He had no time to say more, for at that moment Vink Mitchell came slipping through the doorway behind him with an upraised gun in his fist. Then the gun descended, the heavy steel barrel striking with crushing force on Hunter's head. Hunter groaned once, then slumped to the floor, the six-shooter clattering from his senseless grasp. Vink leaped inside the office, pulling the door closed behind him. Color flowed back into Kane's ashen face.

"You—you came just in time, Vink," Kane gulped.

Vink said, "Christ! What's happened here?"

Kane jerked one trembling hand toward the sheriff. "He was stubborn. I had to kill him. The jig's up, Vink.

215

We're in a bad spot. Hunter was about to kill me when you arrived—"

"What do you mean the jig's up?" Vink demanded swiftly.

"I'll tell you later. Now we've got to think fast. I wonder if anybody heard my shot."

"I doubt it. If they did they wouldn't pay any attention, there's so much noise in town. Our crew has started to whoop things up. I reckon it's a good thing I came down here to see what was keeping you. I saw Hunter enter just ahead of me. When I see him covering you I let him have it. What happened before that?"

"I'll tell you later. We've got to act fast while there's still time." Kane jerked a coiled rope from a peg on one wall, then crossed to the desk and extinguished the lamp, plunging the office into total darkness. "No use taking chances on some passerby glancing in the window. This damn Hunter will probably remain unconscious for some time, but we can't risk too much. I'm going to tie him up—tight. While I'm doing that you slope out and round up our crew. Get 'em back here pronto! I'll be waiting."

"What you aiming to do, Kane?"

"I won't go into details now, but we've got to clear out and lay low for a spell, until this blows over. We'll get out of this jam, but we've got to have time to work. First we're going to ride to the Rocking-A and get that black sombrero—one way or another. If they want to give it up peaceful—well and good. But I'm going to have that hat if I have to wipe out every soul on the Rocking-A outfit. There's only four men and two women there. We'll be eleven strong. I figure our hands have drunk enough by this time to be ready for anything. Now, get out and get them mounted and back here. Hurry!"

"You sound desperate." Vink's voice quavered a trifle in the darkness.

"I am desperate! You'd be too if you knew what I know. Dammit! You turning yellow? Get started for cripes' sakes!"

"I'm on my way." Cautiously Vink opened the door and glanced both ways along the street. There was no one in the immediate vicinity. He slipped stealthily outside and started at a swift run toward the center of town. Most of the boys would be at the Mecca Bar by this time. It wouldn't take long to get them into saddles.

Back in the office Kane Mitchell was fumbling at rope knots over Deputy Hunter's unconscious form. Mitchell's hands still trembled at thought of the narrow escape he'd had. Perspiration stood out on his forehead. Hunter had certainly been ready to blast when Vink arrived. "I was a damn fool to lose my head that-a-way," Mitchell considered, "but maybe this way is best. We've put off things long enough as it is. Now we'll get some action!"

NIGHT RAIDERS

"SO YOU SEE," HUMDRUM WAS SAYING, "IT LOOKS like we've finally got the Mitchells on the run. With the evidence we've got they're licked to a thin frazzle."

They were all sitting before the blazing fireplace in the Rocking-A ranch house—Susan, Johnny, Mecate Humdrum and Dave Franklin. Guadalupe was out in the kitchen, washing the supper dishes. The light on the table shone on the small leather-covered notebook from which Humdrum had secured so much information.

217

"You've done a neat piece of work, Humdrum," Johnny said. He heaved a long sigh of relief. "It's sure good to know that two murder charges have been lifted off my shoulders. At last I can breathe easy again." He glanced at Susan.

"Oh, I'm so glad, Johnny," she said. "Things are clearing up, aren't they? For me as well as for you."

"I reckon," Mecate observed, "that if Mitchell is pulled into court on a charge of killing your pa, Susan, it won't be very hard to get him to confess to rustling our cows. We can throw an attachment on his ranch and one way or t'other we'll get the value of them critters out of him. Now if we could only find that gold the Rocking-A would be on easy street."

"Somehow I've got a hunch we'll find that too," Johnny said.

"I figure," Humdrum put in, "that you'll want to be reinstated in the Border Rangers, Johnny, as soon as possible."

Johnny nodded. "It'll be good to have that disgrace wiped out. I owe that much to my old boss, Steve Sharples, for his faith in me."

"Danged if this all didn't work out just like a book," Dave Franklin put in. "It's nigh as interestin' as that story, *Hamlet,* I've been reading."

"Johnny," Susan said slowly, "if you were reinstated in the Border Rangers that would mean you'd be leaving this part of the country, wouldn't it?"

Johnny looked at the girl and saw a slow warm flush creep into her cheeks. After a moment he said, "I reckon it would. Of course I might be sent over this way on Ranger business sometime."

"We'd want to see you—all of us would—as often as possible—" Susan commenced, then broke off short.

218

Outside the house a sudden rush of hoofs had been heard and the creaking of saddle leather. Johnny leaped to his feet. "Who's that?" he exclaimed, frowning. A startling chorus of wild yells shattered the night silence of the ranch yard.

"Who'd be riding here this time of night?" Susan frowned.

A forty-five six-shooter roared outside and a pane of glass shattered in a window frame across the room. A bullet thudded into the wall.

"What in the devil?" Mecate leaped to his feet.

Johnny threw himself halfway across the room and extinguished the lamplight. He heard a scream of fright from the kitchen as Guadalupe came running into the room. Johnny commenced giving orders through the din of voices that rose outside.

"Guadalupe, get some water and put out that fireplace blaze. We can't have light in here. It looks like a raid! I think I heard Mitchell's voice a minute ago. Move fast, fellows!"

The men hurried to do Johnny's bidding as he snapped orders. There was still a considerable amount of shooting going on outside, though no more shots had been directed at the house. The doors of the ranch house were slammed and bolted. Johnny and Humdrum raced to the kitchen to get the guns they'd left hanging there, then rushed back to the main room, which by now was dark save for the sporadic flashes of gunfire from outside which threw momentary glimpses of light into the room.

A wild yelling lifted in the ranch yard, then Kane Mitchell could be heard ordering the men to be silent. He was bawling out one man for firing that first shot that had entered the window.

Mecate and Dave Franklin were both cursing their luck. "Our guns are down in the bunkhouse," Mecate explained. "Didn't figure we might need 'em—"

"My gun's here," Susan put in swiftly. "And there's three or four guns of Dad's around someplace. I'll find them."

"Take one of my guns." Johnny pressed a six-shooter into Mecate's hand.

Mitchell's voice was heard outside: "You there, Donne?"

Johnny lifted one window but kept well back out of gun range. "What do you want, Mitchell?" Johnny replied angrily.

"We've come for that black sombrero. Are you willing to surrender it peaceful—or have we got to take it?"

"You can't have it!" Johnny snapped back.

"You don't know what you're saying, Donne—you see, I know your real name. You're in a tight spot. You can't stop us. My boys are rarin' to go. It would be best if you listen to reason."

Johnny was commencing to think to himself. Rather than see Susan and the others killed it might be best to give up the black sombrero . . .

Susan had come back into the room, bearing some six-shooters, a Winchester rifle and a shotgun. She said swiftly, "Don't give it to him, Johnny. What guarantee have we that he'd leave peacefully, even if he had that hat?"

"You're right," Johnny said. "We couldn't trust him." He raised his voice again, "Nothing doing, Mitchell."

Mitchell commenced shouting angry orders. Johnny swung around and swept Susan to the floor. "Keep down, everybody!" he called.

220

From the Spur-Bar men spread out around the ranch house came a sudden volley of fire. Windowpanes shattered to the floor, bullets thudded into walls and woodwork. The crazy whine of flying lead sounded through the air. The ranch yard was ablaze with the light from flaming weapons.

Johnny quickly deployed his men near the windows, now totally devoid of glass. "Keep back," he gave swift orders. "Those skunks out there are keeping well back, but shoot at a flash every time you get an opportunity."

He lifted his six-shooter, pointed the barrel around the edge of a windowpane and pulled trigger. His ear caught a loud yelp of pain and he judged he had at least drawn blood. Mecate, Franklin and Humdrum were now firing as fast as they saw something to aim at. Some of the raiders were hidden in brush at the edge of the ranch yard; others had remained in their saddles and from time to time would go charging past the house, firing their guns as they rode.

By this time Guadalupe had recovered from her first fright and was helping Susan reload the guns as fast as Johnny and the others emptied them. The acrid odor of powder smoke filled the room and stung Johnny's eyes and throat and nostrils. Out in the ranch yard a man screamed in pain.

"Got him!" Mecate said triumphantly.

Dave Franklin said, "Let me have that scatter-gun and some buckshot. We'll create some real damage the next time a rider drifts past—" His words ended in a groan and he sank down, as a bullet screamed wildly through the room, ricocheted and found its mark.

"You hurt, Dave?" Johnny asked quickly.

"Got me in the leg," Franklin said. "I don't think it's bad, but I can't stand up. Keep firing, don't worry about me."

Susan made her way across the room. Within a short time she stopped at Franklin's side with water and some freshly torn bed sheets. She made her examination in the dark, her voice coming steadily to the others through the gloom. "The bullet got Dave through the fleshy part of his thigh. I can bind it up."

The fight continued, flashes of orange fire crisscrossing the ranch yard like angry hornets. Johnny and Humdrum stood at either side of the same window frame, firing and reloading, firing and reloading.

Humdrum said suddenly, "My loads are getting plumb low."

"Mine too," Johnny replied grimly. "I was just going to ask for some." He called to Mecate, "How's your ammunition holding out?"

"Ain't got more than a dozen shells left. Susan, you got any more ca'tridges in the house?"

"Not that I know of." By this time Susan had finished bandaging Franklin's leg and had moved him against the wall, out of danger, despite his insistence on continuing the fight. She seized his gun and remaining shells and brought them to Johnny and Humdrum, then hurried back to Mecate's side where she crouched low and commenced loading the shotgun.

"It looks like I'll have to make a run for the bunkhouse and get more ammunition," Humdrum drawled.

"You will?" Johnny snapped. "What's wrong with me doing it?"

"You'd never get through that Spur-Bar fire."

"You couldn't either."

Humdrum calmly triggered a shot from the window and swore when he missed. "I wonder," he said, cocking his gun again, "if I could make those coyotes clear out by showing 'em my badge."

Johnny laughed grimly. "That tin badge of yours might fool Pritchard, but it's too late to have any effect on Mitchell and his wolves."

"I mean my real badge—my Border Ranger badge—the badge I showed Pritchard. You didn't know, Johnny."

"Humdrum, are you really a Border Ranger?" Johnny gasped in the darkness.

"Surest thing you know, cowboy. Steve Sharples had me working on that Domergue case after you resigned from the force. He wanted you cleared: I never did find anything out about that, but I happened to be in El Paso the night George Aldrich was killed. I wired Sharples what had happened. He telegraphed back for me to get on the job and see that you received full protection in anything that came up. That's how come I met up with you. I didn't know anything about you, of course, and that's why I staged that clown stunt about being a mail-order detective—"

"Well, I'll be danged! Humdrum, old scout, it's good to know—" Johnny broke off suddenly as a lead slug whined past his ear. He continued a minute later: "Nope, I don't reckon the Mitchells would pay any attention now to a whole load of badges—"

A scream from Guadalupe sounded suddenly in the vicinity of the kitchen. Johnny whirled away from the window. Dashing from the room, he headed for the kitchen. He found Guadalupe unharmed, heard what she had to say, then hurried back to the others. "It's going to be tougher in a few minutes," he said grimly. "Guadalupe has been watching from the rear window. Those skunks out there have pulled up a couple of corral posts and made a battering ram. They're getting ready to charge the back door. C'mon, we'll have to fight 'em off."

He dashed back to the kitchen, followed by the others. He saw a dark group of men forming about the battering ram, some distance back from the door. He raised one gun—then suddenly hesitated. The others stood tense, listening too.

A fresh group of riders were just entering the ranch yard. Already their guns were commencing to bark. There came sudden, frantic yells from the Mitchell faction. The gunfire was redoubled. Then came a long high-pitched call: "Hold tight, Rocking-A! We're here to help!"

"That was Ed Hunter!" Johnny exclaimed. He listened while excitement rose to fever pitch in the ranch house. "There! I heard Henry Linbauer's voice too. It looks like the Wagon-Wheel has come to our rescue!"

"What are we waiting for?" Humdrum said. "Let's get in on the fun. I'd like to make sure I get me one scut."

The back door was flung open and Johnny and Humdrum dashed out, followed by Mecate Bowen. For a brief moment there was a vicious exchange of gunfire, then suddenly the Spur-Bar men commenced to send up cries for mercy. Within a few minutes it was all over. The fight was ended.

Johnny turned back to the house to tell Susan. He was halfway through the darkened kitchen when he bumped into something warm and soft and clinging. Then Susan's voice, low and tender: "Johnny—is it you? Are you all right?"

"Right as rain," Johnny answered unsteadily.

224

Involuntarily his arms went about her slim form and he held her close. He felt her warm lips close on his own. For the next several minutes neither were conscious of their surroundings. They murmured sweet words that were almost unintelligible to the ear but spoke volumes to the heart. Susan's arms tightened about his neck.

Eventually they drew apart in the gloom, brought back to themselves by the voices outside. Johnny said, "And I only came back to light a lamp." He laughed happily.

"Instead, darling, you seem to have struck a spark." Susan giggled softly. "Go back outside. They'll be waiting for you. I'll light up. Guadalupe is in the other room with Dave Franklin. Hurry back to me, Johnny."

"I won't be an instant longer than I have to," Johnny replied, turning toward the ranch yard again.

He had been gone longer than he thought. Lights burned in the bunkhouse now. A number of grim cow hands sat their ponies not far away from the building, and there were a large number of riderless horses near. Three men came hurrying toward Johnny—Humdrum, Ed Hunter and Henry Linbauer. Hunter was carrying a lantern.

"I was commencing to wonder what had become of you," Humdrum greeted.

"I had important business in the house," Johnny said and turned to say hello to Linbauer and Hunter. "You fellows just got here in the nick of time. We sure owe you plenty—say, Mecate isn't hurt, is he?"

"Got a scratch across the back of one hand," Hunter said. "He's fixing it, himself, in the bunkhouse—"

Humdrum broke in: "Johnny, Sheriff Pritchard is dead—killed by Kane Mitchell."

Johnny said, "No!" unbelievingly.

"I came on him right after he'd killed Nick. I was about to do some blasting myself when I got a gun barrel wrapped over my conk," Deputy Hunter said grimly. "I just learned a few minutes ago it was Vink Mitchell did that. He confessed—"

"Did we get Kane Mitchell?" Johnny asked eagerly.

Hunter shook his head. "I reckon he sloped when the firing got too hot. He made a clean escape."

"That's tough luck," Johnny said grimly.

"He is the only one to escape though," Henry Linbauer said. "Only two prisoners have we taken. Pat Scudder is dead, Vink Mitchell is dead, the rest of the Spur-Bar hands are finished."

Hunter continued, "Vink made a complete confession before he passed off. He told us that Kane had killed the sheriff, but he didn't know why. Kane went hawg-wild apparently and lost his head. It wasn't quite clear to Vink. Oh yes, Vink told us it was Ogallala who killed George Aldrich over in El Paso. Ogallala killed Tony Aldrich about the same time. I didn't get details on that. And the Spur-Bar has been rustling both Wagon-Wheel and Rocking-A cows for a long time. They even blotted Wagon-Wheels on the Rocking-A in the hope of starting a fight between the two outfits—"

"You know, Johnny," Linbauer interrupted excitedly, "how those low-life thieves made a Wagon-Wheel out of the Rocking-A brand? Some more of those brands we find. After you tell me I send my men riding in all directions. Sixteen cows they picked up with that clumsy brand work. I was not sure if Miss Aldrich would believe me when I tell her we are innocent, so I decide to come to town and tell first the sheriff. I bring all my men, so the sheriff can hear their stories firsthand. But when we get to town the office is dark.

226

We hear someone groan. We open the door and find the dead sheriff and Deputy Hunter tied with ropes on the floor. The deputy is just coming to life—"

"Once they got me untied though," Hunter interrupted, "I got busy and rounded up some riders to add to the Wagon-Wheel hands. Someone had seen the Spur-Bars leaving town on the trail that leads here. We followed, pushing our broncs as fast as they'd come and—well, you know the rest, Johnny."

"I know we'd been wiped out if you hadn't got here, you and Henry," Johnny said soberly. "We owe you a heap."

"You don't owe us a thing," Hunter said grimly. "There wa'n't a man of us who didn't relish the thought of a chance at the Spur-Bars—particularly Kane Mitchell. My only regret is that he escaped. Well, there's work to be done around here. Miss Susan wouldn't relish seeing this mess. We'll pick up the dead, take our prisoners and head back for town."

"Someday," Johnny said, half to himself, "Kane Mitchell is due to pay for the deviltry he's done. I aim to square accounts with that bustard, if I have to trail him from here to hell!"

HIDDEN INSTRUCTIONS

IT WASN'T YET NINE-THIRTY THE FOLLOWING MORNING, that all signs of the previous evening's battle had been cleared away, even to the throwing of loose sand on certain dark stains about the ranch yard. Practically the only sign to show that there had been trouble was found in the shattered window frames and certain bullet-pocked spots about the house walls. An hour before

Mecate Bowen had driven the buckboard to town, to carry Dave Franklin to the doctor to have his wound dressed. The wound wasn't serious, but Susan had insisted on Dr. Pickett seeing it. Humdrum had saddled up and gone along with the wagon, with the intention of telegraphing Steve Sharples, head of the Border Rangers, regarding the recent things that had been learned.

Morning sun shone brightly over the range. There wasn't the trace of a cloud in the sky. In the clear air the Sangre de Santos seemed nearer than ever, with Superstition Peak cutting a sharp triangle, above its fellows, against the turquoise heavens. Johnny came walking slowly from the corral where he had just finished replacing the posts taken up by the Spur-Bar men the previous evening. He reached the bunkhouse and dropped down on the long bench that fronted the building. Removing the black sombrero, he mopped perspiration from his face with a blue bandanna.

From the kitchen of the ranch house came Susan's throaty contralto singing a song of the Old West. Something about rain on the prairies making flowers grow. Johnny didn't know the words but he thought the song pretty. After a time her voice fell silent and he guessed she was helping Guadalupe with the breakfast dishes. His gaze strayed to the black sombrero on the bench at his side. "Hat," he muttered, "you've sure made plenty of trouble. I wonder why? What's the connection?"

He wondered, too, where Kane Mitchell had escaped to. "I'd like one more chance at that coyote," Johnny mused, frowning. "Just to line my sights on him once would be worth a heap to me. The dirty, murdering skunk!"

228

"Johnny, what are you frowning about?" Susan had suddenly rounded the corner of the bunkhouse. Her eyes sparkled happily as Johnny rose to take her in his arms.

"You drive all the frowns away," he told her a minute later as she disengaged herself from his arms.

"But I insist on knowing."

"Well," Johnny admitted, "I was thinking about Kane Mitchell and what I'd like to do to him—"

"Johnny! you're downright bloodthirsty. Forget Kane Mitchell. I think we've seen the last of him. He won't dare ride on this range again. It's been made too hot for him."

"And," Johnny went on, "I've been thinking about that gold and wondering where it could be buried."

"I've sort of given up thinking about it. Sometimes I wonder if it wasn't discovered and taken away long ago. So many people knew about it. Somebody must have dug it up."

"Maybe so, but I'm not going to give up trying. I only wish I could have been in that old adobe house the night that Ogallala Mitchell and Tony Aldrich rode in with that gold."

"You weren't, so you'd better forget it for the time being. There were only two people there at the time— Guadalupe and her son, Ramón. Ramón was just a youngster—"

"Susan, come up to the house with me. I'm going to talk to Guadalupe. She might, under questioning reveal some detail she's forgotten to tell other people."

"Sure, we can try it." Susan nodded. She slipped one hand through Johnny's arm. Johnny picked up his hat and together they made their way to the ranch house.

They found Guadalupe in the kitchen, vigorously plying a broom. Susan made her sit down and told her what they wanted. Guadalupe looked questioningly at Johnny.

"I'm tell you everyt'ing I'm remembering, señor," the old Mexican woman said.

Johnny nodded. "First, you saw Ogallala and Tony Aldrich ride in that night the posse was after them. What did they say?"

"Ogallala, he say nothing. He's mighty near dead. The bad wound in his side. Tony, he tell me they have to hide out. He don't say why, but I make the guess. I'm see the pack horse with the box lashed to hees back."

"You're sure you saw that?" Johnny persisted.

Guadalupe's head bobbed. "Is very bright moon that night—almost like daytime. I look out the door and see the three horses. One have the box lashed to hees back. Tony carry Ogallala in the house and put him on bed. Then hees tell me and Ramón we should go to other room. Ogallala he is not talk, only make the groaning. It was ver' bad. Tony give him water, then he step outside, he say to take care of horses—"

"How long was Tony gone?" Johnny cut in.

"Ver', ver' long time. Maybe two hour—maybe more. I'm know that when he takes care of horses he does something else, because I see him, t'rough a window, with a shovel and pick which I have to make the small garden."

"And he was gone for two hours or more," Johnny mused. "Look, Guadalupe, what did he do when he returned to your house?"

Guadalupe considered a moment, casting her memory back over the years. "He comes in the house and goes to see how is Ogallala. He asks for water for Ogallala. I give it to him and go away. Pretty soon I can hear Ogallala talk—ver', ver' feeble. Is hurt ver' bad. They

230

talk some more. After while Tony he come to my room with a pencil in hees hand and ask me for some writing paper—"

"Guadalupe!" Susan exclaimed, "you never told us that before."

The Mexican woman shrugged her shoulders. "I'm not think eet is ver' important. I didn't have the paper so I couldn't give to him—"

"Gosh," Johnny exclaimed, "I'll bet Tony was going to make a map showing where he'd buried the gold."

"No paper, no map," Susan said hopelessly. "That idea is shot to pieces."

"What did Tony do next?" Johnny persisted.

"He say, 'Goddamit!' and go back to room where Ogallala is. I hear them talk ver' low for long time. Then they are quiet. Pret' soon Tony come to my room again and ask for needle to sew up bad hole in Ogallala's side—"

"Wait a minute," Johnny interrupted. "Somehow that doesn't seem logical. As I understand it, Tony was no surgeon. Did he say he was going to sew up the wound in Ogallala's side?"

Guadalupe shook her head. "No, he deed not say theses, but"—indignantly—"for why would he want the needle?"

"I'm danged if I know"—Johnny frowned—"but I'm afraid you've let your imagination run away with you, Guadalupe. You gave him a needle and thread though, eh?"

Guadalupe nodded vigorously. "I'm give him. He had a bullet hole in hees hat. Maybe he wants to sew eet up, no?" she added hopefully.

"I'm afraid not," Johnny said slowly. "Then what happened?"

"Nothing is happen for maybe one hour. Then we hear riders coming near. I hear Tony say goodbye to Ogallala, then Tony, he's go out the window and ride his horse like hell—"

"Guadalupe!" Susan said reprovingly.

"Is true," Guadalupe insisted stubbornly. "Nevair do the law officers catch him. But they take Ogallala away to the jailhouse and for many years he does not come back here."

"And that's all that happened?" Johnny asked.

"Is all." Guadalupe nodded. She sat patiently waiting while Johnny considered the information.

Susan said, "It looks like a brick wall, Johnny darling."

"Maybe." Johnny frowned. "I'm still wondering what Tony wanted a needle for."

"Maybe he was going to do some embroidering to pass the time," Susan said humorously. "Especially if that ever was Ogallala's sombrero you're wearing. He might have wanted to cheer Ogallala up by adding some fancy needlework to the decorations on that hat—"

"Wait!" Johnny interrupted. "I've got an idea!" He swung around to the Mexican woman. "Guadalupe, did Ogallala have on a hat like mine that night?"

Guadalupe nodded. "Ver' much like your sombrero. Maybe eet is same sombrero, no?"

"Maybe. Now remember carefully. What kind of hat did Tony have?"

"Just common gray hat—what you call Stetson—with bullet hole in heem like I tell you. The Stetson is what you call ruin'. I theenk maybe that is why he leave the ruin' hat for Ogallala and take Ogallala's hat when he makes the getaway to ride like hell—"

"Wait, wait, wait!" Johnny said excitedly. "You say

232

Tony took Ogallala's black sombrero, the hat like his, this hat?"

"Sure." Guadalupe looked surprised. "Why not? Ogallala, he's go to jail. Is not right that Tony should leave the so-beautiful black sombrero to go to the jail too—"

"Guadalupe!" Susan said, "you never told us that before."

"No one have ever ask me," Guadalupe said simply.

"We've got it, we've got it, I think," Johnny said swiftly. "Listen, Susan. Tony buries the gold. He has a pencil but no paper to make a map. Now what does he need a needle for?"

"I'm sure I don't know."

"You'll get the idea in a minute. There's no lining in his own Stetson hat, but there's a white silk lining in Ogallala's sombrero. Tony makes his map on the white silk lining, then has to have a needle to sew it back in—"

"Johnny! Do you suppose—"

"We'll find out in a minute." Johnny laughed nervously.

Seizing the black sombrero, he studied the lining inside the crown, then whipped out his pocketknife. Turning back the sweatband, he commenced cutting the stitches that held the lining in place. The knife blade moved swiftly around the circular crown, and an instant later Johnny had removed the round piece of sweat-stained silk. For a moment he hesitated, scarcely daring to turn it over, then took a deep breath and—

"Johnny!" Susan shrieked, "there's writing on it!"

Johnny gulped. "Yes, there is, but it's not a map like I expected." His voice trembled.

They spread the hat lining out on the table. "It's Tony's writing," Susan exclaimed. "And I'll bet it's

233

instructions showing where the gold is buried."

The pencil writing had become somewhat blurred from rubbing over the period of years, but it was still decipherable on the inner, underside of the sombrero lining. Susan read slowly:

"Face west from crack in Ghost Rock. Row of three cottonwoods in line with Superstition Peak. From center tree ten paces west. Five paces south."

The girl's voice shook as she looked doubtfully up at Johnny. "It doesn't say anything about gold being buried and Tony's name isn't signed to it."

Johnny was laughing crazily. He seized Susan's arms and whirled her around the kitchen. "It's instructions though," he cried. "We can't ask for everything." He whirled Susan until she was breathless.

Guadalupe beamed up at the two. "Is good news, no?" she asked uncertainly.

"Is good news, yes!" Johnny exclaimed. "We're getting someplace at last."

Susan's eyes were moist with joy. Johnny released her and she fell into a chair, panting. "Just—as soon— as I get my—breath," she said, "we'll get started."

Johnny stared at her. "Started where?"

"Over to Ghost Rock. I want to see if that gold is there."

"Today?" Johnny asked. "Right now?"

"Right now." Susan nodded emphatically. "I'm not going to take a chance on anyone getting there first."

"It's a good idea at that," Johnny agreed suddenly. "Now I know why Ogallala wanted this hat. It was his hat all right. He knew Tony had written directions in it, but he didn't know what they were. I suppose Tony always expected to get in touch with him again but never did—"

"Johnny," Susan protested, "must you stand talking all day? Please saddle our horses while I change my clothes."

"At once, lady! I'm on my way to the corral now!"

POWDER SMOKE!

THE SUN HAD PASSED MERIDIAN BY THE TIME SUSAN and Johnny pulled their ponies to a halt near the foot of Ghost Rock. Johnny slipped down from the saddle, then helped Susan to the ground. Susan said breathlessly, "Well, we're here, darling. Will it prove to be a wild-goose chase, or do you think—"

"I've quit thinking." Johnny laughed nervously. "Now I'm just hoping."

"I feel shaky," Susan confessed. "Here's Ghost Rock and way over yonder is Superstition Peak. And the sky's so blue. Oh, Johnny! On such a glorious day we surely can't be disappointed. Honestly, if we were I'd feel just like going in that old adobe house there and never coming out."

"Don't get your hopes up too high," Johnny warned. "We can't tell what we've got ahead of us." Now that they had arrived he seemed reluctant to make the start. He didn't know why he first walked over near the old adobe house and cast his eyes around. It was just that he couldn't get over the impression that someone was watching him and Susan. He and the girl circled the old adobe. There were still the signs of the Spur-Bar men about. Picks and shovels lay where they had dropped them. Under the trees near the adobe were hoofprints, two days old.

"Johnny," Susan said, "what are we waiting for?" She looked curiously at him.

"Not a thing." Johnny laughed suddenly. "I reckon I'm afraid to start this search for fear we'll find our hopes dashed. But come on, we've got to start some time." They made their way back to the foot of Ghost Rock and glanced up at its high uneven sides.

"Think we can make to get up there?" Susan smiled.

"We? There's no use both of us climbing up there."

"Cowboy, when I'm wearing overalls I climb any place you do. You're not going to leave me out of one bit of this expedition. Come on, I'll beat you to the top!"

It wasn't difficult climbing. There were natural footholds worn in the great gray granite ridge, and protruding knobs of rock for the hands were plentiful. Now and then bits of rock worked loose and went clattering and tumbling to the earth below, but there was never any danger of either Susan or Johnny falling. Within six or seven minutes their vigorous muscles had carried them, panting and laughing, to the top. They straightened up and glanced about.

Fifty feet below them they could see the roof of the adobe house, and standing near the house were their ponies, looking somewhat smaller from this distance. Johnny glanced along the top of the ridge on which they were standing and judged it to be seventy-five or eighty feet in length, running east and west, and about twelve or fifteen feet wide. "You ever been up here before?" he asked the girl.

Susan nodded. "Dad and I climbed up once, a good many years ago. Come on, I'll show you where that crack is—you know, where the soul of the Great Spirit emerged."

236

"I'm interested in that crack for other reasons."

Johnny followed the girl for about thirty paces until they stopped at a great crack in the granite probably four inches wide, that opened horizontally across the ridge and ran clear through to the bottom. "From here on cowboy," Susan said softly, "we follow Tony's directions."

Johnny pulled from his pocket the circular piece of lining he had removed from the black sombrero and slowly perused the writing. "Face west from crack in Ghost Rock," he read. "Row of three cottonwoods in line with Superstition Peak . . ." He broke off and glanced toward Superstition Peak.

Looking west, the earth sloped away to a great hollow filled with brush and cactus. But standing out above the lower growth, three cottonwood trees lifted their leafy branches toward the sky. Undoubtedly those were the trees Tony Aldrich meant.

"I see the trees," Susan said in a half whisper. "Do you?"

"They'd be hard to miss," Johnny replied. "Gosh, those trees must be nearly an eighth of a mile from here. I don't wonder nobody ever found that gold digging near the adobe house. Tony was wise enough to bury it some distance away. All right, pick out that center tree and don't forget where it stands after we climb down from here. That tree gives us our directions."

"Come on. I won't forget it."

Quickly they turned and ran back along the ridge, then started to climb down. They reached earth, slipping and sliding, in a shower of dust and gravel. Susan brushed off her overalls, while Tony went to the adobe house to secure a pick and shovel. In a minute he was back, the tools slung over one shoulder. They started

237

out, skirting the bottom of Ghost Rock.

Susan said, "Maybe we should take the horses to bring the gold back."

"We'll worry about packing the gold when we find it." Johnny laughed. "Shucks!"—lengthening his stride—"I'm in no state of mind to be held back by a horse now. I want to move!"

Side by side, they hiked down a long incline toward the brush-grown hollow. They couldn't see the cottonwood trees now, but Johnny had the direction pretty well established in his mind. The growth became thicker as they proceeded. Broken slabs of granite impeded their progress. Almost before they realized it they were pushing their way through a veritable jungle of growth—cactus, mesquite, manzanita. There were also sage, stunted scrub oak, cottonwood seedlings and other flora common to the Southwest.

And then quite suddenly they emerged from the thicket into a small clearing where three cottonwood trees, standing in a row, filtered the sunlight from overhead. "There's our trees!" Johnny exclaimed. Again he produced the written instructions on the hat lining and studied them. "From center tree ten paces west. Five paces south," he read. "There you are, Lady Susan. Do you care to pace them off with me?"

"You can't stop me—providing you tell me which way west is. I've lost all sense of direction since we entered this section of growth. All I can see is that center tree."

Johnny glanced up through leafy boughs at the sun, then marched directly to the center tree's trunk and stood on the other side. "I've got the direction. Come on."

Side by side, they paced off ten paces toward the

238

west, then made a left turn and moved five paces to the south. The final step brought them to a small pile of loosely heaped broken rock. "I guess this is it," Johnny said.

"But, Johnny," Susan said dubiously, "all that rock—"

"I figure Tony put it there to sort of hold things in place, in case a cloudburst ever flooded down in this hollow."

He tossed down the pick and shovel and commenced clearing away the rock. Susan helped and before long they had the earth cleared. Johnny lifted his pick and swung it hard. After a time he changed to the shovel and excavated the loosened dirt.

"Wouldn't it be easier working if you took off your gun belts?" Susan asked when he stopped once to mop his brow.

"Who said it was hard work?" Johnny grinned. "This is the most enjoyable labor I ever undertook."

He again started work with the pick. Then the shovel. In time quite a sizable excavation was made, but nothing that in the least resembled buried treasure was to be seen.

"Johnny!" Susan wailed, "I'm afraid something is wrong—"

She stopped suddenly. Johnny had been swinging the pick again, when abruptly the ringing sound of steel against stone and gravel changed to a dull, hollow, thudding sound. Johnny noticed the difference too. He redoubled his efforts. Then the point of the pick unexpectedly sank out of sight. Slowly Johnny withdrew it and straightened up. He tried to hold his voice steady. "I think we've found something, Susan," he said in queer tones and grabbed the shovel.

Only a minute more was required to clear the dirt and

gravel from an old oaken strongbox. The wood had commenced to rot. There was a great hole in the cover where the pick had penetrated. The hinges and metal-reinforced corners were nearly rusted through. There was no padlock on the rusty staple and hasp; that had been removed long since by the men who had robbed the Little Bonanza payroll. Johnny dropped down on his knees beside the box and with the aid of the pick point pried back the cover.

Susan caught her breath, then gave a sudden gasp. "We've found it, Johnny!" A dull glinting of yellow metal met her gaze.

"I reckon you're right," Johnny said unsteadily, as the girl dropped on her knees beside him.

Within the box were several cloth money sacks, moldy with damp and commencing to split apart from the weight of their heavy gold burden. One sack had been already opened and a number of yellow double eagles had spilled out over the other sacks.

"Oh, Johnny, it's really true. We've found it—"

Abruptly Johnny swung away from the box and pressed his hand against Susan's mouth. Shhh!" he whispered swiftly.

Again he listened, noticing now that all around there was a strange silence. There must be someone moving through the thicket when the birds that had been chirping but an instant before suddenly fell silent. Johnny strained his ears. Then off to the left there came the sharp cracking of a broken stick in the undergrowth.

Johnny motioned Susan to silence, then removed his hand from her mouth. He glanced quickly toward the girl's side to make certain she had her gun. Then he raised himself out of the excavation while still retaining a stooping position. Taking the girl's arm, he silently drew her back and pushed her into the brush. "Don't make a move," he said calmly. "Keep low. I'll be back in a minute."

"But, Johnny, what is it?" the girl whispered: "What's wrong? Where are you going?"

He still held his voice low. "There's someone moving through the brush over there. Maybe it's Kane Mitchell. He might have planned to hide out around here, figuring there was a chance of us leading him to the gold." His hand went again to Susan's mouth to stifle her involuntary exclamation. "Now keep down. I'll be back in a minute."

Moving with the stealth of an Apache, Johnny faded noiselessly into the brush. Susan sank down, her heart beating madly. She strained her ears but could hear nothing. The minutes ticked slowly away. She lost all sense of time in the mounting fear that had taken possession of her. She could feel a scream rising in her throat, and her trembling fingers strove to stifle the noise before it emerged. Now and then a twig snapped in the silence.

Then, off to the north some distance, there came the sudden roaring of heavy guns. Susan stumbled up, clutching her six-shooter, and fought her way wildly through the brush in the direction of the sound . . .

After leaving Susan Johnny had pushed swiftly through the undergrowth, working away from the girl as soon as possible. Then he had frozen to silence again, straining his ears for the first sound. Some distance off to his right a heavy boot scuffed dry leaves.

Johnny nodded and brushed quickly through the thicket. Prickly spines and thorns tore at his shirt now as he moved, but he was no longer trying to travel silently. He was being hunted, and he wanted to lure the hunter

241

as far away as possible from the spot at which he'd left Susan.

Loose branches slapped at his face as he made his way through the dense growth, circling wide of the spot where the gold lay. Now he turned once more, this time toward the north, and forced his way through a tangled mesquite thicket. He swung wide around a huge clump of prickly pear and came to a stop, again straining his ears.

After a moment he nodded and a grim smile crossed his face. The hunter was closer now. Johnny plunged on for another hundred yards, wended his way through a scattering of Spanish dagger plants, crossed a small clearing and took up a position behind a small chaparral tree. The brush grew high at his back and overhead, giving the light a greenish cast as the sun's rays worked down through the thick vegetation.

Johnny stood like a statue, waiting. He blended with his surroundings with the cunning of a frightened deer. The snapping of twigs and branches reached him now as the hunter came nearer. Then there was a sudden silence. Johnny knew his pursuer had stopped to listen. Stooping, Johnny found a small bit of rock. He tossed it to fall crashing through branches, a few yards away. Then he strained his ears again. The snapping of twigs and boots on dry leaves was resumed.

The sounds came nearer, then suddenly Kane Mitchell burst from the brush into the small clearing and stood gazing insanely around. The man's eyes were wild and bloodshot. His clothing was torn and he'd lost his hat. His hair was a tangled mass and unshaven whiskers gave his face a smudged, evil appearance. In either hand he clutched a forty-five six-shooter. His head sank down between his shoulders as he peered about, muttering madly to himself.

So well did Johnny blend with his surroundings that Mitchell failed to see him at once. The man cursed in a savage undertone and had started to turn away when Johnny spoke:

"You looking for somebody, Mitchell?" Johnny said quietly.

Mitchell whirled. "Damn you, Donne!" he snarled as his eyes took in Johnny's silently waiting form. The guns in his hands swept up, belching flame and smoke.

Johnny flung himself swiftly to one side, hands stabbing to the holsters at his thighs. A stream of white, hot fire spurted from the vicinity of his hips.

Mitchell cursed again and staggered back, one hand hanging limply at his side. The other was swinging a gun to bear on Johnny. A bullet slashed through the bandanna at Johnny's neck.

Again Johnny shifted position. He felt the heavy Colt gun jump in his grip. Powder smoke made a thick haze before his eyes. Mitchell's shots went wild as he slumped to his knees. The gun dropped from his hand and his fingers tore frantically at his throat.

"Got enough, Mitchell?" Johnny asked grimly.

There was no need to ask. A gurgling cough left Mitchell's lips. His eyes widened, stared wildly at Johnny for a moment, long fingers still tearing at his throat. Then quite suddenly he pitched on his face and died.

Johnny stood over the man a moment. "That squares Nick Pritchard," he said softly. He blew the smoke from his muzzles, reloaded his guns and started back through the thicket.

He hadn't gone far when he heard Susan's frantic cries.

"Take it easy, girl," Johnny called. "I'm coming as fast as possible. It's all right."

He moved more swiftly through the brush now. "Wait where you are." He raised his voice again. "I'm coming!"

"Oh, Johnny, where are you?" Susan wailed.

He changed direction through the dense undergrowth, then through the leafy fronds of the mesquite branch saw the girl's tear-stained face. An instant later she was sobbing in his arms. "I—I was so afraid for you—afraid that it was Kane Mitchell—and—and that he'd kill you—"

"It *was* Kane Mitchell," Johnny said quietly. "He won't bother us any more." He silenced her sobs with his lips, held her close while a long sigh ran through her slender form. Her arms tightened about his neck. They were in a world of their own making now, with the sun's warm light making lacy shadows all about them and the songs of a thousand birds joining the joyous singing in their hearts . . .

We hope that you enjoyed reading this
Sagebrush Large Print Western.
If you would like to read more Sagebrush titles,
ask your librarian or contact the Publishers:

United States and Canada

Thomas T. Beeler, *Publisher*
Post Office Box 659
Hampton Falls, New Hampshire 03844-0659
(800) 818-7574

United Kingdom, Eire, and
the Republic of South Africa

Isis Publishing Ltd
7 Centremead
Osney Mead
Oxford OX2 0ES England
(01865) 250333

Australia and New Zealand

Bolinda Publishing Pty. Ltd.
17 Mohr Street
Tullamarine, 3043, Victoria, Australia
(016103) 9338 0666